CHRISTMAS WISH UPON A STAR

sands press
Brockville, Ontario

CHRISTMAS WISH UPON A STAR

SUSAN BAGBY

sands press

sands press

A Division of 3244601 Canada Inc.
300 Central Avenue West
Brockville, Ontario
K6V 5V2

Toll Free 1-800-563-0911 or 613-345-2687
http://www.sandspress.com

ISBN 978-1-990066-15-3
Copyright © Susan Bagby 2022
All Rights Reserved

For information on bulk purchases of this book or any book published by Sands Press, please call 1-800-563-0911.

To book an author for your live event, please call: 1-800-563-0911

Sands Press is a literary publisher interested in new and established authors wishing to develop and market their product. For more information please visit our website at www.sandspress.com.

For my mom, who inspired my passion for writing romance novels, and for her unconditional love that gave me the courage to follow my dreams.

And for my dad, who believed I could do anything.

Acknowledgments

This book is a dream come true. My passion for writing romance novels has taken flight thanks to Sands Press, my publisher.

I want to thank Perry Prete for making my dream a reality and welcoming me as a new author. You are an awesome publisher!

To Shannon Horsley at Sands Press, for supporting me and for your helpful suggestions on every step from submission to print. I appreciate your friendship.

To Laurie Carter, my editor extraordinaire. You made it easy and thank you for your guidance along the path to the finish line.

To Anne Matter, my first reader—for your invaluable input and humor as I prepared my first manuscript for submission. I value your friendship and willingness to help me, no questions asked.

To Alison Kunkel Johnson, for designing my author logo and helping me launch my presence into social media.

To Jacob Johnson, for the invaluable legal counsel you gave me and encouragement while entering the publishing world.

And all my close friends who have been with me along the way. You know who you are. Thank you.

Chapter One

Wind whipped around her shoulders as Alison got out of the taxi. Shivering, she pulled her coat closer, and with suitcase in tow hurried inside her apartment building. Snow wasn't falling yet, but winter was making her presence felt in Manhattan. She would have loved to stay longer at her parent's house in Connecticut but a couple of days off for Thanksgiving was all she had. Alison worked as a production assistant for a children's television show, which was a far cry from the publishing world, where she would rather be, but at least she was getting some experience for her resume and could pay her bills. She had dreamed of writing children's books, but her demanding job had left her with little time to write. Managing kids on set wasn't quite what she had pictured in her head, but she *was* around children, gifted muse for her inspiration.

As she opened the door, her roommate came to greet her. "Welcome home!" Jenny was a painter and make-up artist and Alison's best friend since college. They had met in New York and solidified their friendship over late night coffee and studying together. They'd both encouraged each other's dreams and become each other's biggest cheerleaders. Jenny reached out to help Alison with her bags. "How were your mom and dad? Did you eat as much as I did?"

"Mom acted as if I'd never eaten. My suitcase is full of leftovers. How was your time with Mike?" Alison liked Jenny's boyfriend. Another artist like herself, Mike had steered towards the digital corporate world and quickly found success. His family lived in New Jersey, and Jenny had been invited to their house for Thanksgiving. Jenny and Mike always found time for each other. Something she lacked lately with her guy.

"Thanksgiving was a blast! Kids were running around, plenty of chefs in the kitchen and enough food to feed an army. They welcomed me with open arms despite the chaos!"

Alison grinned at the image, then looking around, she noticed large boxes strewn on the floor filled with Christmas garlands, ornaments, and crystal figurines. "Are you waiting for me to get your Christmas thing going here?"

"You know it. I thought we could start tonight. We can get a tree later." Jenny and Alison both loved Christmas and looked forward to decorating their home every year.

"Alison heard her phone ding, picked it up, and rolled her eyes once she saw who was texting her.

"Your guy? What's he saying?"

"He's not coming back to the city until late tonight. No holiday plans for us. Says we'll do lunch later this week." Alison felt disappointment. Again. Steve never seemed to be available or make any effort at doing the couple things Alison yearned for with a man. "You know how busy he gets, and he rarely gets to spend time with his family."

"Don't make excuses to me, girlfriend. I see it written all over your face. Maybe it's time you cut the cord and moved on. I don't like the way he treats you."

Alison reflected on Steve's actions or rather lack of action toward her. "Maybe. But enough! Let's eat and then get those fancy garlands out." No matter what, any relationship woes would not deter Alison's Christmas spirit. She had enjoyed a wonderful visit, and her mother had finished sketches for her latest picture book. "And wait until I show you what Mom designed for my book."

Jenny laughed and clapped her hands together. "So much to do!"

Alison adored her friend. Jenny was a dazzling woman with long, curly hair often tied up in colorful scarves. Her olive skin was glowing, and her vibrant, brown eyes never missed a trick. Several years ago, she had been responsible for helping Alison land a job on the television show *Hands-On Kids*. She did hair and makeup for the cast, and when they lost a production assistant, Jenny recommended Alison before they alerted anyone to the vacancy notice. The producer was happy to hire an educated employee, hoping she might last a little longer than the previous one.

"I'll heat up the leftovers and you start on the boxes." Alison was glad for a distraction from her disappointment with Steve. Maybe Jenny was right. Maybe she should just end it and move on. But every time she thought she might, he would show up and do something nice for her. And besides, she was too busy to worry about it.

***

At the Anderson family home in the Berkshires, Jake Sanders headed to the main house to catch his uncle before he returned to the city. It was a sprawling estate and after his wife, Clara, died, his uncle had suggested he and his daughter, Annie, come live in the guest house. Jake had spent summers there as a young child, but when his parents died in a car accident when he was ten, Jim Anderson, his mother's brother, had become his legal guardian. Jake spent the rest of his life living in Jim's majestic home until he went to boarding school and college. He felt blessed his uncle had been so generous with his time and money, even though Jake had acquired wealth from his mother's share of the Anderson fortune. His aunt Martha had died when Jake was in college, and Jim's daughter, Maggy, lived in Los Angeles. A feisty, independent woman, she had followed in her father's footsteps and was a successful television producer and business entrepreneur.

Jake and Annie were looking forward to her visit at Christmas.

It had snowed the night before but Marty, the groundskeeper, always made sure the walkway was clean, so Jake and Annie could get to the main house easily. As he entered the back kitchen, the aroma of Sara's cooking aroused his senses. His uncle's housekeeper for years, she did what she could to support Jake after their tragic loss, and Jake could finally see a spark returning to Annie's young spirit. Luckily, his uncle had a need for his services in one of his companies and hired him to work from a smaller office in town. These last few years had been a hard adjustment, but Jake knew he had made the right decision moving to Maple Ridge.

Stomping his boots to get the excess snow off, Jake exclaimed, "Something sure smells good."

"Daddy! Come here! Look what Sara and I are making!" Annie was small for nine years of age but radiated her mother's essence. She wore her blond hair in a braid and her bright blue eyes were mischievous. Jake was starting to believe everything would eventually be alright.

When they lived in the city, Jake had devoted much of his time to his work and left most of the parenting to Clara. Clara had been a brilliant artist and business woman herself, overseeing the management of a prestigious art gallery in the city. But she always made Annie her priority even when she got sick. Her illness and death had struck Jake's world with a shocking blow, and he would forever be grateful to his uncle and Sara being there for him in a time of need. It had been his uncle who suggested the move, offering a creative, less stressful environment for Jake to work in while he concentrated on healing the loss he and his daughter had endured.

"I'm ready for soup. Let's see what you two have been doing together." At six feet, Jake towered over both of them, but Sara was quick to wave him away with her spoon.

"You go sit at the table and we'll bring you a bowl. Right, Annie?"

"Yes, you sit down, Dad. We've got this covered."

Jake threw up his hands. "I know when I'm beat! Where's Uncle Jim?" Bonding with his uncle during the Thanksgiving holiday helped soothe the void in his heart, but Jake knew he would be returning to the city soon.

"He's in his office. Got an important phone call and said he'd have lunch with us before leaving," answered Sara.

"Somebody looking for me?" A handsome man in his sixties and tall like his nephew walked in and put his hand on Jake's shoulder. "Do you think you and I could talk in the den before lunch?"

"Sure. You guys keep it hot for us, okay?"

"Okay, dad. But don't forget, you said we could decorate the bookstore this afternoon. You need to put up the decorations if you want to draw a holiday crowd."

Laughing, Uncle Jim shook his head. "She's already got a business head like an Anderson! I promise, we won't be long."

Jake and his uncle went into the den, sitting down next to each other in front of the fireplace. Jim looked over at his nephew. "I got a call from Bob Goldberg this morning. He's on the board with me at Sinclair productions. We have a couple television shows filming in the city."

"I remember him. What's up?" Even though Jake had left a high-powered investment firm in Manhattan, he still had his hand in business with running a local bookstore he owned in town and starting up a new imprint for his uncle's publishing company. The imprint would be a brand specializing in children's books. He had set up an office upstairs from the bookstore and was able to apply his skills for numbers and business at a pace enabling him to give Annie all the time and attention she needed.

"Do you know the show *Hands-On Kids*? It's a reality television show focusing on art and literature for kids."

"Yeah, I've seen it before. Annie likes to watch it, but then always tries to get Sara or me involved in one of the projects she sees on the show."

Jim laughed. "They always do a big Christmas show and travel out of the city to a snowy, rural location. They record taped episodes for four or five days, with a live finale airing on Christmas Eve afternoon. The venue they had has fallen through and he wanted to know if I would open Anderson Estates for some of the production team before filming it in Maple Ridge. In the spirit of Christmas, of course."

"What did you say?"

"I wanted to talk to you first. I know you're getting ready to launch your imprint, but I was wondering if you would play host to the producer sent to organize things, maneuver around town and help with the pre-production tasks. I thought Annie would enjoy the excitement. It might ease any sadness she may have at this time of year. What do you think?"

"Sure. Whatever you need. When is the producer coming?" Jake would do anything for his uncle. Even though he was anxious to finish the details for his business, it might be fun for Annie.

"Soon. The producer will need to get a great deal ready for the multiple shoots. I'll call Bob on the way back to New York and get more details. I wanted to run it by you first."

Even though it had been several years since they had lost Clara, this time of year with the holidays was hard for both of them. Jake struggled to hide his sorrow from his daughter, so a little distraction might be welcome.

"Maggy should be here a few days before Christmas and can help too. I'll give her a call." Uncle Jim stood up and they walked back into the kitchen. He lovingly put his hand on Jake's shoulder. "Thanks, Jake. I appreciate this."

"No problem."

Sara looked up. "Who wants soup?"

"We do!" they all chimed in.

"Then to the store, Daddy?"

"Yes, to the store. I have to get the decorations out of the attic first and then I'm all yours to direct as you please." Keeping busy was the best strategy he had to keep his own sadness in check.

***

Alison stepped back to inspect the tiny trinkets placed in evergreen boughs and lights strung around the fireplace mantle and felt the Christmas spirit lifting her mood. Maybe Jenny was right. Maybe it was time to let Steve go and just let the universe handle her love life. *She* wasn't doing such a great job at it. She tilted her head and said, "Now all we need is a tree!"

"I was hoping we could get one this week after work. What do you say?"

"Absolutely. Let's play it by ear since you never know how long our day is going to be." Alison hadn't been used to such long hours at a job and was looking forward to her Christmas break after the last shoot. She wanted to polish her book and hopefully start a new one. Alison stretched her arms in the air and yawned. "I've got to get up early tomorrow. Miss Carolyn likes everything done before she gets in."

Jenny didn't miss Alison's sarcasm. "I know. Maybe she'll be in a better mood since it's Christmas and all."

"I hope so." Alison loved the concept of the show, the kids, and especially the literature part of it, but she didn't like her boss. She was pushy and often not kind. Carolyn had high hopes of moving up the ladder in the television world and would overpower anyone who was in her way. Since Alison didn't have the same aspirations, she kept her head down and nose to the grindstone as they say. One day she'd move on.

Alison smiled at Jenny and lifted her glass. "Here's to Christmas wishes coming true and love filling our hearts." Love. She had yearned for the real thing, but just hadn't found it yet. Or perhaps it hadn't found her. Whatever. Maybe Steve would change. At least she hoped he would.

"Yes, love! I hope you realize you deserve the real thing, Alison."

Alison knew what she meant. Steve had never invited her to spend the holidays with him and his family. He was generally kind and had been there for her whenever she needed work advice, but lately, the romance had been lacking. He did invite her to his corporate parties and events, but Alison knew his boss looked more favorably on staff who were married or in committed relationships. She was beginning to think whatever served his career was the reason behind all the invites. "I know what you mean." Gazing around the room, Alison was satisfied. "I think we did a fabulous job."

"We sure did. And wait until we get our tree!"

Alison felt grateful for her friend and family who supported her writing ambitions. She was hopeful she could finish her book and submit it to publishers and agents. Her happy place was being hunkered down in front of her computer and writing, and she was determined to work hard until her dream came true. Meanwhile, Alison would try her best to be a good assistant producer and enjoy the holiday spirit herself.

As evening ended, Alison closed her eyes in bed, and while becoming still, thought of Steve once more. Then she prayed. "Dear God, if he is the right man for me, please let me know. Give me a sign. If he isn't, please lead me to the man who will love me unconditionally and completely for all of who I am. I trust in you and know your plan is the best one. Just let me know what it is!" She laughed gently to herself. She knew she was supposed to let go and surrender, but there was always a part of herself wanting to control the outcome. This time she was letting go. And she rolled over and turned out the light.

Chapter Two

After dropping Annie off at school Jake drove straight to the bookstore where he had plans of burying himself in work before his host duties began. He had hired a new manager for the store and luckily, she was proficient in the job. She worked hard, kept the store neat and was totally into Christmas. He couldn't have asked for more.

Opening the bookstore, he looked around and smiled at the previous day's accomplishments. His and Annie's. She had talked him into decorating all afternoon even while people came in and shopped. Their customers had seemed to enjoy the festive mood, and Jake made sure to acknowledge the success of her entrepreneur spirit.

Before he could go upstairs, Lucy, his manager came in a few minutes later. She looked around in awe. "This place looks fantastic! How long were you and Annie here last night?"

"Looks pretty decent, huh? We stayed an hour after you left, and I promised we'd get a tree later this week."

"Yes! A tree will be the finishing touch. Who wouldn't want to buy their Christmas presents here? It's full of holiday sparkle and magic!"

Jake knew he had made the right decision when he hired Lucy. She was a young mom herself with a boy about Annie's age, and her husband was currently deployed on a special assignment for the national guard. This would be the first Christmas Lucy and her son, Tim, would spend without him. Therefore, she had no problem spending long hours at the bookstore. It took her mind off worrying about him.

"Glad you're here early. I'm going up to my office to work. I have to get a lot done in the next couple of days because we'll be hosting some hotshot producer from New York. It seems Uncle Jim has offered Anderson Estates for some of the pre-production staff of the children's television show, *Hands-On Kids*. They have a special Christmas production, and it's going to take place in Maple Ridge."

"Timmy loves the show. Will they film here?"

"Not sure yet. Uncle Jim is filling me in later with the details." Jake turned to go upstairs. "Call me if you need anything."

"Will do." Lucy smiled. She was looking forward to some excitement in Maple Ridge and couldn't wait to tell Tim.

Jake entered his office, still impressed with the awesomeness of the space. He had opened it up into a large loft with plenty of light, ideal to house plenty of staff. It was looking a little bare, though, Jake mused. He'd have to bring Annie upstairs to do a little decorating later.

Uncle Jim's name appeared on his cellphone as it rang. "Hey, there. Everything okay?" Jim proceeded to tell him all the show's details and inform him the producer would be arriving by train the day after tomorrow. He would email him a possible itinerary and any more information after he got it from the production staff on the show. The producer would be staying at the house and Sara was ready to do her part as well. Uncle Jim was the most generous guy Jake knew, and he wanted to do an excellent job of playing host even if it meant putting up with an uptight entertainment executive from the city.

***

Alison had arrived at the production set early and was doing her usual prep when one of Carolyn's assistants notified her that she was wanted in her office. Her heart started beating a faster in anticipation. She hoped she wasn't getting fired this close to Christmas!

As Alison walked in, she saw Carolyn wasn't there, but another man was sitting at her desk. He was dressed in a suit, on the phone, and motioned for her to sit down. She found herself visibly shaking.

When he got off the phone, he looked up at Alison. "Hello, my name is George Stevens. I'm another producer for the network and I'm taking on some of Carolyn's duties temporarily. Unfortunately, she had a skiing accident over the Thanksgiving holiday and is unable to come in to work for a bit."

"Is she okay?" Alison wasn't very fond of Carolyn, but she didn't like to hear someone had been hurt.

"Yes, she's fine. Just wounded pride and torn ligaments. She did have surgery and must wear a cast for two weeks without bearing weight on her foot. Afterward, she will have a walking boot, but we can't wait. The reason I asked you here is I need someone to take her place since she won't be able to maneuver around a set."

"Me?" A confused expression spread over Alison's face.

"Yes. As you know, we have a huge off-site Christmas show to be filmed in two to three weeks and have no on-site producer. You were recommended to fill the position if you're interested."

Alison clutched her clipboard to her chest, unconsciously holding her breath. Exhaling, she slowly found her words. "I've never run the show myself. I've been Carolyn's right hand person but never called the shots."

"She seems to think you can do it, so the job's yours if you want it. Of course, there will be more pay, and you have to leave the day after tomorrow."

"The day after tomorrow?" Alison felt like her life was suddenly spinning out of control, and she wasn't sure what to do. But she knew she had to respond without hesitation. Of course, she should do this! And besides, how hard could it be? She knew the makings of the show inside and out and had worked very hard these last few years. "Yes. I'll do it."

"Outstanding!" George stood up and Alison followed suit. "You have an executive planning meeting with the production staff at one o'clock. This morning we will give you someone to train for your duties and then you're finished. I don't need to tell you how important this special is for the company. We receive a lot of revenue from the advertisers for the Christmas extravaganza. You'll leave by train on Wednesday afternoon. Any questions?"

"No, sir. Thank you for the opportunity."

"I hope Carolyn is right. If you get in a jam, she will be available by phone, but I'm sure will be monitoring your every move. Good luck!"

"Thank you." Alison walked out of the office in a daze. *What just happened?* Did she agree to produce the entire show herself? Oh my. She could already feel the stress overtaking her body. *Breathe. You can do this.*

She hurried backstage, looking for Jenny, who should have arrived by now. When Jenny saw her, she said, "What happened to you? You look like you've seen a ghost!"

"You're not going to believe what just happened!" She grabbed Jenny, sat down on a nearby bench and proceeded to tell her the news.

"I can't believe Carolyn gave up her position for this show. She really must be incapacitated. She takes pride in doing the Christmas specials each year—and to let someone else do it?" Jenny whistled, shaking her head. "You won the jackpot, Alison."

"You think I can pull it off?"

"Of course! When do you leave?"

"Wednesday afternoon." Alison suddenly realized what all this meant. "I won't be here to get our tree."

"Don't worry! We got most of the decorations up yesterday. You need to focus on the job at hand. I'm so excited for you. And I'll be up the last week, so you won't be alone too long."

"And what about Steve? We had some plans."

"Forget about him. He can see what he's missing when you're not around."

"You're right. A whole new adventure awaits! Maybe I can even add my own creative spark to the show."

"There you go. Now let's get busy. We still have a job to do today." Jenny hugged her friend. "I'm so proud of you!"

"After the show is over, then you can sing my praises." Alison's head was swimming with so many thoughts of planning and wondering what lay in store ahead of her. And what was Steve going to say? Would he make an effort to see her before she left? She had prayed for a sign and maybe this was it. Maybe.

***

Jake sat down to dinner with Annie and called Sara in to join them. "I have news for you both." Sara winked at him because she already knew.

"What is it, Dad?" Annie's eyes grew large and Jake smiled at her never-ending enthusiasm.

"You know the television show, *Hands-On Kids*?"

"Yes. Mom and I used to watch it all the time."

"They needed somewhere to film their Christmas special and guess what? They're coming to Maple Ridge!"

Annie's eyes lit up like a Christmas tree. "Can we watch?"

"We will actually be hosting some of the crew here at Anderson Estates. And the producer arrives on Wednesday. We'll be helping her prep for the show like what cousin Maggy does."

"Can I help? Please?" Annie could hardly contain herself sitting in her chair.

"Perhaps, when you're not in school." Jake was trying to be as enthusiastic as his daughter, but honestly would rather be working in his office these couple of weeks before Christmas, preparing for the imprint launch.

"Can I be on the show, daddy? Can I?"

"Let's not get ahead of ourselves. We'll see what she has planned, okay?" Jake was beginning to feel this show would consume all of his time. But nothing warmed his heart more than seeing his child's radiant smile. Life had been too tough on her these last few years. He was trying his best, but sometimes his previous work habits crept in. Thank God for Sara. She always filled in when he couldn't.

"What about our trees? We need them soon!"

Jake shook his head. He might as well give up any idea of work until after Christmas. "Why don't we get our trees tomorrow night? But it might take us a couple of days to decorate. One for the store and one for here."

"And maybe the producer lady will want to help us!"

"She'll probably have work to do. We'll see."

Jake looked over at Sara who was smiling at the both of them. It was like she could read his mind. She knew this was going to be a big deal for them and for the town. He might as well surrender now. "Finish your dinner and do your homework. We're not falling behind because it's Christmas. We'll get the tree decorations out tomorrow and figure out which ones we'll take to the store. Satisfied?"

"Yes!" Annie jumped up from the table, put her dishes in the kitchen and ran to get her homework out of her backpack. Jake got his computer and headed towards his uncle's office. The old Jake would have gone back to his office in town, leaving evening parent duties to Sara. But Jake was changing. First out of necessity but as the years passed, he finally felt in his element as a single parent. Annie meant the world to him and he'd do anything to love and protect her.

***

By the time Alison got home, she was exhausted. Jenny had left the set hours ago and was there to greet her. "Welcome home, executive Rockwell!"

"I'm so tired! Can you believe this day? What happened?" She laughed but was dead serious. Her feet were killing her. She plopped down on the couch and Jenny promptly offered her a cup of tea.

"Here you go. I'll tell you what happened. You've been working incredibly hard, and life is giving you a chance to do something bigger. And you deserve it. Even if it's not in the publishing world, this promotion is surely going to open doors for you."

"I hope so. If it doesn't kill me first." Amused, Alison took a sip of tea. She was excited, yes, but scared too. She had never produced a show on her own, let alone one dependent on getting the best ratings ever during the holidays. It was a lot of pressure on her. Today had proved eye opening when she had to attend an executive meeting and realized the show's fate did hinge on how well their Christmas special rated when aired.

"Are there any leftovers? I'm starved."

"Already to pop in the microwave. I've got your back. Just take me with you when you hit the big time!"

"Very funny." Alison shook her head, grinning. "Thanks for dinner. I'm going to eat and then call Steve and tell him the news. I didn't have a chance all day."

"Good luck." Jenny was secretly hoping Alison would see Steve's true colors. She didn't like the way he took her for granted, and perhaps this situation would give Alison clarity she needed to make a change.

Retreating to her room, Alison sat on the edge of her bed and called Steve. He picked up right away. "I was just going to call you. Sorry, we couldn't get together for the holiday, but you know how my parents can be."

Not really, thought Alison, since she barely knew them. She had briefly met them once when they came into the city but had never spent any quality time with them. "I've been busy too. I have something I need to tell you." Alison proceeded to describe the day's events and her plans for the next couple of weeks. Steve listened and was anything but supportive.

"Sounds nice, Alison, but we have some plans too. Did you forget about the firm's Christmas gala on the twenty third? Or the firm's cocktail party tomorrow night with one of our biggest clients? There's a couple more you should have on your calendar too. What about our plans?"

No mention of how he wanted to see her, or he had missed her. Or good luck, this is great for your career. It was all about him. As usual. "Look, Steve. I'm sorry, but I'm going to do this. The time has come to put me first. I'll see if I can get away tomorrow for cocktails, but I have a ton to do to get ready. I hope you understand."

"Alright. Meet me tomorrow and we can talk about this more. I'll text you the address."

They chatted for a couple minutes and then hung up. Alison shook her head. Yes, she had prayed for a sign, and felt like a neon one was flashing in front of her. She sighed, got ready for bed and was out like a light as soon as her head hit the pillow.

***

Alison couldn't believe she was squeezing in a cocktail party with Steve. Just a couple of hours, and then she could return home and finish packing. Eager for the trip, she sensed a new path of creative freedom was opening up in front of her. Plus, no one would be bossing her around like Carolyn did every day.

Arriving at the venue, Alison looked around for Steve. Wearing a stylish, red cocktail dress that clung firmly to her slim figure, she brightly stepped into the bar area and was looking forward to seeing him, even after the recent disappointment. She saw him talking to some clients and walked over. Their eyes met, and he welcomed her into their discussion. After leaning over to kiss her on the cheek, he introduced her. "This is my girlfriend, Alison. I'm so proud of her. She just got a big promotion. Head producer for a television show."

Although Alison was slightly taken back by Steve's sudden support, everyone congratulated her. She smiled as she shook hands with each person. "Thank you. I'm looking forward to doing our annual Christmas special. I leave for the Berkshires tomorrow." Those standing next to her asked questions and seemed genuinely interested. Some members of the firm were entertainment lawyers. She chatted away, and Steve looked proud. Was he honestly proud of her or just happy it was good for his career? After an hour, she looked at her watch and asked Steve if they could go somewhere and talk privately. She wanted to talk about their relationship before she left.

As they found a quiet corner, Steve faced her. "Everyone was impressed by your new promotion."

Alison sighed. "I guess so. But I don't care what others think. I worked hard and did deserve this opportunity."

"Of course. I was just saying…"

"It was good for your image?"

"No, what do you mean? Our relationship is important, and I meant…I'm proud." He gently put his hand on her shoulder as he looked into her eyes.

"I'm not sure our relationship is important to you. I think we should reevaluate what we mean to each other during this time apart. I've thought about it, and I feel we want different things."

"What do you mean, different things?"

"I want a committed relationship. One where we spend more time together. I want to have children someday. Sooner than later."

Steve put his arm around her. "I do too. Just not now. But soon."

Alison looked up at him. This new job had given her the confidence she needed to make a change. "I've decided I want a break. I'll be away until after Christmas, and we can talk about it then." She stepped back from him and looked him square in the eyes. It didn't even matter what his response was going to be. She had made up her mind.

Steve was surprised. "I'm sorry you feel this way, but I think you're making a mistake. We'll have to discuss it after the holiday, and I know you'll change your mind." He grabbed her hand and pulled her closer. "I'm not ready to give up on us, Alison."

His unnerving gaze almost made Alison second guess herself, but she recovered quickly. "Yes, we'll see." Alison leaned up and kissed him on the cheek. "Merry Christmas, Steve." She turned and walked out of the restaurant. She smiled as she hailed a taxi. She liked the new woman she was becoming and was ready for the next adventure.

Chapter Three

Jake took his hand off the mouse and sat back in the chair, scanning the computer screen one last time. If all the numbers were correct, his projections showed a positive income flow within a year for his new imprint focusing on children's books and the latest venture in his Uncle's publishing company. He wanted to name the imprint Starlight Publishing and link it to the bookstore. Win, win for everyone. Yes, this could work.

Jake looked at his watch and realized the train would arrive soon, so he put on his coat and went downstairs. Seeing the store was busy with holiday shoppers, he walked over to Lucy. "I'm off to the station. Thanks for looking after Annie."

"No problem. She and Tim can finish their homework, and then we'll put the final touches on the Christmas decorations down here. I've been so busy today I might have to train one of them on using the cash register!"

"Maybe we need to hire another part-time person for the holidays. Why don't you put an ad together? See if anyone is interested."

"Okay, boss. You better get going! Don't want to be late for your high-level executive from the city!"

"You're right." Jake looked around and felt a sense of great pride. The store was bustling; the tree lights were shimmering; holiday music filled the air; and he knew once more he had made the best decision to leave New York. He wished Clara was here to see the success. A pang of guilt overtook him briefly as he reminisced about his marriage to her. He should have done something like this a long time ago. This town would have been the perfect place to pursue her artistic career. He looked up at the painting on the wall, the inspiration for the bookstore's name. It was her last painting, entitled *Starlight*, a genuinely magical masterpiece. The hope existing in the stars and stirring others to dream grounded him somehow. She would have been proud. He pulled the collar of his winter coat closer to his neck, trying to clear away the gnawing heartbreak still in his chest, then headed for his truck.

***

As Jake pulled into the train station, he wondered what kind of person Alison Rockwell would be. He hoped she was nice and not too power driven. After all, it was a kid's show. He had no idea what she looked like, but luckily Lucy had made a name sign in case a crowd of people were departing the train.

Alison hoped she had everything she needed in her suitcases and computer bag. She would be doing scouting, preparation, auditions of local kids and finishing scores of to-do lists. Supposedly the bookstore owner was picking her up. Anxious to see his shop, she was hoping it would be the perfect place for the literary segment of the show.

Jake walked closer, holding his sign, as people disembarked the train. Alison looked up and saw him. She waved her hand and stepped closer. My, he certainly is handsome, was her first thought. She felt a little butterfly in her stomach as he approached. She hoped he was a nice guy and reached out her hand. "Hi! I'm Alison. You must be the bookstore owner, right?"

"Jake Sanders at your service. My store manager made me a sign, so I could find you." He smiled, taking in this seemingly harmless woman.

Alison couldn't help but notice this man's deep, blue eyes and muscular physique as he hovered over her petite frame. All of a sudden, she felt shy. This is ridiculous. Get a grip, girl. You're here to do a big job. Not drool over your personal guide. "Thank you for picking me up. I just have a couple bags."

Jake grabbed the bags and pointed in the direction of his truck. "I'm over here. Watch your step. These sidewalks can be icy." He noticed she had fancy boots on, just like a New Yorker.

Alison saw him looking at her boots. "Don't worry. I brought work boots. I'll be okay." She slipped on the ice a moment later, but Jake grabbed her arm, so she didn't fall.

"You probably want to put them on soon."

Alison noticed his warm manner as he teased her. He seemed so genuine, yet she sensed an edge about him too.

Jake was surprised Alison was a younger woman. "Here we are. I hope you don't mind but I left the limo at home."

Alison laughed. "I grew up on my parent's farm not far from here in Connecticut. Trucks are better to haul things if needed. You are my guide for the show, right?"

Jake looked at her big, brown eyes and knew this woman was not what he had envisioned. She didn't resemble a snobbish know-it-all but appeared more down to earth. Good. It made his job easier. "Yes, I am. Now off to Anderson Estates and I'll show you around."

As they drove to town, Alison looked out at the landscape. Recent snow had blanketed the mountains and trees like a Currier and Ives' painting. But as Jake turned into the long driveway to the estate, Alison couldn't hold back a slight gasp. "Oh my! This is Anderson Estates?"

"Yep. Pretty impressive, huh? It's been in the Anderson family for generations. He's quite the generous guy, so I'm not surprised he offered his home to you." Jake wasn't sure he wanted her to know Jim was his uncle and part of the family. He liked keeping his personal life to himself.

"This is amazing! I can't believe I'm staying here! Will there be time to look around the town today?"

"First let's get you settled, and I'll introduce you to Sara. She's the housekeeper and will help you during your stay." As they passed the guest house, Jake pointed to it. "I live there, so if you need anything, I won't be far away."

Alison looked over at Jake. This guy was handsome, helpful and even had a sense of humor. Concentrating on her responsibilities could be challenging if he continued to be so kind and chivalrous, she mused to herself. "Good to know."

As they pulled up to the main door, Sara greeted them. "Come in and get out of the cold!" Sara took one of Alison's small bags and Jake took the larger ones. "I'm Sara and I will be your hostess—or one of them—for the next few weeks. Jake, would you put her bags in the last guest room at the end of the hall upstairs? I've got tea in the kitchen."

Jake took the bags upstairs, and Alison followed Sara into the kitchen. It was enormous and had a long breakfast bar at the end. "You sit down, and I'll bring you a cup and a little snack. Dinner won't be ready until six."

Overjoyed her life had taken such a complete turn, Alison climbed up on a chair. She knew she had a lot of responsibility in producing the show, but she already felt comfortable in this giant house. Sara exuded grandmother qualities, and Jake was possibly a distraction. But a welcomed one. Perhaps, he would be the extra push she needed to forget about Steve and make their break more permanent. Time would tell. Alison sat down and sipped her tea.

"Delicious! Thank you."

"My pleasure, dear. You must be tired from your trip, but I want you to know if you need anything, just let me know. I live in the back wing in a small apartment, but I'm usually busy in here."

"Will do." Alison turned her head and saw Jake standing in the hallway.

"I put your bags in your room. We can go over your itinerary later, but I have to get back to the store to pick up Annie, my daughter."

"You have a daughter?" Alison hadn't noticed a wedding ring.

"Yes, you'll meet her soon enough. She's quite excited about the show being filmed here. We'll be back in time for dinner."

Alison didn't feel tired at all. "Do you think I could tag along? I'd love to see the store and start sketching out some ideas."

"Sure, if you're not too tired."

"Are you kidding? I've got too much nervous energy to be tired!" Alison had never felt more alive as she stared into Jake's blue eyes.

Jake thought Alison seemed friendly, earnest, and not at all pretentious. Maybe this hosting gig wouldn't be so bad after all. "We leave in ten minutes. And you might want to change your shoe apparel."

Alison blushed, looking down at her high-heeled boots. "Yes, no problem."

Sara shook her head. "Jake, stop bossing our guest around and go finish whatever you have to finish."

Alison noticed the fondness Sara had for Jake and was starting to relax into her new working environment. And Jake. Definitely was easy on the eyes.

***

The ride into town was short, but Jake freely pointed out some historical sights to Alison. She noticed he took great pride in the city. She wondered if he had lived here long and what his real story was. His chiseled profile and rugged appearance were a fresh change from the busy, uptight men in suits in New York. She did appreciate a nice suit, but there was something very appealing about a man in a flannel shirt, worn jeans and work boots. It gave her some hometown comfort she hadn't experienced since moving to New York.

Alison's lips parted, uttering a tiny gasp as they pulled up to Starlight Books. White twinkling lights and bright, holiday décor lavishly bedecked the window, which framed a toy train sitting among an array of books. "Wow. This is your store?"

"Yep. Don't worry. Plenty of Christmas inside, thanks to my daughter and Lucy. It should work for your show."

As Jake and Alison entered, Annie ran to greet them. "Daddy!" She hugged him and then turned towards Alison, extending her hand. "Hello. My name is Annie Sanders and welcome to our store, Starlight Books. We're happy you're here!"

Jake shook his head, seeing how cordial Annie was being towards Alison. Thank goodness her sweet, perky self was returning.

Lucy stepped forward. "I'm Lucy Barnes, the manager. Anything you need while you're here, just ask me."

Alison eyes widened as she scanned the store. She was taken by surprise as her long-kept desire to be a writer rose from within, teasing her emotions. "It's perfect!"

Jake looked at her face. He was pretty good at reading people and noticed she was genuinely intrigued. There was something else in her eyes. But he couldn't quite figure it out. Something deeper. "Thanks. We like it."

Annie pulled her hand and motioned towards the rest of the

store. "Come on. I'll give you a tour."

Jake looked at Alison warmly. "Be my guest. Annie will take care of you. I need to finish up some details with Lucy. Then we'll head back to the house later for dinner."

Annie gave a grand tour of all the nooks and crannies in the shop. The children's section was in the back, filled with overstuffed chairs, pillows, and enough room to entertain at least thirty children on the floor. Beautiful artwork hung on the wall and one large piece caught Alison's eye. It was a painting of a bright star shining over a majestic mountain scene with a waterfall and other stars gleaming in the night sky. The colors used were ethereal, with an enchanting impression drawing in the beholder. Alison looked at the artist's name written on the bottom. Clara Sanders. "This is exquisite! Who is the artist?"

Annie proudly replied, "My mom."

Was Jake married? "She's an incredible artist. Does she work here, too?" Alison didn't know why, but felt a slight disappointment thinking Jake was a married man.

Annie suddenly looked down at the ground. "No, she died a few years ago."

Alison immediately felt saddened when looking over at Annie. "I'm so sorry." Alison wondered if Jake was still grieving the loss of his wife. She imagined he was struggling to raise a daughter by himself. It couldn't be easy.

"We named the bookstore after this painting. To remember her. We think she looks over us, like the star does in the painting."

Annie looked up at Alison with her effervescent, blue eyes. Alison gently touched her shoulder. "I'm sure she is watching over you like special stars do."

Observing from afar, Jake slowly approached them. "I see you found our children's corner. Do you think it will be big enough for the shoot?"

Alison held tight to her emotions as she looked up at Jake, realizing he was a widower. Her thoughts lingered for a moment, but she brought herself back to reality. "Yes! Let me take some pictures and I'll be ready to head back." She pulled out her phone and went off to gather photos of everything.

Jake watched her for a minute before returning to the front of the store. "Come to the front when you're ready."

"Will do. Thanks." As she took the pictures her mind kept drifting off to the painting. It could have been the cover to her new book, *The Brightest Star*. Was it a sign to keep writing? Seeing the image had given her chills, and whatever the message was, she would have to wait.

***

After dinner, Annie invited Alison to their tree decorating in the living room. "Daddy and I are going to decorate a tree tonight. Do you want to help?"

Jake didn't want Alison to feel pressured into anything. "I'm sure Ms. Rockwell is tired and has plenty to do with her planning."

Alison's holiday obsession could not be hindered. "I'd love to. I had to leave early before I decorated our tree at home. Jenny and I always go all out for the holidays. We love Christmas." She looked over at Jake and found those deep, blue eyes staring at her. Slightly unnerving, it made her blush.

"Who's Jenny?" asked Annie.

"She's my best friend and roommate. In fact, you'll get to meet her. She works on the show and will be here a few days before filming. She does hair and make-up for the cast."

"Cool!" Annie wondered who else would be coming to Maple Ridge.

"Let's clear the dishes for Sara and then we'll get the decorations. You still have school tomorrow, so don't think we're staying up late." Seeing Annie's exuberant expression warmed Jake's heart. He'd have to tell Uncle Jim what a good idea this had been for her.

Jake's sincere father-daughter relationship was attractive to Alison. "You sure have an enthusiastic little girl. She's lovely."

"Thanks. But most of the credit goes to her mom. She was an amazing mother. Thank God she was with us for the first six years of Annie's life. She still remembers her." Jake grabbed some more dishes and headed towards the kitchen, wanting to keep this part of his life still private.

Alison could sense some sadness in Jake's voice. She imagined he tried hard to hide it from Annie, but his feelings were quite visible when the little girl wasn't around. He was still in pain. Celebrating the holidays without his wife couldn't be easy.

Jake came out of the kitchen and proceeded to bring boxes into the living room. The three of them engaged in opening boxes, stringing lights, laughed and hanging ornaments. Annie made sure to show Alison all of her favorites. Sara put Christmas music on and brought in hot cocoa with cookies when they were almost finished. "Here you go. You've been hard-working elves and deserve a break soon."

They sat down on the couch, grabbed a mug and admired their work. "Now, it looks like Christmas!" Annie said.

Jake noticed how easily Alison talked with Annie and how relaxed she seemed with children. He guessed he should have known, since she was a producer of a children's show, but high-level executives can be tense and annoying. She had none of those qualities.

Alison realized Jake was staring at her. She avoided his glance before he could see her cheeks flushing red. So far, this trip had been nothing like she thought it would be. And it was only the first night. What an adventure this was turning out to be. Even with all of the stress and work ahead of her.

Jake looked at his watch. "Time for bed. School tomorrow."

"I know, Dad."

"Let's get your things and say goodnight to Miss Rockwell."

"Please. Call me Alison." Alison wasn't used to such formality, but suspected she better get used to it.

Annie got her things, put on her coat and came over to Alison. She hugged her and said, "Thanks, Alison for helping us decorate"

Jake walked over and said, "Thanks for helping out. You didn't have to, but I'm glad you did." His eyes locked onto hers and didn't waver. "Listen, get some sleep, and tomorrow morning I'll help you set up a production office in the library. I think it will suit your needs."

"Thank you." Alison felt those butterflies again in her stomach. *What was happening?*

After the two of them left, Sara came out of the kitchen. "Let me know if you need anything in your room. I'm sure I'll be up before you, so come on down when you're ready for coffee."

"Thanks for everything, Sara. All of you have been wonderful hosts."

"No problem. Get some rest."

Rest. All of a sudden, she was feeling drained. Emotional energy was surging throughout her body with no place to go. Tomorrow she knew she had to hit the ground running. She needed to get a reality check, because she knew this whole production wasn't going to be easy.

Chapter Four

Alison awoke to the smell of fresh coffee and something delicious originating from downstairs. Walking into the kitchen, she found Sara at the stove counter, whipping ingredients together for a healthy breakfast. "Good morning! Have a seat. Coffee?"

Alison slid into the comfy chair at the breakfast bar. "Yes, please. I'm going to need it today." She looked around and wondered if Jake was around.

Sara must have read her mind. "Jake took Annie to school and will be back shortly to help you set up your production office. Now, what do you want for breakfast? Eggs? Pancakes?"

"Eggs and toast would be great. Thanks. You sure you don't want any help?"

"Absolutely not. This is my job and I love it. How did you sleep?"

"Like a rock. All the excitement must have worn me out, but I'm ready to get started on all the prep work." Alison was curious to find out more information about Jake. "Annie seems like a great kid. Did they always live in Maple Ridge?"

"No. When Clara was alive, they lived in Manhattan. I'd say Jake was a different man then. He worked at a prominent investment firm in the city and was consumed by a fast-paced lifestyle. He and Clara loved each other immensely but I think he regrets not spending enough time with them as a family. He often worked late, but Clara always supported him. She understood his drive to succeed and made sure Annie was loved and cared for emotionally, even in his absence at times. Clara's death was devastating for him, and he realized he needed to make a big change to be a reliable parent for Annie. So, they moved here—where he has some childhood memories and could establish a more stable lifestyle for his daughter."

"He was an investment banker?" Alison certainly had a different picture in her mind meeting him now.

"Put an MBA to use right out of graduate school. He was fast tracked quickly and became very successful at a large investment company. But losing a loved one can change a person." Sara looked up and saw Jake's truck pulling into the back driveway. "Here he is now."

Alison was beginning to see a whole new side of this man. She wondered how he felt about going from a high-end job to running a bookstore? Did he feel a sadness or loss?

The door opened, and Jake walked in. "Brrr. That cold air is nippy. Hope you got your winter clothes unpacked." He looked straight at Alison.

A slight tingle went up Alison's spine. "I think I have everything I need. If not, I'm sure you have a store in this town, right?" She laughed.

"It's not New York, but we manage." He realized he was actually enjoying Alison's company and felt lighter these last twenty-four hours. "I'll unload my truck and start setting you up in the library. I brought a white board and some office materials for you, but I imagine the network is providing you with supplies as well."

"They shipped everything, like a printer, supplies, and other stuff to the post office. Do you think we could swing by there, later?"

"Sure. Finish your breakfast and I'll show you the library."

"Thank you." Her phone rang. Carolyn didn't waste any time checking up on her. Alison looked up at Jake. "I've got to take this. It's my boss."

"The library is down the hall to the left if you need privacy."

Alison jumped up and headed towards the library, closing the door behind her. "Hi, Carolyn. How are you feeling?"

"I'm fine. I'm fine. Just can't move around too well with this cast. I just want to make sure we're on track with everything up there. Do you have a production timeline ready, yet? You know, this is the biggest show of the year, and everything has to be perfect. I'm counting on you and don't forget my name is still on this show."

Alison's neck muscles tightened. Here we go. Even with the distance between them, Carolyn quickly rattled off her demands. "Yes, we're setting up as you speak. Jake is taking me to pick up supplies and I should have a timeline in place by tomorrow." Even though she was feeling a new confidence, Carolyn had a way of messing with her self-esteem. But Alison was determined not to be bullied by her now.

"Who's Jake?"

"My host the network hired. He's a local and has been very kind so far. He owns the bookstore where we'll film the finale. I'll send you some pictures later. It's perfect."

"I may be at home, but I'm going to be involved as much as I can, understand? Let me know the moment you run into any problems."

"I will. I have to go. Jake is bringing in supplies now."

"Good. Talk to you later." Then she hung up.

As Jake walked into the library, he noticed the look on Alison's face. Her bright, cheery demeanor had morphed into to a worried frown. "Everything alright?"

"Yes. It's just, my boss—can be a little overbearing. And not so nice." She didn't know if she should open up to Jake, although she was beginning to feel very comfortable around him.

"Don't worry. We have everything under control."

We. Alison noticed he used the word *we*, to reassure her she wasn't in this alone. She took a deep breath. "Right! Let me help you with the board." She suddenly noticed the beauty of the room. Hundreds of books lined the shelves, while large sofas with velvet pillows and over-stuffed chairs were arranged neatly upon elegant oriental rugs woven in rich hues. A large fireplace with an elaborate, ornate design of brocaded brass around its mantel edges made the room even more enticing. "This room is beyond beautiful! Are you sure Mr. Anderson is okay with us using it?"

"He's totally fine. He even suggested it."

"I've never met him, but he has a great reputation."

Jake thought about telling Alison who Jim Anderson really was to him but decided against it. At least for now.

Alison wanted to make sure there was a calculated flow to the room, so the production staff could move freely around and not get in each other's way. She turned to Jake. "Do you think we can pick up the supplies now? I'd like to get everything in here, so I can start mapping out the shoot." Keeping busy would make her less stressed. As long as she was moving, she couldn't doubt herself.

"Let me call Lucy and let her know I'll be in later. We're hiring an extra staff person for the holiday rush, so I'm all yours." A big grin spread over his face and Alison felt the butterflies again. She couldn't deny the feelings stirring inside of her. The attention she received from him was a welcomed gift. It had been a long time since a man acted so thoughtful towards her. Even if it was just for work.

While Jake was out of the room, Jenny called. "There's my friend! I've been worried about you! Is everything okay? What's our host like? Did you see any of the town yet?"

"Yes, A picturesque town, kind people, and a helpful host. Jake and I are picking up supplies, so I can't chat long. I can't wait until you get here!"

"Jake? Tell me more! Is he a nice guy?"

"Yes, and rather handsome, too. But I can't talk now. I'll call you tonight."

"You better! I want to hear all about it. And this Jake guy. More details please."

Alison laughed. "Of course."

No sooner had she hung up when Jake appeared at the doorway. "Ready?"

Alison looked up at him. "Yes, just let me get my coat and purse upstairs. Thank you for doing this."

"No problem. I'll be in the truck."

It was a short ride to the post office and everything had arrived on time. Jake and Alison chatted about the show, her plans, and places she needed to line up for the multiple shoots. When they got back to the house, Jake helped her set up tables and arrange the computers and work stations. The network was sending a film crew with a mobile unit to oversee most of the editing. This temporary office was mainly for pre-production.

When everything had been set up, Jake asked, "Do you have everything you need?"

Alison marveled at how quickly they had set it all up. "Should more than suffice. Thank you so much." She looked over at the roaring fire Sara had prepared and smiled at the coziness of the room. "Much better than a cold, stark office in the city!"

Jake nodded his head. "Be careful. You may get spoiled working in the country," he said, giving her an amused look.

"I know. Don't tempt me!" She laughed. "I need to look over my plans, but can we scout out some more places this afternoon?"

"Sure, but I need to pick up Annie today. Can't make Lucy do all my work.

"I'll be organized so we can do it quickly. Annie can come along with us if we don't get done."

"She'd love to, but don't let her get in your way. She can be overly zealous at times."

"Remember, this is a children's show. It would be helpful to get a child's perspective if I need it. She can be an honorary consultant." Alison was beaming and loved being in charge.

"I'm starved. Sara made lunch so let's take a break."

"I'll be right there." Alison needed a moment to herself. Working closely with Jake made it tough to focus at times. She wanted to make sure she didn't forget any details.

***

Alison and Jake drove to the recreation center next to the church, jointly owned by the church and the city. Jake thought it would be an ideal place for auditions and possibly more. Marilyn, the center's director, was waiting for them when they arrived.

"Come on in and I'll show you around. Jake told me all about your show and we're ready to help." Marilyn was a spunky, middle-aged woman with never-ending energy. She had lost her husband ten years ago and had found much needed solace and fulfillment in her job at the center.

As Alison walked in, she knew immediately it would be a significant filming site. The largest room was adorned with Christmas lights threaded in pine boughs holding red velvet bows and homemade ornaments scattered on the tables and walls, reflecting a celebratory mood. "Your space is lovely!" She looked at Jake with a big grin. He appeared pleased with himself.

"Jake, why don't you show her around? I have some business to attend to in my office, so come find me when you're ready."

"I already know I want to film a couple activities here, so yes, we'll come find you."

Jake pointed towards the back. "Right this way." He realized playing host to this vibrant woman made facing the holidays a tad bit easier. Clara had loved Christmas and always made sure to create an atmosphere in their home filled with fun and laughter for Annie and himself. Just the thought of her brought a heaviness to his heart. After several years, he still felt an aching that seemed to linger on no matter how much he tried to let it go.

As they walked around, Alison noticed a bulletin board in the back of the main room with a poster describing the town's annual toy drive. It gave her an idea. She turned to Jake. "What's this?"

"The fire and police department come together with the town every year to sponsor a toy drive for less fortunate kids. Gifts are distributed to a children's home on the outskirts of town, and other families. Why?"

"What if we make a service project part of the show this year? We've never done it, and I think it could be inspiring!"

"How so?" Jake was intrigued.

"For one, we could bring the kids here to help wrap presents. And maybe our arts and crafts section could be about making gifts and ornaments for those in need. What do you think?"

"I think it's an awesome idea." On top of everything else, this woman had a big heart, too.

"I guess with a new idea I'll have to run it by the network, but I think they might like it." Letting her artistic talents find an outlet was exhilarating. Even if it wasn't writing, it gave Alison a sense of satisfaction. Following her dream but making a creative detour along the way.

Jake pointed toward the large kitchen. "You could do a cooking segment here, but there's a bakery in town you might like. The owner is a friend of mine, and the exposure could help her business. We'll stop there too."

"You haven't steered me wrong yet." As they came out of the kitchen, she noticed large wooden doors in the back. "Where do those go?"

"A walkway into the church next door. Want to see it?"

"Yes!"

Alison followed Jake through the doors and down a hallway. He opened a second set of doors and she found herself standing in a quiet alcove with pine wreaths draped on magnificent mahogany beams, lit candles and more holiday adornment. "Right through there is the church and down the hall is Reverend Michael's office. There's much more on the other side of the church, like the Sunday school and other offices. Most people in town attend this church and love the Reverend."

"Can we go inside the church?" Alison missed going to a small-town church like this one. She had never found a church in New York with a community feeling like the one she grew up attending in Connecticut.

Jake nodded and proceeded through the alcove.

"Do you mind if I light a candle?" Once inside, a spiritual serenity surrounded Alison, reminding her of the true meaning of Christmas.

"I'll wait here," said Jake.

Alison walked towards the back of the church, looking up at the exquisite paintings of holy scenes. She lit a candle, closed her eyes and silently said a prayer. She was genuinely grateful for this opportunity to express herself and for meeting such wonderful people as Jake, Sara and Annie. Jake. Asking for support and guidance, she knew she needed help from a higher power to manage this vast undertaking successfully.

Moving toward Jake, she noticed he was staring at her again. She responded with a warm glance. "I'm ready to go. I just wanted to pray for a successful production. Before things get crazy as I know they will."

"Definitely can't hurt." He was discovering this woman had faith in addition to being sweet. Jake looked at his watch. "Sorry, but we have to go, or we'll be late picking up Annie. I can bring you back here tomorrow if you like."

"Yes, thanks."

***

Annie's sapphire eyes widened even further as she climbed into the back of the truck, ready to join Alison and her dad on an adventure. "Where are we going now?"

Jake laughed at his precocious little girl. Even though she was only nine, she seemed mature in many ways. Going through a tragedy changes a young person, or any person. But she was still a little girl, and Jake wanted to make sure she experienced all the joys of a normal childhood.

"I thought we could take Alison to the Sweet Ridge Bakery to look at their kitchen and facility. What do you think?"

Annie's face beamed as she looked at Alison. "They have the best gingerbread cookies ever!"

Alison was finding Annie more and more endearing and wanted her to be part of the main cast for the show. Even if it might show favoritism. After all, it was show biz. "I love gingerbread cookies. Let's go!"

When they entered the bakery, Alison was engulfed by the aromas of fresh baked goods, coffee and hot chocolate. The ambience was lovely and if the kitchen was big enough, it might work for the show's cooking segment. She wanted to do a piece on different kinds of Christmas cookies, including gingerbread characters. Jake approached the counter and asked to see Christine, the owner.

A couple of minutes later, an attractive woman in her early thirties walked out of the kitchen and when she saw Jake, she immediately went over and gave him a big hug. "Jake! I didn't know when you were coming. I would have prepared a professional tasting for the producer." Alison noticed she had touched Jake's arm and her smile was bordering flirtatious. Was this Jake's girlfriend? Or was she just reading into something?

Jake raised his hand toward Alison. "This is Alison Rockwell, the show's producer." Then he motioned to Christine. "And Christine Murphy. Baker extraordinaire!"

She smiled at him and then faced Alison. "Very nice to meet you. Jake told me he might bring you by since you were scouting different locations for your show. Feel free to try anything you see, and then come to the kitchen, the most important part. Annie can recommend her favorites to you." It was apparent they already had a relationship.

Annie looked up at Alison. "You and dad sit down, and I'll pick out a few things to sample."

Christine spoke to her staff behind the counter. "And bring them our house specialty gingerbread."

Jake and Alison sat at a table while Annie brought them treats. Alison nibbled bites of the different cookies, sighing with contented pleasure. "These are delicious! Does she do all the baking herself?" Alison was curious to find out more about this charming baker.

"She does most of it, or at least all the recipes. This was her mother's bakery, and when her mother passed away five years ago, she took over. It's been in their family for generations. She definitely knows what she's doing." Jake was amused watching Alison swoon over the baked goods. "She wants to expand into an online business with some specialty items. She just finished a re-model of the kitchen, so I think you will be pleasantly surprised when you see it."

Annie piped in. "She taught me how to make the gingerbread cookies and sometimes I come here after school." She looked at her dad. "If he lets me."

"Yes, if she doesn't have any homework. Christine has been very generous with her time since we moved here. Annie loves baking."

Alison imagined Christine had more in mind than helping Annie. She saw the way she looked at Jake. Any woman would notice. "Let's go take a look then. I don't need to eat all of the cookies in here!"

When they entered the kitchen, Alison's mouth fell open. For a small-town bakery, she thought it would be small. But they had expanded out the back, making it large enough to become a commercial bakery. "I'm impressed. I would never have guessed it looked like this." Alison walked through, taking notes and photos while Jake and Christine stood and chatted. Alison was still wondering about their relationship and if they were interested in each other. But she couldn't let herself become distracted more than she already was. When she finished, she joined them.

"I think this could work. I have to go back to the house and look at everything, but I can let you know this weekend."

"We feel fortunate to be considered for the cooking part." Christine placing her hand on Jake's arm. "And this guy has been helping me with my expansion. His business sense came in handy. I would never have been able to do it without his help."

"He seems to have many talents." Yes, she was definitely into him.

"Enough about me. We better head over to the house. I'll bring you back whenever you want, Alison." Jake had been spending time with Christine, but he hadn't been interested in dating her. He sensed she was interested, but Jake wasn't ready yet. He enjoyed her company, but he found he only missed Clara more when he was alone. With such a profound loss, he wondered if he would ever indeed be happy again. He found he was more concerned for Annie's emotional well-being and figured his could wait. At night though, he would find himself lying in bed with overwhelming feelings of sadness, but he kept his emotions in check during the day. At least he thought he did.

Alison was ready to go, too. "Thanks, Jake. I almost forgot. I have to get back to the house for a conference call. It was nice meeting you, Christine. I'll be in touch." She gathered up her notebook and turned to leave. Annie was there to greet her with a bag of cookies.

"Just in case we get hungry!"

Alison laughed. "Yes, thank you." Alison and Annie got in the truck and Jake followed after them.

"I think we had a successful day, don't you, Miss Rockwell?" Jake looked over at Alison and then at Annie in the back seat who was grinning ear to ear.

"Yes, we did, Mr. Sanders. Yes, we did." Alison's heart seemed to flutter like crazy with every interaction with Jake. And she didn't want it to stop.

"Now off to Anderson Estates. Sara will wonder where we are!" Alison appreciated the time and care Jake was giving her. She had to remind herself he was probably being paid a nice sum to do so. She hadn't even looked at the budget yet. She needed to buckle down tomorrow in her office and make sure her timeline was going to work. Carolyn would most likely be calling her soon, and often. Even though she was directly reporting to George Stevens for this show, Carolyn wasn't going to let anything slip by her. And Alison knew there was more at stake with this Christmas special. It had been made clear to her at the meeting before she left. Ratings had been slipping and if the ratings weren't high enough, the show might be canceled. And Alison wasn't going to let that happen. Not on her watch.

Chapter Five

Staring out her window, Carolyn contemplated her involvement with *Hands-On Kids*. After researching this Jake guy, she discovered he was Jim Anderson's nephew and decided she needed to have a little chat with him. At this point, Alison probably had no clue who Jake was, and she could use it to her advantage to develop her relationship with him. Let him know who the real boss was.

Snickering to herself, she phoned the bookstore where he worked, and Jake picked up. Carolyn mustered all her niceness possible to schmooze Mr. Anderson's nephew. "Hello, Mr. Sanders. I wanted to introduce myself to you. I'm Carolyn Parks, the main producer for *Hands-On Kids*. Alison Rockwell is helping me out while I'm healing from a silly ski accident."

A warning signal coiled inside Jake. "Yes, I've heard your name from Alison. What can I do for you?"

"I wanted to give you my contact information in case you had any questions or concerns while my show is filming in your community. We want to do our best for your uncle." Carolyn proceeded to outline her distinguished history in the production world while Jake squirmed in his chair, anxious to end the call. "Tell your uncle not to worry. I'm still very involved." Satisfaction roused a cunning expression to spread slowly across her face.

"From what I've seen, you needn't have any worries."

"Nice to hear."

"I'll transfer you to my assistant, and she can take your information. Take care."

"I will. Nice chatting with you."

A strange premonition lodged in Jake's gut. He wanted to tell

Alison about the phone call but couldn't because he hadn't discussed his personal life with her yet. Time was ticking.

***

Alison's head was bent over, scouring documents, budgets, schedules and timelines spread out on her desk. Jake had agreed to take her to the community center after lunch to set up Saturday's auditions. Absorbed in her thoughts, she barely moved when a knock came at the door. "Come in," she said.

Alison kept working, thinking Sara was coming in with another mug of fresh coffee and then noticed Jake looming above her. "Are you ready?"

Startled, she found herself gazing at Jake's friendly glance. "Oh, my gosh! What time is it? I completely lost track of time." She started to gather her papers and clean up, quickly trying to get ready.

"No worries. I can see you're busy."

"Yes, but I want to go to the center. I have to."

Jake turned towards the door but stopped and looked back at Alison. "I haven't eaten yet and I suppose you haven't either. How about I get Sara to make us a couple sandwiches before we leave?"

He seemed to think of everything. "Yes, I'm starving. I'll be there in a minute."

Alison organized her mess, then found Jake setting the kitchen bar table with their sandwiches, chips and drinks. "Sara made chicken salad. Hope you like it."

Alison plopped down into the comfort of her bar chair. "This is perfect! I'm famished. I guess I've been so busy I overlooked the time." She looked up at Jake. Hard to think of him as a high-power businessman like Steve with an intense drive for advancing his career.

He seemed so laid back, yet extremely capable. She wondered if Steve would ever be this thoughtful and giving to her, although she knew it was unfair to compare the two. Jake was very different from Steve. Watching him with his daughter, Sara, and the friends in town, she knew relationships of all kinds were important to him. But there were moments when she imagined he was not done grieving the loss of his wife.

As they ate, Alison described her plans for the auditions on Saturday. Jake offered to help in any way. "How many shows have you done for this company? Is this always what you wanted to do?" he inquired.

"There's something I need to tell you, but I'm going to ask that you keep it to yourself." Alison paused, then decided perhaps she should open up to Jake and let him know the truth. After all, he was helping her, and she was beginning to trust him.

Jake put down his sandwich, giving Alison his full attention.

Alison bit her bottom lip, then lifted her eyes to meet his gaze. "This is my first show as head producer. I've assisted Carolyn for several years and when she injured her leg in a skiing accident, the network selected me to take her place for this episode. I guess Carolyn suggested me because she knew she could control me better than if they brought in a seasoned producer." She laughed at herself. "I've been working on the show for a few years, so I know what takes place, but I've never been responsible for the whole thing. Of course, the crew knows, but I need all the new contacts to think I've been doing this for a long time. So, they'll respect me. But working closely with you, I feel it's only fair if I tell you the whole truth. If I start to flounder or look unusually stressed, you'll understand."

Now all of Jake's previous thoughts about her made sense. She was a young woman with a new opportunity and a chance to express herself. To be successful while still innocent and full of wonder pursuing a new career. It just made him want to help her more. "Thanks for telling me. But watching you these last couple days, I can honestly say, you've got this. I appreciate you being so honest with me." Jake knew he needed to share his secret about his identity as well. Soon, but not quite yet. But Carolyn's call haunted him.

"Thank you. Now you know the reality behind the scenes. So far, everything seems to be running smoothly. But anything can happen!" She hoped she hadn't made a mistake by telling him the truth of the situation, but she believed being honest was the best way to live.

"I understand. Let's finish up here and head over to the center. I called earlier, and Marilyn will be waiting."

"If you aren't careful, you could end up as an associate producer on the show. I'll even give you a credit." She playfully joked.

"As I said before, whatever you need."

"You may be sorry later." The bantering between the two of them seemed effortless.

"I certainly hope not." Jake grinned. "Let's get going before I change my mind."

"Okay. I wouldn't want you to bale on me now."

As Alison stood up to go, Jake reached over and picked up her coat for her. As he held it, his hand accidentally touched her hair and face. It was quite innocent, but Alison felt a tingle up her spine as he came so close to her. Better hurry to the truck she thought. Definitely need some fresh air. With two and half weeks to go, she needed to pace herself and her emotions.

***

Marilyn, happy to help organize the event, was waiting for them when they arrived. It was more excitement than they had seen in ages. She had one room set up for private auditions, with registration tables in the larger space.

"Probably all the kids in town will be coming. You may be overwhelmed with a response. Are you prepared?" Marilyn was concerned Alison would be flooded with giggling, rambunctious children of all ages, anxious to be on television.

"Believe me. I know what can happen. Back in New York they can be lined up around the block when we have an extra call like this. But eventually we sort it out. I have one of my production assistants arriving later tonight, so I won't be alone. Would you mind volunteering as well? Perhaps you know one or two parents who would be willing to help? It's too cold to wait outside, so everyone will have to wait in here. I have the call times staggered out by age groups which will help. We need to get the child's personal information, make some notes about personality and desires, and then figure it out back in the office with a master plan. You'll see. I'm hoping all those interested will get to do something. But I will need a core group of two to three kids in every segment with our New York cast."

Alison eyes rested on Jake who was just staring at her. "Will you help me set up the tables in the small room? I want to make it as comfortable as possible for the kids. So, they're not nervous."

"I'm right behind you. Show me what you want me to do."

Jake and Alison efficiently worked together, arranging the tables and chairs, creating a more intimate space for the kids and their interviews. When they were done, Alison said, "I have to order some refreshments for the main hall and in here. Let's talk to Marilyn."

"She's done this kind of thing a hundred times before." Jake liked watching Alison work. She was kind to others, energetic and, so far, didn't even seem stressed.

Alison discussed the rest of the details with Marilyn and was satisfied everything would be in order tomorrow. When she got a phone call from her office, she stepped aside to take it. "Hi, Henry! What's up? Are you still coming tonight?"

Henry was her favorite production partner. They had worked seamlessly together for a few years as assistants and associate producers on the show. Being his boss, she was hoping nothing would change between the two of them. "I'll be there around eight. I've got directions to the inn so no need to wait up for me. I don't know what the traffic will be like coming out of the city. Anything else you want me to bring?"

"I'll email you a few more things I need and send you directions to the center. But I may be able to pick you up in the morning. I have to check with Jake first." She didn't want to appear as if she expected him to be there for her every whim and desire.

"Who's Jake?"

"Jake is the man the network hired to be our host. He's been wonderful. You'll like him. Text me when you get in, and I'll see you in the morning."

Henry was looking forward to getting out of the city and working with Alison. A welcomed reprieve from Carolyn.

Alison found Jake standing in the back with Marilyn. He looked up at her when she approached. "Everything alright?"

"Yes. Henry, my assistant will be here later tonight and will be staying at the inn. Do you think we could pick him up tomorrow when we come back?"

"Sure. I've got the day planned to be here. We'll have to put Annie to work, though." He knew she would be too hyper to stay home.

Marilyn spoke up. "She can help me with the refreshments. Believe me, there will be plenty to do."

"Wonderful! I think we have our team in place." Alison couldn't believe how much she was actually enjoying her job. Being around Jake enhanced matters, but whatever the reason, she was glad.

"I have to go to the bookstore after this. Annie went there after school with her friend, Tim. Hope you don't mind." Jake wanted to make sure he could keep his personal life in order regardless of the extra responsibility of taking care of Alison.

"Of course. I want to make sure I have my calculations correct as to how many kids we can get in there for the last shoot."

"Lucy can help if you need it. She's been in charge of book signings and readings. We don't do many of them, but I hope to do more in the new year." Jake wanted to expand doing readings with his new imprint and tie it to the bookstore.

Alison bent her head to one side as she paused for a second, imagining her favorite part of the show. "Yes, I can use any help I can get."

***

Annie was helping Lucy at the register, bagging customer's purchases. Tim was in the back, helping the new girl unpack boxes of books to put on the shelves. Jake laughed when he saw his daughter. "Am I going to have to start paying you, too?"

Annie looked up at them. "If you want to. I mean I could always use the money." She flashed a mischievous grin at her dad.

Annie had an amusing personality, and Jake knew it was starting to resurface again. The death of her mother had hit her hard and for the last few years, with the help of Sara, his uncle and the bookstore, he had seen her emerge from a dark cloud of deep despair. Moving to Maple Ridge had been the best decision for both of them. Perhaps he could take a lesson on healing from his own daughter. "Let me think about it. How's her skills, Lucy?"

Lucy placed her hand on Annie's shoulder. "Better than most. Not a lazy bone in her body!"

"Did you do your homework?"

"Dad!" she protested. "It's the weekend! I'll do it later. Please?"

"Okay, but this is going to be a busy weekend. Auditions for the show are tomorrow at the center and we are both helping Alison."

"Really?" Annie looked up at Alison. "What do I do?"

Alison was happy Marilyn had thought of a job for her. She would be too busy with the interviews. "Marilyn thought you could help with the refreshments."

"Can I audition?" Annie's eyes were wide with anticipation.

Alison had already made a decision to put Annie in most of the segments as a town regular. "I do know the producer. I think I may be able to get you in."

Annie ran around the counter and wrapped her arms around Alison in a huge hug. "Thank you! You won't be sorry!"

Alison put her hand on the girl's shoulder affectionately. "I'm sure I won't." In reality, Annie had the perfect personality for one of the regular spots.

Meanwhile, Jake had been watching the two of them together. His heart began to melt as he saw Annie reach out to Alison, soaking in all of her nurturing qualities. A female touch was sorely missing for his daughter these last few years. "Let's let Miss Rockwell finish her work, and then we'll all go home for dinner."

Annie released her hold on Alison. "I'll be in the back with my tape measure. And Lucy, if you don't mind, can you show me how you normally set up for readings?"

"Let me get Cindy on the register and I'll be right there."

Jake said, "I'll be upstairs in my office if you need me. I have a few things to attend to before we go back to the house."

Relishing the atmosphere of children's books, Alison began measuring. Lucy made suggestions for moving furniture around and opening up the space. As she finished her notes, Jake came around the corner.

"Get everything you need?"

"I think so. I'll work on a floorplan this weekend." She looked around again. "I love this store and space, Jake. You have something very special here."

"I think so too. I'm looking forward to expanding the business."

"I'd love to hear about it sometime. I miss the literary world." Being in the store reminded Alison of her true dream. To be an author of children's books.

"You do? I thought you were into television production and climbing that ladder of success."

Alison looked up at him with her innocent, brown eyes. "Oh, no. Don't tell anyone but my real love entails books. I always wanted to be a children's author. I studied literature in college and always planned to get an entry job at a publishing company in New York. But nothing was available, and bills were mounting. Jenny was able to get me a job on this television show, so I decided to put my dream on hold for a while. But don't get me wrong. Producing is a great gig. And with this promotion, I'm getting to use my artistic abilities, which I'm grateful for. Someday I'll get back to my literary dreams."

"Do you still want to write?" Jake was more than intrigued now.

"I still do. When I have the time. I just finished a children's picture book and my mother has given me some drawings that may be perfect for the illustrations. Hopefully, I'll get a little break after this production and finish it."

"I'd love to see it if you don't mind." Maybe there was more than one reason their paths had crossed.

"I did bring it, in case I had time to write. Crazy idea since I've got enough on my plate." She lifted a brow with a smile lurking at the corners of her mouth.

"Either way, I still want to see what you have. If you're ready." Jake didn't want to push her, but he wanted to see if she had as much talent writing as she did in producing television.

Alison tilted her head. "I could be. Let's see how it goes." Alison wasn't sure she was ready to show her work yet, but she was beginning to trust Jake more and more. After all, he was a bookstore owner. He had to know something about book publishing.

***

After dinner, Alison was deep into the planning process, crouched over her desk with papers strewn in front of her, when Jenny called. Rubbing the back of her neck, she dropped her pen and gladly picked up the call. "Hi! I miss you. I can't wait until you come."

"Are you kidding? I'm counting the days. I almost jumped in the car with Henry." She tossed her long curly hair back, laughing to herself. "And Jake. It sounds like you may have some other interest in him. I hear a lilt in your voice whenever you've mentioned him to me."

"No distractions while I'm working, so don't get any ideas!" Alison knew her friend was right, but she was determined to keep her feelings in check, producing the best show she could do.

"I guess I'll have to see for myself. Listen, I have to go, but I'll talk to you this week."

"Thanks, Jen. I've arranged for you to stay with me at the Anderson Estate. The rest of the crew will be at the inn in town. One of the perks of being the boss!"

"Awesome!"

"See you soon." As Alison hung up the phone, she caught a glimpse of Jake poking his head around the door.

"Just checking to see if you need anything else tonight. I've got to put Annie to bed or at least try. She may be too excited to sleep." Jake chuckled. He realized he was getting used to Alison living in the big house, and he liked it.

"No, I think I'm good. Listen, thank you for today and everything you've done over the last few days. You've made it easier for me. And I hope you will keep the personal things I've shared with you to yourself. I don't need the network knowing I have other aspirations than television!" She laughed.

"Your secret is safe with me." Jake started to leave but glanced over his shoulder before going. "I'll see you in the morning. I know you'll want to get an early start."

"You're getting to know me." Her dazzling eyes locked into his for a brief moment, lingering in the air with some underlying expectancy. "Henry texted me a few minutes ago and he's all settled at the inn. He's an awesome guy. You'll like him. Goodnight."

"Goodnight."

And then he left. Exhaustion saturated Alison's body as her thoughts drifted to Jake. Jake. No denying. There was a stirring of emotions whenever she was around him, and she didn't want it to stop.

Chapter Six

Sara had cooked a hearty breakfast and was insisting everyone eat. "Good morning, Alison. Coffee is made, and I just told Jake that you three need to eat before running off. Sustenance is essential!"

Jake pointed to a chair. "There's no use arguing. Come and sit down. We have surrendered."

"Definitely need coffee!" Alison hopped up onto one of the breakfast chairs next to Annie. "Smells good." She reached for a piece of toast. "I'm anxious to go to the center. Marilyn texted me and all of the refreshments have arrived, so I think we're set."

Annie gleamed with enthusiasm. "Am I one of your production assistants now?"

"Why, of course. I think you have been ever since I arrived here." She laughed.

"Will I get to audition too?"

"Yes! I have no doubt you'd be a natural in front of the camera. And besides, you have an in with the head producer."

Annie's eyes sparkled as she replied, "Thank you!"

"Just have fun today."

"Let's finish and get going then."

Alison couldn't hide her amusement. "Okay, boss!" She noticed Jake had been staring at her again. It made her slightly nervous, but she liked his attention.

Jake stood up. "You finish up here, and I'll warm up the car. I've got the SUV today, so we can fit Henry in too."

"Thanks Jake. We'll be there in ten." Alison finished her coffee and toast. She was looking forward to working with Henry again.

***

Marilyn and her volunteers were bustling about, setting up tables and refreshments, organizing waiting areas and making the place feel as comfortable as possible. Christmas music was playing in the background. The holiday surroundings were an incredible sight to behold and very different from the bare, uninviting rooms in the city. Alison was more than pleased and Henry was impressed.

"Wow. How'd you get everyone to work so hard? I may not have anything to do here." He looked over at Alison. "I always knew you would make a great producer."

"Don't worry, I need you. Marilyn and Jake can handle this out here. You're with me in the audition room. I need your expertise in selecting kids."

Alison noticed Christine was in the back and had already made her way towards Jake. She saw them laughing, talking, and another hand touching his arm. It was apparent Christine was interested in more than friendship. She wondered if Jake knew? He must. He'd have to be an idiot if he didn't. And Jake didn't strike her as being naïve.

As she went into the audition room with Henry, she couldn't believe her eyes. Marilyn had set up a Christmas tree with additional wreaths and ornaments around the tables and windows. Unbelievable! She hardly had to lift a finger, and magic happened all around her.

Henry looked around. "You did a great job in here, too."

Alison looked at him. "I didn't do any of this. Just some tables and chairs were here when I left last night. I swear Marilyn must have a stash of elves somewhere."

Henry put his arm around her. "The miracles of Christmas!"

Alison and Henry became very busy as almost every child in the town was arriving for a chance to be on television. Alison had never seen such open, innocent personalities. In New York, she was used to getting the kids who were striving to be stars either on the stage or film, and most with an underlying air of entitlement. But children in Maple Ridge were truly appreciative of participating. Motivated by fun and adventure, their enthusiasm was refreshing.

Around one o'clock Jake appeared with a tray of food. "Time for a break. Marilyn prepared your lunch, and I insist you eat. No arguments. She shut the entrance for a bit and told everyone to come back in about an hour."

Alison looked up. Did he think of everything? "I'm famished. Thank you. Come in. Why don't you join us?"

Henry could sense the spark between the two of them. He had sensed it almost immediately. "Yeah, tell us what's been going on out there and we'll debrief you about our morning." Henry liked this guy.

"There's plenty here, so I guess I could join you. Annie is engaged with Marilyn, helping to set up for the afternoon rush, so she won't miss me."

Alison motioned for him to sit next to her and he willingly complied. She was excited to share her thoughts with him. She was getting used to his company. "As you know, we have two regular kids coming for the week from New York. Sean, the boy is a hoot. He's hilarious and always has something funny to say. Melissa, the other child, can be rather pretentious, but fearless behind the camera. I want to select two regulars from Maple Ridge as well. Depending on how much room we have, the rest of the kids will be scattered throughout the days and probably only be in one segment. Everyone can come to the town's tree lighting of course, but the last scene will be special and more tightly spaced in the bookstore."

"Any ideas for the town regulars?"

"I would like Annie to be one, if you agree."

"Are you sure? Just because she's my daughter and I'm helping you, I don't want anyone to think we're pulling favors."

"I understand. If I didn't know she was your daughter, I'd still pick her. She has all the qualities we look for. She's smart, inquisitive, sweet and willing to do anything I ask her." Alison laughed. "I don't think she'll have a problem being filmed."

Jake paused for a moment. "I hope not. She just came out of a period of being very shy and even withdrawn. I'm going to trust if you see her not having fun or shutting down, you pull her from the show."

"Yes, I'll keep my eye on Melissa and let Annie know if any negative words get spread on set, she can come immediately to me. Melissa can be rather territorial. I have an idea for the second child, but I want to wait until after all of the auditions before I make a decision."

"Sounds like a plan." Jake looked at his watch. "You've got about fifteen minutes before you start again. If you want to stretch your legs or get some fresh air, do it now. I'll take the trays back to the kitchen. Good luck."

"Thanks." Alison watched him as he left.

Henry didn't miss a beat. "You like him! Don't you?"

"Yes. I like him. He's a great guy. But we have a strictly professional relationship. Nothing more. Don't get any ideas." She grinned, shaking her head in denial. "I'm going to take a little walk. Meet you back here in ten." Alison knew where she wanted to go.

As she walked through the center, she noticed Christine was still there. Most likely, trying to spend as much time with Jake as she could. She was a pretty woman and as sweet as all of her baked goods. Alison could see how Jake might be attracted to her. And she had a caring relationship with Annie as well.

As Alison stepped into the church foyer, she tipped her head back, closing her eyes for a moment letting the precious silence fill her soul. She then walked toward the prayer alcove to light a candle and meditate for a few minutes. She needed the stillness of the sanctuary to remind her who really was in charge of her life and relax into knowing everything was being taken care of in a wonderful way.

Coming out of meditation, she heard the door open from the rear walkway. She took a deep breath, offered her thanks and stood up. As she looked around, Jake was walking towards her. They were the only ones in the church. "I thought I might find you here. Everything okay?"

"Now they are. Just needed a few minutes of calm. And prayer. Is everything alright out there?"

"Yes. Henry was looking for you. I had a hunch where you might be. Hope I didn't disturb you." Alison's beauty in the glow of candlelight took Jake's breath away.

"No, you didn't disturb me. I'm ready to go back." Alison found herself wanting to reach out and grab Jake's hand. Make a connection of more than friends. But she knew she couldn't. Not now.

"You know, you could come to church with us tomorrow. You might enjoy it. And you're getting to know some of the town folks, so you wouldn't feel like a stranger."

Alison's face lit up. "I would love to come. Thank you for the invitation." Returning back to reality she started to walk. "Let's go. I'm sure Henry is pacing the room." She laughed.

Jake put his hand on her back, guiding her towards the door. "You're probably right."

***

Alison and Henry buckled down in the library with a fire blazing to strategize their audition results. "Are you sure you don't want me to stay until Monday?" Henry was concerned Alison might try to do too much. "You know, you are the boss."

Alison smiled at him. "No, I've got this. And I know you have tickets for a play tomorrow night. And a big date!" Alison liked Henry's boyfriend.

"Yeah, Nathan might be bummed if I back out!"

"Besides, you'll soon be with me full time. Might as well celebrate the holidays with him in the city before we get too busy. You can finalize the lists and make phone calls from New York. We can work remotely, and before you know it, you'll be back here."

Henry looked at his watch. "It's late. Are we done? Suddenly I'm beat."

"Yes. Go back to the hotel and get some rest. You deserve it. Working together was fun, wasn't it?"

"Very different from our usual atmosphere. How many times did Carolyn call you?" He laughed.

"Three. But it's easier to deal with her in this position. And so physically far away," she said, as a grin spread across her face.

Henry stood up and gathered his materials to take back to New York. "I'll call you before I leave. I may sleep in and then grab breakfast at the bakery."

"I'm going to church with Jake and Annie tomorrow, so if I miss you, you know how much I appreciate you, right?"

Henry looked at her. "Church, huh? With Jake? Hmm. Part of your preproduction planning?" He couldn't resist teasing her.

"No. I just want to go to church. Now, get out of here." Alison stood up and gave her friend a big hug. "Tell Jenny I miss her and can't wait until she arrives."

"Will do, boss."

"And stop calling me boss." Alison enjoyed being in charge, but she didn't want anything to change in her relationship with Henry. They had been through too much together under the wrath of Carolyn.

Alison was cleaning up her desk when Jake peeked his head around the door. "Didn't want to disturb you but do you still want to go to church with us tomorrow?"

"Yes. I guess I'll see you at breakfast? Bright and early?"

"We usually eat breakfast around eight thirty and head over around nine thirty. Service is at ten. Not too early."

"I'll be there."

"See you then." He paused. "Today went quite well, don't you agree?" Jake knew his uncle would be calling him this weekend to get a report. He wanted to make sure Alison felt the same way as he did about their progress.

"Beyond my expectations, for sure. Thanks again for your support."

"My pleasure. See you in the morning."

"Goodnight, Jake." Their eyes locked for a moment, and then he was gone.

Lying in bed that night, Alison went over the day's events in her mind. She was grateful everything was running smoothly. She had managed to get out her proposal to George for a new twist on the Christmas special. She wanted to get his input first before showing it to Carolyn. She felt he had more of an open mind and viewed her as a real producer, whereas Carolyn just saw her as her assistant filling in for her. But the idea of a giving back theme resonated with her strongly. She wanted to accentuate more than arts and crafts and books and hoped children and their families would feel inspired to help others and give freely at this time of year. Sleep came easily as her final thoughts drifted to Jake, bringing a smile to her face as she slipped into a calming slumber.

Chapter Seven

On the way to church the following day, Annie barely took a breath while asking Alison a slew of questions about the production. Jake looked over and noticed Alison didn't even seem to mind the inquiry. Her positive attitude was steady, remaining kind, but Jake wanted to stop the interrogation, so he interrupted. "Let's give Alison a break this morning. I'm sure she would like a little peace and quiet. After all, we are going to church."

Alison was touched that Jake seemed honestly concerned about her. It felt like more than just doing his job. Something was different. "Annie can talk to me anytime. I don't mind."

"Alright, dad. But I think Alison likes my ideas." Her infectious smile was undeniable.

"If you say so." Jake knew when not to argue. "And here we are. Just in time."

Walking into the church, Alison was greeted by familiar faces. She realized she was starting to feel like a part of their community in such a short time. She knew she was bringing something special to their town, and everyone was willing to help and participate. As Alison sat down, she noticed Christine across the aisle from them. She waved to Jake with eyes sparkling in adoration. Yes, she was definitely into him.

Annie sat between the two of them and every once in a while, Alison looked over and exchanged glances with Jake. It felt natural to be in church with him. Almost as if they were a family of husband, wife and child. She shook her head to wake herself up out of such a daydream. Instead, she decided to stay focused on the minister's sermon. Giving to others, even if you feel you have nothing to offer—a perfect motif. Without knowing it, he was warming up the entire town to prepare for the new theme of her show. Her show. Yes, this would be her first show. She felt more courageous each day with a new sense of believing in herself. She hoped she could maintain the feeling through Christmas.

After church, Alison and Jake mingled with other parishioners, chatting to Marilyn and people she knew. Jake approached, gently putting his hand on Alison's shoulder. She found herself in close proximity to him, gazing up at his intense blue eyes while a shiver shot up her spine.

"Annie wants to spend the day with her friend, Tim, so do you mind if I drop her off after we eat lunch. I didn't know if you needed anything today involving your chauffeur." A wide grin broadened across his cheeks.

"Please, take the day off, Jake. I insist. You've done so much for me already." Again, a special caring beyond the duty of a good host. Was she reading too much into his kindness? She made a mental note to look over the budget more closely. Maybe he was getting paid more than what she had imagined. "I'm ready when you are."

After lunch, Alison secluded herself in the library. Sara had already lit a fire and brought her some tea. She was getting spoiled living in this house. She kind of liked it.

When her mom's ringtone sounded, she picked up. "Hi, Mom! How are you?"

"I'm fine, but I want to know how you are! How's the production going? Are you getting enough sleep? And food to eat? You know, as a mother I worry about these things."

Alison quickly reassured her. "Yes, Mom. I'm being taken care of remarkably well. The house is incredible where I'm staying, and my office is in the library. I have a roaring fire and Sara brings me tea or coffee whenever I need it. And she's a great cook."

"How are you feeling about the show?"

"So far, so good. But this is just the preproduction stage. Everything gets a little crazy once the cameras start rolling. And my host, Jake, has been very helpful."

"Jake? Hmm. What's he like? Does he live local?"

"Yes. He and his daughter live on the property. He owns the bookstore in town where we will be filming the last segment."

"Does his wife live there, too?"

"He's a widower, Mom. He used to live in the city but moved here to give Annie a better life in a small town after his wife died."

"Do you like him?" Mrs. Rockwell wasn't going to let her daughter keep any secrets from her. She was hoping the break with Steve would become permanent. She never thought he was good enough for Alison or appreciated her worth.

"Yes, Mom. I like him. He's a nice guy, but I'm not getting involved with anyone while I'm working. I've got too much at stake. So, stop asking me." Alison laughed. Her mother had a sixth sense about these things. Her radar was finely tuned.

"Do try and enjoy yourself. Your time to shine is now. Don't forget!"

"Thanks, Mom. Are you guys going to be able to come up for part of the filming, at least Christmas Eve?"

"We wouldn't miss it. We booked a room at the inn a couple of days before Christmas. Then hopefully we can take you back to the house on Christmas morning for a well-deserved vacation."

"Sounds wonderful. Believe me, I'll be ready."

"Are you finding any time to work on your book?"

"Not yet. But I brought it with me. Maybe I'll go get it now. I have a lovely space to work."

"Remember, you need creative moments to yourself. These moments are nourishment for your soul." Mrs. Rockwell, being an artist herself, had always supported Alison's artistic talents and pursuit of her dreams. She knew her innermost passion was books and writing. She wasn't going to let her forget and get swept up in the world of television production.

"Thanks for the reminder, Mom."

"Now, get to writing and we'll talk soon. I love you."

"Love you too, Mom."

Alison ran upstairs to grab her manuscript and drawings. She wanted to put them together in a mock book form to see how it looked, and in her office, she had plenty of room to do so. Alison hummed along with holiday tunes playing in the background as the flames in the fireplace crackled and arranged her mother's drawings with the written words on the pages. An hour passed, and she didn't even notice. Her mother was right. She needed this.

Alison had left the door open and didn't notice Jake was standing there until he cleared his throat to get her attention. "Hope I'm not disturbing you. Got a minute?" He wanted to see if she was interested in helping them get a Christmas tree for their cottage. Even though the larger one was in the Anderson house, Annie had been bugging him for one in the cottage. He didn't want to disappoint her.

"No, come in. I'm just working on a personal project." Alison wasn't sure she was ready for anyone to see her work yet.

Jake walked closer to her. "What's this?"

"A mock lay-out for my children's picture book, *The Brightest Star*. I'm not sure if it's finished." Mounting tension between her shoulder blades intensified, signaling her insecurities were trying to get the best of her.

Jake walked around the table and stood next to Alison, curious to see her work. His proximity made her stomach tingle. He knew she was probably nervous about revealing her writing. "Do you mind?"

Alison slowly shook her head. "No, I guess I need to show my work if I ever want to get published." And I trust you, she thought to herself. "You can be a practice run. And please, be honest. You own a bookstore, so I know you have some experience."

Alison stepped aside and let Jake begin browsing through the pages, one at a time, reading and perusing. Nerves got the better of her, so she decided to leave him for a minute. "I'll get us some coffee. Be right back. I can't watch you."

Jake understood. "Alison, don't worry about what I think." Jake knew this was hard for her and wanted to be as gentle as possible. After all, with his new imprint he would be dealing with plenty of new authors, and needed to support their creative aspirations.

Alison returned and saw Jake sitting in one of the large, overstuffed armchairs in front of the fire with her book on his lap. He looked up, inviting her to join him.

Alison walked over, handed him his coffee, and sat down next to him in the other chair. "Go ahead. I can take it. Give me your best critique." Her stomach was tied in a knot, but she didn't want him to know. She tried to appear calm and relaxed. After all, she was a professional.

"Actually, I don't have much criticism. I found the story enticing and the message uplifting. Exactly what kids need these days. You are a talented writer, Alison Rockwell. You should be pursuing this as another career. I look for this kind of book when stocking my children's section. And your mother's illustrations are gorgeous. Bright, colorful and very appealing to the eye. Can't wait to see this published." Jake could see a wave of relief sweeping over Alison's face.

Alison's face brightened as she put her coffee mug on the table and brought her hands together, looking into Jake's captivating blue eyes. "Really?"

"Really."

"You're not just trying to make me feel good?"

"It's the honest to God truth." Jake suddenly remembered he hadn't been a hundred percent honest with her about who he was. He knew it was time to tell her, but not in this moment. This moment belonged to her.

Alison sensed a shift inside herself as she took in everything Jake had said. Maybe it was time to send it out into the world and see what happened. He was staring at her with such compassionate eyes. It was as if he knew how she felt and was creating safe space between the two of them. And supporting her so she could muster up the strength to go after her dream. Slowly, she spoke. "Okay. No more procrastinating. After the holidays, I will start sending out the manuscript to publishers and agents. You're right. It's ready. I think I knew, but I needed another pair of eyes on it. Someone, who I trusted would be honest with me." She felt herself softening inside with a new feeling beyond butterflies and tingling. A comfort she had never known with a man. A comfort her heart had been yearning for, for a very long time.

Jake had a similar feeling. But his was ridden with guilt. Perhaps the right time to tell her the complete truth was now. "Alison, there's something—"

Suddenly her phone buzzed with Carolyn's name flashing. Gee whiz. On a Sunday? Really? "I'm sorry. I have to take this."

"Sure."

"I'll only be a minute." Alison stood up and walked over to her desk. Jake stayed in the chair, staring at the fire, contemplating his next move.

When Alison came back, she detected his quiet introspection. "Did you have something you wanted to tell me?"

Jake wasn't ready. Being the wealthy nephew of Jim Anderson had been a blessing all of his life. But it had also overshadowed some of his relationships. He never knew when people were genuinely interested in him or his money. He wanted to hang on a bit longer to this feeling with Alison—a possible relationship developing without the pretense or expectations of his wealth and status. "Uh, I wondered if you wanted to go with Annie and me to get a tree for the cottage. She was asking if you would help decorate it. I didn't want to disturb you, but I told her I would ask."

"Sounds like fun. As you know, I love decorating. And besides, I have an idea I want to run by you and may need your help."

Jake stood up, knowing their intimate moment had ended. "Of course, anything you need."

***

After finding the perfect tree at a local tree farm, Jake pulled up to the cottage and looked over at Alison. "Do you think the two of us can get this inside, or should I call Marty?"

"Are you kidding? I'm a strong woman, Jake Sanders. Bring it on!" She playfully grinned at him.

"Yeah, Dad! Girl power! How can you even doubt us?" Annie piped up from the back.

"Well then, wonder women, let's go!"

Alison and Annie were a comical sight, bringing up the rear with the tree. But they got it into the cottage, wobbling and giggling. Alison was keen on seeing the inside of their home. Perhaps she'd gain insight into this man who kept his cards close to his chest. She had revealed her fears and dreams to him and didn't even know what deep desires he held in his heart. Did he want more than owning a bookstore? Was there a special woman he had his eye on?

As they set the tree down in the corner, Jake motioned with his hand. "Welcome to our humble abode. It's not grand like the Anderson place, but we find it very cozy."

Alison admired the beautiful furniture in the dining room and the hand-built stone fireplace in the living room. In addition, she saw a stairway leading to the bedrooms and a kitchen with all new appliances and tiled floor. This place looked like it belonged to a millionaire, not a bookstore owner. Maybe Jake had secrets he wasn't telling her, but it was none of her business, she told herself.

"Jake, your home is beautiful. Did you do all of this work yourself?"

Jake stood tall with his shoulders held back and a gleam in his eye. "I designed it, but I had a contractor do most of the work. It's perfect for Annie and me. Besides, we eat many meals at the Anderson house. Sara is always inviting us, and since you've been here, we seem to find ourselves over there all the time." Jake's eyes locked with Alison's and didn't waver. He sensed their potential chemistry was only getting stronger and he realized his heart indeed beat faster when she was around.

Alison felt the energy between them and decided to get busy. "Let's get to it! This tree is begging for some ornaments." She took off her coat and placed her phone on the table. She needed to be on call twenty-four seven.

Annie carried the box of ornaments to the tree. "Sara brought us banana bread and hot cider. She left them on the counter."

Jake made a mental note to tell his uncle how very right he had been about having the production occur in Maple Ridge. Annie was the happiest he had seen in a long time. And even at Christmas, when missing her mom was usually the most difficult. "Alright, but no eating until we do some decorating. I'll put on the music."

Jake went over to his audio system and keyed up his favorite holiday selections. As he walked past the table where Alison had left her phone, it rang. He looked down and saw it was a man named, Steve.

Alison turned her head towards the phone, and asked, "Who is it? Can you tell me the name?" She didn't want to stop decorating if she didn't have to.

"Says Steve. Do you need to get it?"

An uncomfortable sensation hit her. "No, no. Let it go to voicemail. Not important." She would deal with him later. He had called more than once this week. "Come help me with the lights before I create a disaster!" She was eager to redirect the moment back to the task at hand.

Jake wondered who Steve was, but decided to let it go. Probably some production guy. But on a Sunday night? It seemed more personal. He looked over at Alison. "I don't think anything you do could be a disaster."

Alison blushed. "You don't know everything about me yet."

Yes, I guess I don't thought Jake. "On my way to the rescue then."

As the evening progressed, the three of them laughed and joked as they worked together to produce a masterpiece. Soon they found themselves sitting on the couch, hot cider in hand, admiring their work.

"Magnificent tree," Alison said, looking at Jake.

"We had much more fun having you help us. Right, Annie?" Jake wondered if Alison had a boyfriend back in New York missing her during the holidays.

"Absolutely." Annie was grinning with delight. "And you're very good at it, too."

"Why, thank you." Alison laughed. She looked down at her watch. "I better go. I have a couple of emails I need to send before I call it a night."

Jake put his arm around Annie. "And it's bedtime for you little one."

"Can Alison read with me before she leaves?"

"I don't think she has time, honey. She has more work to do tonight." Jake didn't want Alison to feel pressured into any additional duties. He was supposed to be making her job easier, not more complicated.

But Alison couldn't resist reading to a child. "I would love to. Just one and then I have to scoot." After all, it was why she loved writing. She loved to see the joy in a child's eyes when a story came to life.

"Teeth brushed and pajamas on first. Alison will be up in a minute."

Annie scurried up the stairs, excited to have a story read by her new friend.

Jake wanted to make sure that Alison wasn't feeling pressured. "She's a good reader herself, but at bedtime she still enjoys someone reading to her."

Alison rose and started to clean up the plates and cups in the kitchen.

"Hey, you don't have to do dishes! I'll finish. You've done enough."

"I guess it's a habit. I'm always the one cleaning up at home. Jenny isn't, how do I say this, the neatest person?" She laughed.

Jake walked over and gently put his hand on hers. "Really. Stop. I can do this." A magnetism was pulling him closer to this woman. He wanted to kiss her but knew it was too soon and not appropriate. So, he playfully grabbed the towel away from her and said, "Now, go upstairs. I'm sure Annie is waiting for you. But don't let her talk you into two books. The network won't be pleased with me if they find out I'm keeping you from your duties!"

"Come get me if I'm not down in fifteen minutes." As she turned to walk up the stairs, her knees were wobbly. Was it just her, or did they just have a moment now? Was he thinking of kissing her? When his hand touched hers, she sensed something more coming from him. No, she must be crazy. Or was she?

Jake cleaned up the kitchen and put the extra decorations away in the closet. He looked at his watch. Twenty minutes had passed, so he climbed up the stairs. Jake stopped and listened to Alison's animated voice as he approached Annie's room. He peeked in and saw Annie, lying in bed, looking up at Alison with adoring eyes. His heart fluttered seeing the two of them together. His sense of loss seemed easier to bear these last few days, and he was grateful. But it was time for Miss Rockwell to go home. She must be exhausted.

"Okay, you two. I think you need to wrap this up. Remember, it's still a school night. You still have another week and a half before vacation."

Alison gazed at Jake and then quickly caught herself. "And time for me to finish my emails and get to bed, too." She pulled the covers up over Annie, as if she had been doing it for years. "Sweet dreams, and I'm sure I'll see you around!"

Annie was starting to wind down and Jake could see she was visibly tired. "Thanks, Alison."

Jake nodded to Alison. "I'll be down in a minute."

When Jake came down, Alison was putting on her coat. Time to leave. The energy between the two of them was getting a little too intense for the professional relationship she needed to keep. "Thanks for an awesome night. I needed a break."

Jake could sense her urgency. "And thank you for helping. And reading to Annie. My heart is lighter seeing her so carefree. This television production has helped lift her out of a very dark place, thanks to you." As he reached out to open the door, he turned once more to her. "Was there something you wanted to discuss about the show? I forgot you had something you wanted to ask me."

Alison wanted to run her idea of including Fairside Manor in the show, but the closeness of Jake's body next to hers was interfering with her thoughts. "Yes, there was something, but we can talk about it tomorrow. Why don't you come to my office after you take Annie to school and check on your store? It can wait."

Jake nodded his head. "I'll see you then. Goodnight, Alison."

"Goodnight, Jake." She turned quickly and made it outside to walk the short path to the main estate house. She needed a walk to clear her head. She allowed the cold, crisp air to fill her lungs, and with each breath out, she tried to let go of all the feelings, little by little. Too many feelings. Tonight, had been fun. No doubt about it.

Her phone vibrated in her pocket and when she pulled it out, she saw it was Steve again. She would have to call him back. Tomorrow. Tonight, she needed to send George Stevens a very detailed proposal of her new idea. She needed approval before she could implement any action. And she had a good feeling about this idea. It may be just the thing that could help boost ratings for the network. She wanted to send it directly to George first since he had hired her for this job. She knew Carolyn wanted to be informed about every detail, but she wanted to explore this idea on her own without any negative feedback. After all, this show would have her name on it, too. Sink or swim, she was ready to take full responsibility producing *Hands-On Kids* by herself.

Alison looked up at the sky and saw the brightest star shining down on her. She closed her eyes and made a wish. Like her story said, the star would hold her wish until the time was right to release it and come true. She believed this with all of her heart.

Chapter Eight

Alison had spent a late night crafting her proposal for George and was now in a wait and see mode. After waking up, she got dressed and looked out her bedroom window. Several inches of fresh snow had fallen during the night, and the tree branches coated in white glistened in the sunlight. She could get used to spending more time in the country. The hustle and bustle of New York City could be intense, but in Maple Ridge, she could hear her own thoughts and feel more like herself. She looked at her watch and saw the time was nearing for her conference call with Henry.

After grabbling some toast and coffee from the kitchen, Alison organized her day. She was looking forward to discussing her new idea with Jake. She wanted to see the children's home and talk with the executive director if possible, even if plans weren't approved yet. The more information she had, the better. Especially if George needed to be swayed in any way. She was feeling a little guilty about not including Carolyn on the email but was clear she didn't want any resistance invading her space to create.

As she ended the call with Henry, she looked up and saw Jake standing in her doorway. Her stomach did a flip. As usual. He rambled in with an air of gentle assurance Alison found very appealing.

"Didn't want to disturb your call, but I'm ready whenever you are."

"Thanks for coming. I want to run this idea by you. Pull up a chair." Sitting close together, side by side, Alison outlined and described the proposal she had sent to George. Jake watched her from the side. He could tell she enjoyed this creative process, which inspired him. When she was done, she looked over at him. "What do you think?"

"I think it's brilliant. Might be the perfect idea to help boost ratings for the show."

Alison glanced at him with a puzzled look. "How did you know about the ratings?"

Jake realized Alison had never told him about the show's trouble. His uncle had, and he quickly tried to cover up his mistake. "I just thought every television program worries about ratings. Especially Christmas specials. I know they depend on their advertisers." He was hoping she wouldn't suspect anything.

Alison appeared pensive for a moment. "I guess you're right. But I will tell you another secret. The network is concerned about our ratings. In fact, at my first production meeting in New York, I was sternly instructed this special may be the deciding factor as to whether the show gets picked up again for another season. No pressure, huh?"

"No pressure!" Jake tried to make light of the topic, relieved she hadn't pursued any more questions about his comment. "Don't worry. This new idea could give it the fresh twist it needs."

"I hope so."

Jake knew he was beginning to let his guard down around Alison. He was enjoying the slow momentum of getting to know her first. But part of him still wasn't ready for a relationship and he knew it.

"Can you take me out to Fairside Manor today? I want to look around and meet with the executive director if possible. I haven't called her but could do so now."

"Why don't you let me make the first call, or we can do it together? I know her, and I could make an introduction for you."

Of course, he knows her, Alison thought. "Great! I have the number. Let's do it."

Jake pulled out his phone and dialed. He had known Karen Thompson for years. His uncle had been a prominent supporter of the facility. Even though the kids came from all over the state, Maple Ridge was used to taking them under their wing, so to speak, whenever the need arose. Jake knew his uncle would love this idea. He had to tell Alison the truth soon. "Karen, this is Jake Sanders." He looked over at Alison. She was wide-eyed and leaning into him, ready to speak. "Yes, everything is fine with Annie and me. I want to tell you about a possible new venture for the manor." Jake explained the idea in general and then handed the phone over to Alison.

Alison continued with details and Karen was more than enthused about the prospect of her children getting well-deserved attention. Especially during the Christmas holidays. She invited Jake and her to come over as soon as possible. She understood Alison had not received the green light yet, but chances were in their favor. When Alison got off the phone, she was beaming as she looked at Jake. "I have a good feeling about this. I'm getting more and more ideas as I think about it. Can we go now?"

"Absolutely. Listen, there's something—"

The sound of Alison's phone cut him short. She glanced at the display and saw it was Henry. "I've got to take this, sorry!" She and Henry talked for about ten minutes, working out a glitch in the schedule. After hanging up, she asked, "You were saying something?"

Jake decided to tell her later. "Nothing. Let me get my coat and I'll be ready in five."

Alison wondered what it was he wanted to tell her. He was so mysterious at times. She grabbed her notebook and went upstairs to get her coat. Her heart felt full. Even her book had possibilities.

***

As Alison and Jake drove out to the manor, they brainstormed more ideas for the service component of the show. A long, winding private road lined with sweeping trees and manicured shrubbery led to the main house sitting on palatial grounds. The manor's structure was similar to Anderson Estates and Alison was blown away. "How in the world did they obtain such a massive property?" she asked Jake.

Jake knew his uncle's family, or rather his own family, had played a significant role in setting up Fairside. Still, he didn't want Alison to know until he explained his personal history. He had telephoned Karen in private before he left and asked her to keep his identity confidential for now. "They had and still have large donors who take care of the maintenance and upkeep. The state provides some money, but the town usually holds fundraisers when they need something extra. Your idea is perfect. It's a win-win situation for everyone."

Karen was there to greet them as they pulled up. She was an attractive woman in her fifties and physically fit in order to keep up with all of the children. Karen had plenty of staff, but she liked to be hands-on whenever she could. As Alison and Jake walked into the foyer, she motioned towards her office. "Let's go in here first. Then I'll give you the grand tour."

As Alison looked around, she noticed the manor had an overwhelming coziness and a family atmosphere. The things children needed the most. Handmade pictures of Santa, reindeer and Christmas trees, snowflake ornaments, as well as paper wreaths, hung on the walls and from the ceiling, most of them homemade.

Karen had hot tea waiting for them, and the three of them

engaged in talking about details for the show. Afterward, Karen led them on a tour but soon got an important phone call, so she sent Alison off with Jake to finish. "Jake has been here before and knows the layout. My staff can answer any questions and I'll catch up with you in a bit."

Alison ruminated on how many children the manor must accommodate as she strolled through the many rooms. They walked outside, and she saw about a dozen large bungalows positioned in a semi-circle close to the manor.

"The main house was overflowing with too many kids, so these were built to house the older kids. They get to feel like they have their own space yet are close enough so that staff can watch them. Fortunately, there's enough staff to have house managers in each building. Karen is trying to develop an after-foster care program for these local orphans and other foster kids who turn eighteen with an opportunity to become a house manager for a year as part of a transition plan. They get room, board and a small salary. She hopes to set up the second step of transitional housing and jobs in the community. We're lucky most business owners are open to the idea, but as you can imagine, it all takes money. Your idea is very appealing for this reason. It will give exposure to the needs and an online presence for fundraising, which is what the manor is missing."

Alison felt her heart opening to this man who seemed to genuinely care about people. She gently put her hand on his arm and said, "I never imagined this little idea might have such an impact on so many. Thank you for bringing me out here today."

Jake put his hand over hers. "At this point, Alison, we're in this together. I'm committed to helping Fairside as much as possible."

Before Alison could say or do anything else, her phone went off. She had to break away from Jake as she knew she was on-call for work. It was Henry again. She looked back at Jake and whispered, "Sorry."

Jake waved his hand, communicating for her to take the call.

Luckily, it was only a question or two and she was able to resume the tour. But the special moment between the two of them was over. A chill passed through Alison as a cool breeze came through the trees. "Let's get back to the main house. It's pretty cold out here."

Seeing her visibly chilled, Jake felt an urge to place his arm around her shoulder and pull her close, but he restrained himself. "Karen should be available to answer any more questions you may have."

She thought, back to business as usual, but little did she know what was going on his mind. It wasn't business.

***

Karen was ready for them and waiting in her office. "What do you think? Can it work?"

Alison sat down in front of her. "Yes! Seeing your facility and getting to know about your programs and visions, I'm committed to getting approval from the network. Whatever it takes!" Alison hoped she could convince the executive producers and network board, but she also knew the reality of television, and money would be a deciding factor. She would have to look for ways to cut costs wherever she could. Maybe she should show the spreadsheets to Jake and ask for his help. After all, he did have an MBA.

Alison didn't want to get Karen's hopes up until she heard from the network. "I will do everything I can, but remember, until I get approval, we can't move forward."

"I understand. I will keep it our secret until I hear from you again." Karen reached out for Alison's hand. "Any help I get with these children is a blessing. Many of them have had a rough little life so far. Tragedy, loss, heartbreak. It all goes hand in hand when coming to a place like this."

"I should know within a few days. I will call you as soon as I get word. If this flies, we will be swamped these next couple of weeks. So, rest up!" Alison laughed.

Karen laughed with her. "Yes, indeed!"

Alison gathered up her notebooks and stood next to Jake. "I'm ready. Thank you again."

"No problem. Let's head to town, grab a bite and then if you don't mind, I have to go to the bookstore. Annie will be there after school with Tim."

"I've made my decision on the second child to work with the New York cast. It's Tim. Henry received approval from Lucy and you already gave me yours for Annie so, I can tell them together."

"Perfect choices if I must say so myself." Jake grinned at her.

Alison had tried to separate her feelings from the fact she was beginning to feel close to both Jake and Annie, but Annie had indeed been the right choice. Even Henry had thought so. Alison's mischievous eyes sparkled. "Yes, I thought you'd agree." They both laughed.

Alison was passionate during lunch as she discussed her ideas for the manor being incorporated into the show. Jake wanted to call Uncle Jim soon and put in a good word. He didn't want Alison to be disappointed.

After eating, Alison looked over at Jake and became very serious all of a sudden. She wanted his help with the budget and wasn't sure it was appropriate. But she decided to bring it up anyway. "Jake…"

He looked at her and noticed her posture had changed. "What?

Is something wrong?"

"No, but I need to ask you something."

"Sure. Shoot."

"I know you're supposed to be just my host for this production, but with your background, I was wondering…" She was beginning to falter.

"Go on. What is it, Alison?" Jake could see her struggling to get her words out, which was unlike her.

"I was wondering if you could look at my spreadsheets and budget this week to see if we could cut it or move things around to keep costs down. I know this new idea may be out of my budget, and I thought, perhaps you might have some creative ideas." Alison looked up at Jake, all doe-eyed, almost pleading, but still innocent.

How could he say no? "Of course, I can look at them. It would be my pleasure."

"Really?"

"Yes. Just tell me when. We'll fit it into our schedule."

Alison jumped up from her seat and ran over to Jake. She unexpectedly hugged him and said, "Thank you! I think this part may be over my head. And I don't want anyone to know."

Jake was surprised by her sudden affectionate gesture, but he could see she was genuinely appreciative. "No problem. This stuff is easy for me." The closeness of her body aroused a longing for more, but he pushed the feeling away and decided it was time to go to the bookstore. "Settled. Now let's get going. I've got to pick up Annie and do a few things at the store."

"I want to call Henry and give him a verbal report of what we saw." Alison breathed a sigh of relief, knowing Jake was going to help. Managing her budget was the one area where she felt insecure.

***

Alison found a quiet corner to make phone calls back at Starlight Books while Jake went to his office upstairs. She wondered what his office looked like but figured it must be small. She suspected there were other business tenants in the building inhabiting the back space. Luckily, both Tim and Annie were waiting for Jake, and Alison asked them to join her. She explained after finishing the interviews, it was decided the two of them would join the main cast from New York as guest hosts from Maple Ridge. Annie jumped up from her seat and put her arms around Alison. "Thank you! You won't be sorry! Right, Tim?"

"You can count on us!"

Alison laughed at the two of them. "Remember the important thing is to have fun. And forget about the cameras. Be yourself."

"We will!" Annie's eyes were dancing with merriment.

"But I do have to warn you. If anything happens making you feel uncomfortable or upset, you must promise to come to me right away. The two children from the New York cast have been doing this for several years, and they may act, how do I say, somewhat territorial. They're used to being recognized as the stars, and I'm not sure how they may act in sharing the limelight. Understand?"

"We'll be fine." Annie looked confident for her young age of nine years. "And besides, I've got my friend, Tim, with me."

Tim knew his dad would be so proud. He wished he could be there for the filming.

"Come on, Tim. Let's go get some cookies to celebrate!" Annie saw her dad approaching. "Can we go to Sweet Ridge Bakery? Please?"

Jake could rarely refuse his daughter's pleading gestures. And he was proud of her for getting a leading role in the show. "I guess we could make a stop on the way home." Jake looked at Alison with a questioning glance.

"Who can turn down hot cocoa and a cookie?" Alison was getting used to being part of this small family. She didn't know if it was a good idea or not, but it just seemed to happen. "Work can wait." She stared right back at Jake, holding the gaze for an extra instant. What was he feeling? Was he enjoying their time together as much as she was? She reminded herself she had too much to do in the next couple weeks to let her heart lead her astray. Somehow, she had to reign in her feelings. If it was possible.

Walking into Sweet Ridge, Alison got another phone call. She looked at Jake and said, "Let me take this. I'll meet you guys inside." It was Steve. She had been ignoring his calls for too long. She might as well see what he wanted. He wasn't leaving any voicemails. "Hi, Steve."

"Alison! I've been worried. You haven't returned my calls. I know we said we were taking a break, but I didn't think you'd ignore me. Are you okay?"

"Yes. I'm fine. And I'm sorry I haven't returned your calls. I've been crazy busy. I only have a few minutes now because I'm at a possible location site. How are you?"

"I'm good. Big projects have been coming my way, but I've been thinking about you a lot. Any chance you're coming back to New York before the shoot?"

"I'm not sure. I just put in a new proposal to the executives, and I'm waiting on their approval. Then I will have a better idea of my schedule in these next few weeks."

"I want to see you, Alison, if you do. I want to talk. I think we still have a chance to be together. For many reasons. I'll explain when I see you."

Same Steve. Didn't even ask how she was feeling—just plowing forward because of what was best for him. Alison shook her head. She couldn't deal with this now. "Listen, Steve. I can't talk about us on the phone now. I'll let you know if I come back to New York in the next couple of weeks."

"Alright. I'm up for a new promotion and it could give us everything we ever wanted."

"Sounds wonderful for you, Steve but I've got to go. I'll call you when I know something."

"Be sure you do. I miss you, Alison."

"Take care, and I'll talk to you soon, Steve." Then she hung up. Alison wasn't sure she missed him. She knew Steve too well. There was some underlying reason he was reaching out to her now. And it wasn't about love.

Alison turned and walked into the bakery, still chilled from the cold outside. Christine was intently talking to Jake, batting her eyelashes and laughing while Annie and Tim were at a table by themselves enjoying their treats. She needed something hot. "Hi, Christine. Can I trouble you for some hot cocoa?"

"I already got you some." Jake reached up on the counter and handed a steaming mug to her. "You're shaking." He took off his scarf and wrapped it around her neck. "Until you warm up in here."

Alison couldn't help but see the look she got from Christine, who noticed Jake's chivalrous gesture. But she wasn't here to compete. "Thanks. I'm going to sit down if you don't mind."

"How about some cookies?" Christine liked Alison and knew no matter what, keeping a friendly and professional relationship with her was best for her business.

"Would love some." Alison found a seat in the corner. As she opened up her notebook, Jake approached her table.

"Everything okay?" He'd noticed she seemed distracted when she came in.

"Yes. Nothing about the show. Something personal needing to be resolved. It can wait." She wasn't about to share this part of her life with Jake. "Sit down. Let me show you some new ideas for the manor shoots. If we get the green light."

Jake wanted to ask her about her personal life but felt doing so was inappropriate. Maybe another time. He looked over at the kids, and several of their classmates had joined them, making it livelier inside the bakery. Clara would be happy, wherever she may be. Often, Jake felt her spirit watching over them, giving him some peace of mind during his sorrowful days. He let his thoughts drift then refocused on the woman in front of him. "Let's hear what you're thinking. I think the kids can entertain themselves for a bit."

"I think you're right." She discussed some of her ideas, places best for shoots, and the possible online fundraising occurring from the events.

Jake wanted to help in any way he could. Tonight, he would give his uncle a call and then remembered it was still a school night. "I have to help Annie with something for school. Do you mind leaving soon?"

Alison closed her notebook. "No, I have a lot to do and some phone calls to make." Alison knew Jake made her feel something Steve never did. A sense of contentment and ease. Always. Every day. This feeling was different from anything she had felt with a man. And somewhat foreign. She breathed deeply into her gut, trying not to dwell on it. "Yes, let's go."

All were in good spirits as they dropped Tim off at his house and went on to Anderson Estates. As Jake pulled up to the main house to drop Alison off, he said, "If you need anything, I'm just over there." He pointed in the direction of his cottage.

"I do appreciate your help with everything." Alison felt very lucky to have Jake guiding her around town and sharing the tasks she needed to complete. He was one special guy for sure.

"Let me know when you want me to look at your expense books. I'm busy tonight and tomorrow morning I have a meeting at the store. But afterwards, I'm free."

"Will do."

Annie was still glowing. "And thank you for picking me for the show."

"You're quite welcome, Annie. Remember, the most important thing is to have fun." Alison hopped out of the car.

Jake twisted his head towards Alison. "Goodnight, Miss Rockwell. Pleasant dreams." She seemed to bring out the playful side in him that he had long forgotten.

"And pleasant dreams to you, Mr. Sanders." She grinned to herself as she walked into the house.

***

Sara was putting on her coat while standing in the kitchen. "There you are. I didn't know when you would be back, so I made a large pot of soup. There's a salad in the refrigerator and some fresh bread and butter on the table. Help yourself whenever you're hungry. I have to go to choir practice tonight at the church. Marty built you a fire in your office because I thought you'd probably be working." Sara was delighted to have another female in the house, especially one so kind and considerate.

"Thank you, Sara. You're getting to know me all too well. I'm going to change my clothes and then dive into work. Enjoy your evening."

Alison made a tray for herself and hunkered down at her desk. No sooner had she sat, George called. Uh, oh. Kind of late for him to be calling. She picked up. "Hello?"

"Alison, it's George Stevens. Hope I didn't catch you at a bad time."

"Oh, no. I'm sitting in my office going over some things. What can I do for you?"

"I got your proposal and sent it upstairs to my boss. Everyone loves it."

"Wonderful!" Alison knew she hadn't crunched the numbers yet. She had been hoping to the next day with Jake. "I just have to work out some of the numbers."

"We agree, so I'm sending a car for you first thing tomorrow morning. We want you in our office for a couple days. You should still have plenty of time to prep preproduction when you return to Maple Ridge on Thursday. What do you say?"

Alison knew there was nothing to say. "Of course, Mr. Stevens. What time should I be ready?"

"The car will be there at seven thirty. Can you be ready? Bring everything you have with you. We have a ten o'clock meeting with the finance and head production staff. Some of the network executives want to meet with you as well. This could be just what *Hand-On Kids* needs to boost our numbers. And it goes with a holiday theme of giving. Everything about it is positive as far as I'm concerned. Excellent job!"

"Thank you, sir."

"See you tomorrow." George had immediately liked Alison's proposal, but he knew everything would be authorized when Jim Anderson called him an hour ago. As president of the network, Jim was a powerful man. When he wanted something, he got it. His nephew must have given him a heads up.

"Yes, see you tomorrow." Alison hung up and was numb for a minute. *What just happened?* Her heart raced with mounting enthusiasm. Her idea was going to work! And she would get to orchestrate the entire creation. Maybe she should have included Carolyn in the loop, but too late now. Things were moving fast, and her to-do list just exploded!

Chapter Nine

Double-checking her computer bag and dragging her suitcase to the foyer, Alison was promptly ready when the car pulled up. Her stomach was doing flip-flops anticipating her journey ahead. Grabbing a coffee for the road, she let Sara know her change in plans. She'd texted Jenny earlier and would text Jake in the car and let him know she would be gone for a few days. As the car drove away, Alison looked back at the house, realizing a piece of her heart remained at Anderson Estates.

***

As Jake pulled up to the main house, he had hoped to be there a little earlier but had been caught up with bookstore business. Sales were booming, and Lucy was pretty much handling everything on her own. Jake was reassured she could take over day to day affairs when he launched his imprint. He had decided today was the day he would reveal his true identity to Alison, but that wasn't going to happen now. On the way over he had received a disconcerting text from her, causing a sinking feeling in his stomach.

Sara was at the kitchen sink, prepping vegetables. "Hello there. Did Alison text you? They sent a car early this morning and she left right after you took Annie to school. She asked me to tell you she'd most likely be back on Thursday. She was excited, so they must have liked her proposal." Sara didn't know all of the details but knew their guest had been working on an idea which included Fairside Manor. She liked Alison and was more than pleased Jake's and Annie's moods had improved since she arrived.

Jake reflected on the meaning of her trip, but knew she would probably find out from someone about who he was and might feel betrayed by him. The trust they had been building working together could be in jeopardy. He was kicking himself for waiting so long. But there was nothing he could do about it now. She would find out and he would have to deal with it. He shook his head. The fact he even cared so much about what she thought was foreign to him. It had been a very long time since he cared what another woman thought about him.

"What's wrong, Jake?" Sara noticed the troubled look on his face. She had always thought of Jake as a son ever since he was a child.

A feeling of regret was gnawing his insides. He couldn't hide any feelings from her. Never could. "It's just—I think I made a mistake."

"A mistake?"

"Alison doesn't know Jim is my uncle, and I'm part of Anderson Estates and its empire. I didn't want her to know so she'd be herself. I like just being the local guy who's helping her out. I didn't think she'd share so many personal things with me about her dreams and this job. She's going to hate me when she finds out."

"I doubt she will hate you, but don't worry about it. If she does find out, you can talk to her when she returns. And explain. She seems to be an understanding woman, and she may surprise you."

"I hope you're right. I didn't mean to deceive her. I was going to tell her eventually, but then we got so busy. I never dreamed she'd be whisked off to New York."

"Did you talk to your uncle about her proposal?"

"Yes. I wanted to put in a good word for her. It's a great idea. I knew he'd love it."

"See, not a bad thing. Don't worry. You're going to have to let this one go, Jake. Things always have a way of sorting themselves out."

"I hope you're right." Jake wasn't so sure, though. But Sara was right. There was nothing he could do about it now.

"How about a sandwich before you go back to work?" Sara didn't like to see him upset.

"Sounds good." Jake rolled his shoulders in a circular motion, trying to release any anguish in his body. "I guess this will give me an extra couple of days to work on my launch. Seems to be coming together."

"I have no doubt. Sit down at the counter and tell me all about it." Sara knew work would take his mind off worrying if he had muddled his friendship with Alison. She could see they both liked each other, but she noticed they were both cautious. Maybe to a fault. But she had faith people who were meant to be together, were always brought together in some destined way.

Jake sat down on the breakfast chair and explained the next steps for his imprint launch. Work had always given him great comfort in his grieving process, and now was the refuge he needed. He'd talk to Alison when she returned. He couldn't think about it now. There was much to do, and he had to stay focused on Annie and her happiness. She was his priority and would remain so.

***

When Alison arrived in New York, she went straight to the office and was swept up in production meetings. The energy was high, and everyone was on board for the new concept. Sitting at the table, Alison rubbed her neck, trying to free the lodged tension in her muscles from thoughts of all the work to come. And she had to brainstorm ideas on how to keep the costs down. She had been hoping Jake could have helped her before she had a meeting with George. Little did she know she would end up back at his office in

New York. She thought they would review the proposal on the phone, but things turned out differently.

By the end of the day, exhaustion had overpowered her. It had been exhilarating but stressful at the same time. All she wanted to do was go home, take a bath, pour a glass of wine and catch up with Jenny. And sleep in her bed.

She was about to leave when George called her to his office. They had been together in meetings part of the day with other staff, but never alone, just the two of them. Alison looked at her watch, then picked up her notebook. Duty calls.

Upon entering his office, George was definitely in a good mood. After meeting with Jim Anderson earlier, he knew if this new direction was successful, he would be in line for a promotion. He motioned to Alison. "Come in. Sit down. You must be worn out!"

"Thanks, Mr. Stevens. Yes, I can honestly say, I'm pretty tired." Then she laughed. "But invigorated at the same time, if possible."

"I know what you mean. It was the way I used to feel when I was producing my first shows. Now I sit up here in an office and only get to feel the excitement on a day like today, when we're in the planning mode of something new. Excellent job, by the way. Everyone is quite pleased. Especially Jim Anderson."

"I've never met him but hear great things about him."

"Yes, his nephew must be like him. He was very impressed with your work. He called Jim last night, so we got the go-ahead quickly. Good strategy on getting things done, Miss Rockwell."

Confusion spun around Alison's brain like a top. "Nephew? Who's his nephew?"

"Why Jake Sanders, of course!"

A tightening squeezed in her stomach. "Jake is Jim Anderson's nephew?"

"Yes. You didn't know? I thought swaying Jake was part of your strategy. Either way, it worked. You got his support and he relayed his enthusiasm on to Jim. Brilliant scheme if I do say so myself." George sat back in his chair, very pleased at how things were playing out. This probably would never have happened if Carolyn were at the helm. He knew she worked hard, but often could be rather cold and distant with her staff. He'd heard rumors.

All Alison wanted to do was run out of George's office. Multiple feelings erupted inside of her. Confusion, deception, and sadness. She thought Jake was different. Was he just like the other men in her life? All she could say was, "Jake has been helpful."

George pulled himself up erect in his chair. "You deserve some rest. Go home and enjoy the evening. I'll see you back here tomorrow morning to discuss budget issues. Don't worry. I'll help you in this area."

Alison stood up, but her legs were wobbly. "Thank you, Mr. Stevens. See you in the morning."

"Yes, and great job so far. We have much to do."

Alison could only nod with a forced smile as she left his office. She needed to get home. She realized she had no idea who Jake Sanders was.

***

Opening the door to her apartment, Alison couldn't wait to kick off her shoes, and curl up in front of the fire. Why was she so bothered? Jake didn't owe her any explanations of his private life, but she wondered why he had kept his identity a secret. And she had shared some of her most personal thoughts and dreams with him. For some reason, she felt foolish. She had opened up her heart to him, thinking it was safe. And she had trusted him. And for him not to tell her an essential piece of his life, well, she felt hurt. And people would think she manipulated a personal relationship to get what she wanted. She shook her head. Maybe she was being silly. They had just met and were only new friends. He must have had his reasons.

When she heard Alison coming in, Jenny leaped from the couch. "You're home! Yay! I've missed you, Al!" Even though they had seen each other at work, Jenny had been busy with the last shoot of the series before the Christmas special, and Alison had been in meetings most of the day. She hugged her friend and helped with her luggage. "I got our favorite Thai take-out and there's a bottle of pinot opened and waiting."

Alison had never been so happy to see her friend. A bath could wait. Food and drink and a lengthy discussion was what the doctor ordered. "Sounds lovely!"

Alison and Jenny grabbed their dinner and drinks and plopped down on the couch in front of a roaring fire. Jenny lifted her glass for a toast. "Here's to my friend, the producer! I'm so proud of you. Everyone was talking about your new ideas and the relaxed vibe you'll bring to the set."

Alison rubbed the tight muscles in the back of her neck, mulling over her exhaustion and the day. "Thanks, Jen. But remember, this has been only the pre-production stage. Being in the trenches, I could become a tyrant."

"I don't think so, friend. I know you too well. Now, tell me everything."

Alison described everything since she first arrived in Maple Ridge, including all her encounters with Jake. Up to the bombshell dropped in her lap this evening. "Am I crazy? Why do I feel so betrayed? Or sad? Like I've lost something?"

Jenny shook her head, sighing. "Because, my friend, you have feelings for this guy! And more so than what you want to believe. I haven't seen you this enamored with someone since you first met Steve. But this Jake guy seems different somehow. I'll have to meet him to get a full assessment of the situation."

"Maybe you're right. I do have feelings from him. And, it reminded me of disappointment all over again. Of course, I don't know how he feels about me, but we did have some intimate moments. And he almost kissed me once. Or at least I thought he was going to." She took a big gulp of the pinot hoping to soothe her nerves. But it wasn't working. "I don't know. What am I doing, Jen? Am I crazy? I can't get involved with anyone now. But should I be angry with him? For not being more honest?"

"Look. You don't know why he kept his identity a secret. There could be a very sane, logical reason having nothing to do with you. From what you've told me he seems like a good guy. And he's been through a lot with the loss of his wife and being a single parent."

Alison ran her fingers through her hair, gazing down into her wine glass. "Maybe you're right."

"Why not give him the benefit of the doubt? So what, if he helped you out a little by calling Jim Anderson? It means he believes in you. He doesn't have anything to gain. Heck, he's probably not even getting paid for the work he's doing with you. Is he?"

"Funny. I looked at the budget and couldn't find a consulting fee or part-time salary for him for this position. But I got so busy I just let it go. I figured it was buried in another column somewhere on my spreadsheets."

"See? He's a good guy. And you don't know what his reasoning is for keeping such a big secret."

"Letting him know my feelings is important, though. We've

been spending too much time together not to be honest in our relationship, friend or otherwise."

"I understand. You'll know what to do. I'm sure of it." Jenny started dishing out the food. "Let's eat and then you can take a bubble bath and go to bed. You're going to need your rest."

"I've been dreaming of a bath all day." Alison laughed and then looked down at her phone as a text pinged from Steve. Perhaps she should talk to him while she was in town. After all, they had dated for a couple years, and she didn't want to blow him off if he had something important to say.

"Steve?"

Alison told her about their last conversation. "Maybe I'll have coffee or a drink with him tomorrow. If I can get away."

"Do whatever gives you peace of mind, I always say." Jenny knew Steve was unreliable at times but could also see her friend was in a much stronger place. Maybe she would finalize the break-up.

"I'll text him and then take a bath." Alison reached over and squeezed Jenny's hand. "What would I do without you?"

"And what would I do without you? Now go take your bath. I'll clean up the mess. Things will look brighter tomorrow. They always do."

"Yes, they always do." Alison felt better. Her talk with Jenny had helped. Her intense feelings of hurt and confusion were starting to subside, along with embarrassment at what others might think about her. Tomorrow she'd be too busy to even think about Jake. Or maybe not. But it didn't matter. She had faith in herself that she would know what to do when the time came.

Chapter Ten

Pieces were falling into place for Starlight Books publishing. Jake had hired an editor in the city who was moving from New York to Maple Ridge after the first of the year, and a woman who was top-notch in the marketing field was arriving later from Boston for an interview. With tons of social media experience, she could be invaluable for launching the imprint and its first books.

Shuffling papers and crunching numbers, he didn't hear Lucy approach. "Jake, your interview is here. Can I bring her up?"

"Yes, I lost track of time. Let me come down so I can show her around the store. Be right there." Jake was hoping he liked her in person as much as he did on paper. Being a small imprint, having the right chemistry of people working together was important—personalities fitting with the same drive and ambition to launch a new business. Commitment was key.

Liza Stall straightened her posture while browsing books, anxious to meet Jake Sanders. The prospect of working in his company could be the perfect opportunity for her. Trying to calm herself, she knew she had an impressive presentation assembled to demonstrate her capability. As he walked down the stairs to the front of the store, she could see he looked just like the photos she had seen online. And more handsome in real life.

Jake reached out his hand. "Nice to meet you. Thanks for driving over to Maple Ridge. I thought it was important you saw the store and the work space upstairs."

Liza presented herself as friendly yet professional. "No problem. I have family close to here, so I'm staying with them."

"Really? Who?"

"My sister and her husband live a few miles east of here. It was one of the reasons I was interested in relocating."

Jake nodded his head. With family close by, she would probably be more committed. "Let me give you a tour, then we'll head upstairs. I'm eager to see your presentation."

Liza followed Jake and became utterly absorbed in his vibrant words and vision. His openness and tone of voice confirmed her assumption that he was a man with a determined intention for his enterprise. She knew about his wife's passing, but she wondered if he had a girlfriend.

The new office was still rather bare bones but had much potential for being an inspiring place to work. Jake wanted to keep it small at first and let it organically grow as the business did. He had a gut feeling it would be successful. "I know it looks empty, but we just finished the expansion and remodeled the space last month. We'll increase the size as we need to. What do you think?"

"It's perfect!"

Jake looked pleased. "Let's see your presentation. My office is over here." He pointed to an extensive space, with floor-to-ceiling windows and a killer view of the mountain range in the distance.

"The view from this office is amazing." Liza's voice brimmed over with enthusiasm as she envisioned the possibility of working for Jake.

"It beats a city office, for sure. Have a seat and show me what you have." Jake already knew that he would hire her if the presentation was topnotch. She had the kind of energy he was looking for in an employee.

Jake spent the next hour listening and looking at the materials Liza presented. When she finished, he said, "I like everything I'm seeing. If you want the job, it's yours."

Liza bolted upright in her chair. "Yes! Yes, I want it! Thank you!"

"I'll hammer out a contract and send it to you by Friday. Look it over, then let's discuss it on Monday."

"Perfect! And thank you. You won't be sorry you hired me. I'm a hard worker and I understand your vision. My sister is going to be so excited."

"Any questions?" Jake needed to get back to work.

"No. And I'll probably be in town next week in case you want to meet with me. I'm coming for the holidays."

"Good to know. I may be tied up with this television production thing. Do you know that show, *Hands-On Kids*?"

"Yes. My niece and nephew watch it." He had peaked Liza's curiosity.

"They're doing a live Christmas special here the week leading up to Christmas. I'll tell you more when I have a schedule."

"If you need any help, count me in." Liza was looking forward to any extra time she could spend with Jake. This interview confirmed all her fantasies about him. But she would be the best employee ever. And keep it professional. But who knew? Many relationships start with a strong foundation of friendship.

"We may recruit you." Jake stood up. "I'll walk you downstairs. Thank you for coming out this way, and I look forward to you being on the team."

"So do I." Liza's heart was beating rapidly, anticipating the change to come in her life.

After she left, Jake turned to Lucy. "What do you think? Will she fit in?"

Lucy could see the woman was infatuated with Jake, but who wasn't? "She's got high energy and if she's got the skills, fantastic. I trust your judgement, Jake, when it comes to people."

"Thanks, Lucy. I hope so. I'm getting excited to get this whole business up and running."

"Any news on Alison's return yet?"

Jake took a breath. "Not yet." He paused. "She might be upset with me."

"Why in the world would Alison Rockwell be upset with you?"

"Because I kept my true identity from her. And I know she probably found out the truth in New York. She may not like that I was deceptive with her."

"I don't know if deceptive is the right word. Keeping your privacy intact has been important to you, and no-fault for doing so."

Jake was pensive. "I hope you're right."

"In the short amount of time I've known Alison, I think she will understand. Don't worry about her. Things always have a way of working themselves out. You'll see." Lucy cared a great deal about Jake and didn't like to see him disturbed about anything. He had been through too much.

Jake's frown was loosening. "Sara said the same thing. Hope you're both right, Lucy." The bells jingled as a customer came through the front door, distracting him. "I'll be upstairs if you need me." He would try to explain his reasoning when Alison returned. He liked her too much. Uncharted waters lay ahead in those feelings, and he didn't know if he was ready to enter them. Yet.

***

Alison's feet were killing her. Wearing heels as an executive was painful. She wasn't used to the miles she amassed navigating another whirlwind day in New York. Better get used to her new norm. She had made plans to have a drink with Steve right after work and would hear him out. But she already knew her heart had lost interest. In her mind, she kept comparing him to Jake, although she knew doing so was unfair. She still had unsettling feelings about that man and his secrets. But Jenny was right. She should at least hear his side of the story.

One last meeting with George confirming her budget and production schedule, and she would be ready to leave. A car would take her back to Maple Ridge in the morning, so she hoped to go home, pack, spend time with Jenny and, hopefully, get a good night's rest. As she was cleaning up her office, her phone rang. She got a tightening in her stomach seeing Carolyn's name. She had probably heard of all the changes from George and wouldn't be happy she was cut out of the loop.

"Hi, Carolyn. How are you feeling?"

"I would feel better if you had run some of your new ideas past me first. The fact that I had to hear them from George was disappointing." Carolyn was more than disappointed. She was livid. How dare this assistant of hers think she could take over her job. But being temporarily off duty, she couldn't enforce her power. George had made it very clear. She had to get her doctor's release, so she could make an appearance on the set before it was too late. Before Alison took all the credit—in case it was a smashing success.

"I'm sorry, Carolyn. But everything happened so quickly. I just sent a proposal in by email to get George's opinion, and before I knew it, I was back here in New York setting it all up. I was going to send you the final budget and outline later tonight. We just finished it. I'm hoping you approve, and any suggestions would be greatly appreciated." Alison knew she could only fight nastiness with honey.

"I'm glad to know where your loyalty lies. I'll be happy to look at it and get back to you tomorrow." Carolyn was hoping she could find some flaws in the project and come up with the solutions and secure her notice by the network. It was time she got back to work. Injured or not, she was recovering fine and could be mobile within a week or two. Her career was not going to be derailed by this gung-ho, amateur assistant.

An uneasiness gnawed at Alison's stomach. She had a hunch Carolyn was going to show up in person. And soon. Nothing she could do about it but keep moving forward. Her nervous energy lessened when remembering what she had accomplished thus far. No one could deny her progress. She gathered her things and went to meet Steve.

Walking into the restaurant, Alison looked around and saw Steve sitting at the bar. He saw her too and waved. "Sorry, I'm a little late. Kept getting phone calls." A fleeting moment of doubt flooded Alison's thoughts, triggered by Steve's appealing charm. But she also knew his track record for being a boyfriend, which had many letdowns. Mainly, she had never felt like she was important to him. Even though they both had been career driven, she knew now she needed more, a realization only magnified while staying in Maple Ridge.

"Thanks for meeting me." Seeing Alison in all her power validated what he had been feeling. He had been a fool to let her go. "You look amazing, Alison. How's everything going?" He was curious to know what her latest role entailed in the show.

"Still lots to do, but I'm encouraged about the new direction we are going in. I'm getting a lot of support from the network for my ideas, which is a welcome change." Alison knew prestige was essential to Steve. His apparent listening had been a quality she had sorely missed while they were dating. "What's your news?"

"Very exciting. I'm up for a big promotion, and I'd love you to be here for my holiday events. Some of the people may be worthwhile meeting for your career." Steve knew Alison was probably meeting executives in the television network who could be potential clients for him.

"Very thoughtful of you, Steve, but I'm too busy until after this shoot. Congratulations on your possible promotion. You'll probably get it. Your instincts are usually right on about these things."

Steve knew he had to appeal to her emotional side. He wasn't stupid. "On a personal note, I've missed you Alison. We were good together. Don't you agree?"

"We've had some fun, but honestly, I feel like you don't know me. You never cared enough to really listen to my needs. Or share me with your family. Or take time away from work for romantic adventures. After spending some time in Maple Ridge, a simple small town, my priorities are changing, and I'm quite clear. I don't feel like you love me or want a future with me."

"Not true, Alison. I do love you. I just thought we were on the same timeline. Let's spend more time together and see where this goes. What do you say?"

Alison knew in her gut that a relationship with Steve would never work. She needed to end it now. "I'm sorry, Steve. I appreciate you reaching out to me, but I think you should start dating other women. Somebody out there is more suited for you. But not me, Steve. Do you understand?"

Steve couldn't believe Alison was ending the relationship. "I can't argue with how you feel, Alison, but I still think you should think about it over the next couple weeks."

Alison stood up, grabbed her coat and said, "I have thought about it, Steve." She leaned over and kissed him on the cheek. "Have a wonderful holiday. And good luck with your promotion." She turned and left.

Steve was dumbfounded. Not getting his way was foreign to him. He would have to think about another strategy to get her back. Giving up was not his style.

***

Alison exhaled a sigh of relief, stepping out of the car in front of Anderson Estates. Maple Ridge was starting to feel more like home than New York. Sara opened the door. "How was your trip? We missed you around here."

"Quite a flurry of activity but productive. The network loved my ideas, and we're all systems go."

"Wonderful. Lunch will be ready in about an hour. I have fresh coffee and lit the fire in your office. Let me know if there's anything else you need." Sara was glad to have Alison in the Anderson house again. It felt like she belonged there.

Alison hadn't noticed Jake's truck in the driveway. "Is Jake around?"

"I think he's at the store, but I let him know you would be here by lunch time. Why don't you call him?" Sara knew he was anxious about seeing Alison again.

"I'll catch him when he's free. I need to discuss next steps with him." Alison was determined to stay open to Jake and not let her feelings interfere with her duties. She needed him for the production.

***

Organizing her production calendar, she realized Jake was a significant asset to its success. Engaging in her new ideas from the beginning, he had felt more like a partner than just a host. Until she

115

found out the truth of who he was. But should it matter? Had she mixed personal, emotional feelings of desired intimacy with this man with professional ones? Was that the reason she felt hurt? As Jenny said, he may have had perfectly good reasons for not sharing everything with her. Whatever the reason, she knew she had to hear him out.

As Jake pulled up to the Anderson house, he rehearsed what he would say to Alison in his head. He would apologize and explain his reasoning as a need for privacy. She should surely understand that. But the personal moments they had shared had made this secret slightly more complicated. This he knew. She had shared dreams. Private ones. They had worked and even played closely together in the holiday spirit. If he wasn't mistaken, she had feelings for him. And he was struggling with his feelings for her.

Walking into the kitchen, Sara said, "Hello, dear. She's in her office. Do you want some coffee?" Sara knew he was uneasy about the conversation he was about to have with Alison.

"Yes, please."

Jake's furrowed brow did not go unnoticed. "Speak from your heart. It will be okay." She smiled as she gave him his mug.

Jake knew she was right. "Thanks."

As his knuckles grazed the library door, he heard her voice from inside.

"Come in." Alison's stomach quivered like a leaf in the wind. But when she looked at him, all of her anger subsided. How could she be angry with this man? He had been more than generous with her and attentive in countless ways.

Jake put down his mug and came closer to Alison. "How was your trip?" Looking at her long, wavy hair swept up in a messy bun, and her large, innocent eyes as she lifted her head, his heart beat faster.

Alison put her pen down. Should she be curt and businesslike or let him know her true feelings? "They loved my ideas and authorized everything." Then she looked him squarely in the eyes. "But, of course, you knew." She decided not to back down. Whatever came out of her mouth next, she wasn't going to stop it. Life was too short.

Jake shifted his position and pulled up a chair in front of her. "Listen, Alison. I'm sorry I didn't tell you who I was, but I've been so used to hiding my true identity for multiple reasons. Mostly to protect my privacy. And Annie's. Although everyone in town knows who I am." Then he realized he'd said the wrong thing.

"Wonderful! Everyone knew except me! Doesn't make me feel better." Alison fidgeted in her chair, uneasy with their encounter.

"I wanted to tell you. In fact, a couple of times I started to, but we were interrupted by a phone call or something else."

Alison recalled when he had tried to share something, but her phone rang. "Your private affairs are none of my business, but not knowing made me feel rather foolish with George Stevens. He thought I had orchestrated your support to get your uncle, Jim Anderson, on board with my new ideas and manipulated the situation with you to get what I wanted. I just found out before I left. And I imagine other people are going to think the same thing. People in this industry can be cruel."

"Not telling you was never my intention, Alison." Jake began to see it from her perspective. He had screwed up.

Alison bit her lip as she shifted in the chair, trying to let go of her pent-up anger and hurt. "And on a personal note, I've shared some private information with you. I thought you would trust me enough to share some of yourself as well. I guess I was wrong." There, she had said it. She had opened the door for a more genuine relationship, be it friend or something deeper.

Jake reached out, touched her hand and looked into her eyes. "I know you trusted me. Please, believe me. I wasn't trying to keep something from you. I was just stupid. And time kept passing, and we got so busy. Can you forgive me?" Jake wasn't sure what her reaction would be, but at least he had done his best to speak from his heart.

The warmth of Jake's hand on hers began to melt away the anxiety inside. She couldn't stay angry, and she couldn't hold grudges. Tears started welling up uncontrollably. Her heart was pounding against her chest, but she couldn't let him see all of her emotion. Not yet. Trust had to be regained. She blinked her eyes and hoped he didn't see the held-back tears. She gently pulled her hand away and said, "Of course, I forgive you. I respect your privacy and, for whatever reason, I've grown to respect you. Can we just move forward and agree to be completely honest with each other? We have a lot of work to do, and I need you."

Jake uttered a sigh of relief. "I'm yours to order around as you please." He had noticed she looked as if she was about to cry a moment ago. His gut told him she did have feelings for him. "And, I will tell you everything you want to know about me and my relationship to Uncle Jim. No more secrets!" He knew he had to make an effort in rebuilding their trust for each other.

"It's up to you. It's none of my business unless it pertains to this show. You're free to tell me whatever you want." Alison wanted to release him of any guilt sharing. If he wanted to share aspects of his life with her, she wanted it to be authentic. And because he cared about her.

"One more thing. Carolyn called me a couple of days after you arrived. She figured out who I was and wanted to make sure I knew who was in charge. Secretly hoping I'd put in a good word to my uncle most likely." He waited for her response.

Alison tilted her head, then said, "I can't control Carolyn. Now, pull up a chair and let's get to work."

Jake felt a heavy load had been lifted off his shoulders and from his heart. He would make this up to her. And he knew precisely how. He pulled up a chair next to her and his blue eyes locked in with hers, sensing he could salvage the relationship. "Let's see what you got, Miss Rockwell."

Alison went into producer mode and began to outline the upcoming events. As Jake observed her animated enthusiasm and deeper sense of caring for her work, it validated his feelings for this woman. What to do next was still unclear, but he had faith, he would know soon enough.

Chapter Eleven

Jake and Alison, both in sync with their common goal, drove up the long driveway to Fairside Manor. Entering the large foyer, Karen was waiting for them. She was ready to coordinate activities but was concerned she didn't have anyone to do an online fundraising plan. With national exposure, she didn't want to miss any opportunities. If agreeable, Jake had decided to put Liza on the project until after the New Year. It was one item Alison knew she didn't have the budget for in her production account. She wondered what Jake's business entailed. It must be more than a bookstore. "Very generous of you, Jake. You know, I don't have funds for this piece."

"I have some funds set aside for non-profit organizations. It will be a tax write-off for me. Don't worry. I'll explain everything later." Jake was going to be an open book from now on.

Alison looked at him and realized he was making an effort to be more forthcoming. "Whatever you say." Still felt somewhat guarded, she knew it wasn't going to last long. This man had sincerely touched her, and she wanted to trust him.

The next stop was the bookstore, where they found Annie bagging a gift for a customer. "You're back! We missed you!" She ran over and hugged Alison.

This little girl did pull at her heart strings. "Yes, I am. And glad to be back." Yes, she was happy to return to Maple Ridge.

Jake looked at Lucy and noticed his new hire was nowhere to be seen. "Where's Cindy?"

"We ran out of room in the back to wrap ordered gifts for Christmas, so I set up a table upstairs to finish the work. I hope you don't mind, but we needed the extra room. She and Tim are busy up there." With news around town that *Hands-On Kids* would be filming there, Starlight Books had seen an influx of customers. "I ordered more books, too. We were running low."

The business was flourishing, and with communication getting back on track with Alison, Jake was feeling freer to pursue whatever changes came his way, be it business or personal. "Would you mind if I did a little work before we head back to the house? I won't be long."

"I'll find a space in the back. I need to make some phone calls." Alison wanted to check in with Henry and go over some new details.

Jake thought for a second. He knew sharing part of his personal life would help mend Alison's distrust with him. "Would you like to see my office space? I could find you a desk and it may be quieter."

For a second, Alison got lost in the depth of Jake's blue eyes and recognized the effort he was making. "I'd love to." And she followed him up the stairs.

After turning the doorknob, Jake's arm swept open, making a grand gesture. "Voila! Welcome to Starlight Books publishing. My next adventure." He angled his head, awaiting her reaction.

Alison's eyes grew wide as she grasped the enormity of the space. Built as a loft style with high ceilings and glass windows bordering the entire floor, the views of the mountains and countryside stretched out as far as the eye could see. Several desks were strategically placed with plenty of room for more. "Did you say Starlight Books publishing? Are you expanding the store?"

"Yes and no. Yes, we're hoping to expand an online presence for the store, but I am also developing a new publishing imprint for children's books. Thus, the name Starlight Books publishing. The imprint will be part of my uncle's larger publishing house, Anderson Fields. I hope to be up and running in the new year on a small scale, and then evolve from there. What do you think?"

Alison's heart rate accelerated. She knew of Anderson Fields, but never put two and two together. The corners of her mouth spread wide across her face. "Who knew Jake Sanders was in the publishing world? I thought you were just a bookstore owner."

"Just a bookstore owner, huh?"

A rosy hue filled Alison's cheeks. "You know what I mean."

"Of course, I do. No worries. I'm teasing you. Let me give you a grand tour." Jake proceeded to describe his vision for the office space and growth of the company. He pointed to a desk and office space ready for Liza. "You can work here." He watched her taking it all in, and his chest breathed easier. Earning her trust was worth the effort.

"Jake?"

"Yes?"

"Congratulations. I know you'll be successful. Thank you for sharing this with me." Alison had a whole new perception of the depth and skills of this man. She exhaled slowly, feeling the butterflies return to her gut. A relationship with Jake may have a chance. If only she knew how he felt.

"You're welcome." His gaze lingered for a moment before he strode back to his desk.

Later, he could hear Annie's petite frame bouncing up the stairs. Bursting into Jake's office, she announced Sara had cooked dinner and was waiting for them at home. Jake looked at his watch and realized he had let time slip away, occupied in numbers for his imprint. "Right there, sweetie. Go see if Alison is ready."

Alison looked up from her desk as Annie appeared next to her. "I heard you, and I'll be ready in a jiffy. I'm starved. Are you?"

"Yes. I'll be downstairs waiting for you guys."

As the three of them rode in the car back to Anderson Estates, Alison had made a decision. She was willing to take a risk with Jake. Whatever that meant.

***

Curled up in one of the oversized, upholstered chairs, Alison was writing in her notebook while soaking in the warmth of the fire after dinner. Ready to doze off, she heard a sound across the room.

Jake's rugged physique hovered by the entrance. "Have a minute?"

Seeing his robust presence sent a shiver up her spinal column. "Sure."

"Annie is finishing up her homework. Anything else you need?" Jake knew he was beginning to care for this woman. Beyond just being a good host.

"No, thank you. I'm finishing up some production notes and will probably call it a night. Can we go over the schedule for tomorrow? I may need you to take me a couple of places for last minute arrangements."

"Anything you want. What time?"

"I need to make a stop at the bakery and talk to Christine. Also, the community center. Maybe right after lunch we could go out? I'll talk to them in the morning to confirm. They're both expecting me."

"Sure thing." Jake needed the morning to work in his office, so the schedule worked out for him.

Alison was still curious about his relationship with Jim Anderson. She wanted him to tell her, but wasn't quite sure of how to ask him without appearing nosey. Maybe she should just drop it.

"Something else on your mind?"

A knot tightened in her stomach, but she continued. "Were you the reason my ideas for the show were approved? Did you really sway your uncle?"

"No." Keeping secrets from Alison had almost cost him his relationship, be it friendship or otherwise. "I just told him you had good ideas, and he should take a look at your proposal. George Stevens was sold on the idea after he read it. Remember, he called you to New York before I spoke to Uncle Jim. You did this all on your own."

Alison wanted to believe Jake. "I guess, it didn't hurt then when Jim Anderson liked the idea and urged George to move forward with my plan."

Jake laughed. "No, it didn't. Don't worry." He reached out his hand, placing it over Alison's. "Everything's in motion, and you're doing a superb job. No more secrets from you."

Alison smoothed out the crease in her pants to keep her other hand from trembling. Then placed it over his. "And I will be frank and transparent with you."

Their moment held in the air until they heard a tiny voice. "Dad! Are you in here?"

Jake and Alison pulled their hands back, and Jake said, "In here, honey."

"I'm done! Can we go home?" She plopped down in a chair. "Are you guys still working?"

Alison responded, "No, we were just finishing."

Jake took hold of Annie's hand. "Come on, let's leave Miss Rockwell in peace."

Annie cocked her head toward Alison. "Can you read me a story tonight?"

Before Alison could speak, Jake said, "I'm sure Alison is tired from a very long day. Maybe another time."

Alison's hand went up to her mouth, trying to fend off a yawn. She was definitely exhausted. "Yes, I promise to read to you another night. Perhaps this weekend?"

Annie appeared satisfied. "Okay." Then she saw Alison's mock-up of her book on the table. "What's this?"

"Alison's book. One she wrote herself." Jake's chest swelled with genuine regard for her work.

"Can you read me your book? Please?" Annie begged.

How could Alison say no? "If you want. This weekend. It's a date."

Jake put his arm around Annie. "I think she will like it."

Giggling, Annie squeezed his hand and started pulling him. "Come on, daddy. Let's go."

Jake reached down and tickled Annie until she let go of his arm. Jake made one last glance at Alison. The magnetic energy between them was stronger than ever. "See you tomorrow." And then he was gone.

Alison slowly ran her fingers through her hair and stared into the fire. She wasn't sure what was going on between the two of them, but it felt right. Whatever happened, she would handle it. Jenny arrived in a few days, and she couldn't wait. Her best friend would have the insight she needed. She always did.

Chapter Twelve

Like clockwork, Jake arrived at the house after lunch. They were both in high spirits with the prospect of success in view for each of them. Alison jumped into Jake's truck and greeted him with a lilt in her voice. "Thanks for being my chauffeur. I could get used to this."

"Oh, yeah? Forget my company. Maybe it could be a full-time job for me to be your slave." They were definitely flirting now.

"I would always treat you well, just so you know." Alison blushed, realizing a hidden meaning could be lurking behind her words.

For an instant, Jake's brow curled up, pondering her response but brushed it aside. "Good to know. Where to?"

"Community center first and then to the bakery to meet with Christine. I'll go to Fairside Manor tomorrow. I think we have to start working weekends. If you're available." Alison didn't want to take Jake for granted.

"I figured. No problem." Jake was content to help Alison in any way she needed. A sinking feeling in his belly warned him their time together would end soon. The pressure was mounting. Decisions needed to be made.

Marilyn was ready for them and had prepared her outline for the flow of the shoot. Arts and crafts would happen first, and the supplies had already arrived. An overflow of volunteers from the Maple Ridge community had signed up to help, which unexpectedly touched Alison's heart. After perusing the outline and floor plan for activities, she looked at Marilyn. "Excellent. Better than I could have imagined. Tina and Justin Rogers, our hosts, will appreciate the organizational work you have put in. Thank you!" Tina and Justin Rogers were a young couple with degrees in education. After teaching in the public schools, they decided they needed a change. When an opportunity came along for hosts with their kind of background, they jumped at the idea. Their personalities were charismatic, upbeat and creative. They had been a cornerstone of the show for five years, and everyone loved them.

"You're more than welcome. I've enjoyed the challenge. The community center is perfect for holiday festivities."

"My assistants will be here Monday to go over final details, but if anything comes up before then please call me. I'm available twenty-four seven now." Alison stepped closer to Jake. "I'm ready. Next stop, the bakery."

Jake led the way, holding the door for Alison. "After you."

"Why, thank you!" Chivalry is still alive, mused Alison and climbed into the truck.

***

As they entered Sweet Ridge Bakery, Alison was acutely aware of the looks and energy Christine put out to Jake. She wondered why Jake wasn't dating her. She was a beautiful woman and definitely interested. "Come on back to the kitchen. Do you want some coffee or gingerbread cookies?" Alison couldn't begrudge her much, since she was a sweet person. Just like the name of her store.

"Coffee would be great, thank you," said Alison,

"Me too." Jake freely bestowed his infectious smile to all he encountered. It was one of the things Alison liked about him.

The three of them entered the kitchen, and like Marilyn, Christine was also prepared. She had ordered all the supplies with the budget she was given, and the freezer was full of ingredients.

Christine had been busy making prepared dough ahead of time in case they needed it. Like Marilyn, she had recruited volunteers from town.

"Christine, you've done a fantastic job. I think we should have plenty of room to invite some extra kids from Fairside, too. What do you think?"

"Thanks to Jake, I have the room. I never imagined my first job in our kitchen addition would be for television!" Christine had always hoped her working relationship with Jake would turn into more. So far, it hadn't, but she was content to spend time with him as a friend.

Alison looked at Christine and realized it was hard not to like her. "Funny how life works, isn't it?"

Christine laughed. "Yes, it is."

"Are we almost finished, ladies? I need to get back to the store. Liza, my new hire will be arriving soon."

Christine reached out and lightly touched Jake's arm. "Are you taking Annie to the ice- skating party tonight? Everyone is going, and I volunteered to take my niece. My sister has to work." Christine was hoping he would be there.

"I almost forgot about it. Thanks for reminding me. You can be sure we'll be there. She and her mother used to love ice-skating." Suddenly he got quiet, turning away. "I'll be in the truck."

Alison and Christine both noticed that Jake's demeanor had quickly changed when he mentioned Clara. They looked at each other with an unspoken understanding, knowing he still carried unresolved pain.

"Right behind you." Alison made sure to give him some emotional space.

As they pulled up to Starlight Books, Jake muttered, "Sorry I was abrupt back there."

She reached out her hand to touch his arm. "No problem. Forget about it." Changing the subject, she said, "I'm anxious to meet Liza. Do you really think she will be able to pull this off?"

"From what I've seen of her work, yes. She's young but very knowledgeable."

Christmas music resounded from the bookstore when they opened the door. Lucy was busy with a customer as Jake approached. "Have you heard from Liza?"

"She got here about fifteen minutes ago. I took her upstairs. She was eager to set up her new office space."

Jake saw Annie in a corner arranging books. "Hi, sweetie. Are you okay down here while I go upstairs?"

"Yes, Dad. Lucy needs my help. And don't forget about our skating party tonight!" Annie couldn't wait to skate, although she knew it would remind her and her dad of wonderful times with her mom. It was something they always did in New York throughout the holiday season. "Alison, can you come with us?"

"Maybe. I don't know." Alison hesitated. This might be something Jake needed to do alone without her tagging along.

"Please," Annie pleaded. "Everyone's going to be there. Don't you know how to skate?"

"It's been a while."

Jake realized he did want Alison with them. It had been several years since Clara's death, and he had to stop feeling guilty. Guilty he wasn't around enough. Guilty he might want to date again. "Yes, come if you weren't planning on working." Jake would leave it up to her.

Alison put her hand on Annie's shoulder, relieved Jake had asked her. "Work can wait. Yes. I'd love to come. But I have to warn you.

I may be pretty rusty on the ice."

"We'll help you. Right, Dad?"

Jake locked eyes with Alison. "Right."

"Settled. Ice-skating it is." Alison was acutely aware she was letting herself get closer to Jake and Annie. A rippling of fear set into her pores as she wondered if she was making a mistake. She didn't want to get hurt but also knew occasionally risks needed to be taken.

"Let me introduce you to Liza."

Alison snapped out of her thoughts, following him.

They found Liza at her new desk, setting up her computer and organizing some files. She suspected the other woman was the television producer. Close to her own age and very pretty, she was surprised she was so young. Most executives were older. "Hope you didn't mind but I wanted to get set up as soon as possible. We don't have much time to get this website up and running."

Jake was thrilled she had taken the initiative. His gut told him he had been right about her. "No problem. In fact, I couldn't be more pleased. Make yourself at home." He motioned to Alison. "This is Alison Rockwell, our head producer. You'll be working closely with her."

Alison reached out her hand. "Nice to meet you. Welcome aboard. And yes, we don't have much time, but Jake thinks you'll be able to do the job."

"I'm certainly going to give it my best shot."

"I'll let you two get better acquainted. We have about an hour, and then we have to leave for dinner and get ready for the skating party."

"The annual town skating party?" asked Liza. "My sister told me about it. I'm going with her and my nephew and niece. They're very excited."

Alison noticed her captivated look when eyeing Jake. Great. Another one. Another beautiful woman vying for Jake Sander's attention. Even if Alison did start dating him, she would have to live with the reality Jake was a charismatic guy and would attract most single women. Get used to it.

Jake shrugged his shoulders while raising his hands in the air. "Yeah, I guess we'll all be there."

Once he left, Alison put her professional hat on, pulled up a chair, and proceeded to outline her plans and hopes for the online presence of Fairside Manor. After an hour of working with Liza, she felt confident she had the skills to do it. "I have to go soon, but could you come over to my office tomorrow? I wasn't sure if you were available on the weekend."

"No problem. Just text me a time and address." Liza did like this woman. She was intelligent, organized and easy to work with, so far. "I best be going too. My sister will wonder where I am."

"Thanks for your help. I'll sleep better tonight knowing we made progress on this."

"You're welcome. I'm looking forward to meeting some of the town folk this evening. I think I'm going to like living in a smaller town."

Alison's reflection in the glass outlined her face gazing out towards the snow-covered trees. She also liked this small town and wasn't sure she wanted to return to New York. "You will. It's a wonderful community."

Riding in the car with Jake and Annie, Alison tried to keep her sadness at bay. Sorrow for when this adventure would all come to an end. She visualized Jake working on his new imprint and Liza helping him. And she would no longer be in the picture. Somewhat disheartened, Alison pondered her situation. Nothing she could do about it. At least, not now.

She tried to shake the earlier dampened spirit and get back to the present moment, getting ready for the skating party. Yes, enjoy the festivities and her time left with Jake as much as possible. No telling how this story would turn out.

***

A frozen pond was cleared of snow and glowing fires were burning in large metal containers for skaters and spectators. A tent was set up with outdoor heaters and tables were filled with an assortment of holiday desserts, hot chocolate and coffee. Glittering white lights were strung around the tent, and upbeat Christmas music played on speakers as the townspeople reveled in the merrymaking.

"Jake, I'm going to walk around first and take some photos."

"Come join us when you're done. I'm sure we'll be on the ice." His kind expression did not go unnoticed.

As Alison observed the event, the excitement in the air seemed to envelop her, coaxing her to imagine all the possibilities for change in her life. Could she honestly spend the rest of her life in a town like this? Even though she had a high-powered, stressful job to do, she felt an inner calm and contentment in Maple Ridge that she rarely felt in New York. There was always rushing and striving to go somewhere. Do something. Be somebody. Here she felt she was enough. Enough to be accepted and liked for whoever she was. For whatever she did. Plain and simple.

When she had finished, she went to the booth for skate rentals. Putting on her skates she looked out and tried to spot Jake. She quickly found him and could see Christine was skating with him. They were goofing around, playing tag with Annie and others, and

Liza was close by with her sister's family. Alison observed it all, in awe of the close-knit community.

"Are you going to get out there or just sit on this bench?"

Alison turned around and saw Reverend Michael. An older man with greying hair, he was handsome, tall and very fit for his age.

"Hi, Reverend. I was just admiring the view before I ventured out."

"This party is quite a sight. Mind if I join you for a minute?"

"Of course not."

Michael sat down next to Alison and started to put on his skates. He noticed she was looking out towards Jake and the others. "You've made quite a few friends here already, haven't you?"

"Yes. This whole experience has been so unexpected. In a good way, I mean."

"Yes, God works in mysterious ways." He noticed she was more quiet than usual. "Is there anything bothering you?"

"Not really. I think I'm going to miss this town when everything is over. Next week will be a nonstop adventure, but afterwards, it's done."

Michael knew she had been spending a lot of time with Jake and anyone could see the spark between them. He wondered if he was part of why she was deliberating the uncertainties of her future.

"Maple Ridge could be your home. You can always make such a choice." He paused and intently looked at her. "Unless there's another reason."

Alison took a breath. Maybe she needed to talk to someone. She had been waiting for Jenny to arrive, but the Reverend seemed like a good option. "Whatever I share with you is confidential, right?"

"Guaranteed in my job."

"I think I have feelings for someone here. But I don't want to mix my business and personal life. And I don't know how the other person feels about me."

"Have you asked him?"

"No! Of course not!" Alison was mortified at the thought. "It wouldn't be right. It's too complicated. I'll just forget it." Saying it all out loud suddenly sounded silly. Alison wasn't sure she should have opened up to the Reverend.

But Michael wasn't going to let it go. "What are you afraid of?"

Alison contemplated a moment. "I guess I'm afraid the other person has been nice to me because he's a nice guy to everyone. Not because he has feelings for me. He has a job to do working close to me, and the outcome of the production will benefit him as well." There. She had said it. She quietly looked up at Reverend Michael to see his reaction.

"And can't someone be kind and have feelings of his own as well?"

"I guess so."

"And can't complications be overcome?"

"Yes. Sometimes."

"What does your heart say, Alison?"

Alison closed her eyes. She knew what it was saying. She heard it loud and clear. "My heart is ready to fall in love. Plain and simple." She looked up at Michael. "What am I going to do?"

Michael gently touched her shoulder. "My dear, just keep your heart open and trust. I suspect you have faith, so know there's always someone listening, and the answers will come. You just have to be patient."

She knew Michael was right. She had to be patient. This stuff was bigger than her little brain could handle. It wasn't something she could produce or organize. She didn't have control over the situation.

The only person she had control over was herself and how she reacted to things. "You're right, Reverend. Patience is difficult sometimes." She paused. "But I can do it."

"Patience can be challenging for anyone, Alison." He looked out at the pond. "Now, what do you say we get out there and join the others?"

Alison stood up, suddenly feeling renewed. She had made the right decision in talking to the Reverend. She had needed the reminder of what was in her heart and what she already knew. She would keep her heart open and trust. Patience was key. "I'm ready. Let's go!"

Michael was pleased her mood had changed. He knew she was talking about Jake, and he suspected Jake was going through the same dilemma in his head as well. He would remember to put the two of them in his prayers. He knew true love always finds a way even when it's complicated.

As Alison and Michael headed out on the ice, Jake glanced up and saw her coming. She looked a little shaky, so he glided over the ice to lend a hand. Alison's attention was on her feet not anywhere else because it had been ages since she had skated. Jake slowly approached her. "You have to look where you're going, too." He laughed.

Alison raised her head, startled, since she'd been preoccupied in staying upright. "I'm trying to get the hang of it again. It's been a long time."

Jake reached out his hand. "Here, let me help you."

Alison couldn't refuse. She was remembering she never had been a good skater anyway. "Thanks. I guess I do need some assistance."

Jake moved in closer and made sure he would be there if she started to fall. "Don't worry. I'm right next to you. Relax and see if you can feel the rhythm. Like this." And he proceeded to gently guide her in the back and forth motion of her legs and body. "See. Not so hard."

On top of her clumsy ineptness in skating, Alison found it challenging to pay attention. Jake was so close she could smell his cologne and feel the heat of his body next to hers as they skated. A current of warmth engulfed her body as she slowly got into the rhythm with him. They felt like one body moving. Not separate. She was relaxing more and more until she was skating with ease but still with his help. It was like a dance the two of them were doing together, fluid and flawless without restriction.

Jake could smell the scent of Alison's perfume as she leaned into him. "You've got it. Piece of cake."

"Don't let go. It could be disastrous."

"Don't worry. I've got you." Alison's petite figure easily molded into Jake's arms as if she belonged there as they skated. At least it felt that way to him.

Christine glanced out at the pond. She had been in love with Jake for over a year and had always hoped their friendship would become more. But it never had. But she liked Alison. If Alison lived in Maple Ridge, they would probably become close friends. Christine embraced the night air while looking up at the sky and prayed for the right man to come along someday soon for her as well. Content in her faith, she began to skate again and returned to join in the fun with neighbors and friends.

After Jake and Alison had finished skating, he excused himself to go find Annie. As she walked around, she found herself floating on air. The closeness with Jake had intoxicated her. She didn't know if it meant anything, but she would try to be patient as the Reverend had advised. Plenty of time remained before she had to go back to

New York. She sighed. New York. *Was it still her home?*

As the party started winding down, Jake found Annie and then looked around for Alison. He saw her talking to Liza in a corner and joined them. Jake was still relishing the closeness he had experienced with Alison. He looked at Liza. "Did you enjoy yourself?"

"I couldn't be happier. My sister is over the moon I'm moving here; the people are awesome; and I landed my dream job. What more could I want?" Liza's body had been buzzing for days with extra energy. Good thing she had somewhere to put it.

"Glad to hear it. I like an employee who sticks around."

"Alison, what time do you want me to come over tomorrow?"

"Ten o'clock? I have some early morning phone calls, but we'll have enough time to work. Then I want to head out to Fairside Manor in the afternoon. Can you spare most of the day?" A trace of guilt crept into Alison's thoughts for taking over Jake's new employee, but she pushed it away. She needed Liza.

"I'm here to help," Liza said, and smiled at Jake.

"Do you ladies need me to drive you out there?" Jake had promised Annie he would take her Christmas shopping and was hoping he didn't have to break his promise.

Liza spoke up immediately. "No need. I have a car."

"Great," Alison said. "I think Jake could use a break from chauffeuring me around every day."

Jake gently placed his hand on Alison's shoulder. "I've enjoyed every minute, but I did tell Annie I would take her shopping. I don't want to disappoint her."

Alison laughed. "Consider this your day off!" The light banter did not go unnoticed by Liza. She wondered if there was something going on between the two of them.

Pulling up to the main house, Jake reminisced about the evening.

His heart was tingling with awakening energy that had long been dormant. Looking over at Alison in the moonlight, he was awestruck by her beauty reflected in her pink rosy cheeks and sparkling eyes. She was special. And he knew it. "I'm going to drop you off and get Annie to bed. If you do need anything tomorrow, don't hesitate to call."

"I had a blast tonight. Thank you for teaching me to skate again." Her heart overflowed, bathing her soul with hope. She had nothing left to say but, "Goodnight, Jake."

"Goodnight. See you tomorrow."

Alison hopped out and waved to Jake as he drove towards his home. Looking up at the stars, she could see thousands of them shining in the clear night sky. She closed her eyes and made another wish for true love to come her way at the right time. Satisfied all would be taken care of in the big picture, she reached for the doorknob and drifted inside.

Chapter Thirteen

Alison had hardly had a moment to think about Jake since the previous evening's encounter. Probably a good thing. Too much to do now with the crew arriving soon. Sara informed her extra staff would come later to assist with house duties, so Alison needn't worry about anything.

Liza was right on schedule. The impressive estate had left her speechless while driving along the winding, tree-lined driveway leading to the grand mansion. Looking out she could see endless hills expanding to meet the edges of the mountains. She could imagine what it looked like in the spring and summer when the majestic trees and wildflowers were blooming outside. Inside, the exquisite art added to the magnificence of well-defined architecture like a museum holding a reverent space in time.

"This place is incredible! Beyond my wildest expectations."

"I know. I feel quite blessed to be working from here. Have a seat. Let's get started."

Liza pulled up a chair, opened her computer, and the two of them got busy. Time flew by, and before they knew it, Sara was at the door announcing lunch in the dining room. Sara preferred offering guest meals there rather than in the kitchen, which was reserved for small family meals. And she had considered Alison like family from the beginning.

Alison knew Liza would be a worthy asset to Jake's company. She was a wee bit envious of her working for him, but she tried to shake it off. After all, she was returning to New York. Maple Ridge had been great, but she had a life in the city. Or at least she used to. An undeniable longing was pulling her towards the tight-knit community. And Jake.

One of Sara's staff came out and asked if they wanted anything else. Alison looked at Liza. "More coffee? Anything else?"

"I'm stuffed and ready to go. I'm excited to see Fairside Manor."

Liza pointed to the tiny house close to the estate as they pulled out of the driveway. "Who lives there? A guest house?"

"Jake and Annie's home. Charming, isn't it?" Alison had loved the over-sized cottage from the beginning. "And the inside is as magnificent as the Anderson mansion. Just on a smaller scale. Jake has quite an eye for architecture and interior design."

"I guess it makes sense for him to live on the property. After all, one day this entire estate will belong to him. And Maggy. Jim Anderson's daughter. Do you know her?"

Alison was taken aback for a moment at how much Liza knew about Jake's family. She hadn't even had time to do her own research on him. "No, I don't know her."

"She's a big-shot television producer in Los Angeles. Took after her dad in a big way. She'll probably be here before Christmas." Liza had done her homework when it came to the Anderson dynasty.

"I'm sure you're right." Before Alison could contemplate any underlying intentions Liza might be harboring, they arrived at the manor. "Here we are."

"This looks so similar to the Anderson estate—only smaller. Doesn't it?" Liza was impressed.

"Yes, the land and property were donated years ago," said Alison. She wondered if Jim Anderson was responsible. "Let's go inside."

As the two women entered Fairside, Alison looked around and noticed the halls were much livelier than before since all the children were home. As usual, Karen was her most hospitable self and had fresh coffee and cookies waiting. "Bringing *Hands-On Kids* to Maple

Ridge has been such a blessing. I've never seen the town and children so inspired to come together for the holidays. We can't thank you enough."

"I think the real person to thank for everything is Jim Anderson. And of course, Jake, for loaning us Liza. I could never do what she does!"

"The worthy project is easy for me, and I love a challenge. Let's catch you up and get your input if you don't mind." Liza began to explain what they had accomplished so far.

Karen had made sure the children who had been interested in auditioning had come to the Saturday event. As they worked, Alison decided to leave them alone. She wanted to wander the building and grounds and take some pictures herself. One little girl recognized Alison as she came into the recreation room and rushed over to her.

"Hi! My name is Jolene. I know who you are!"

"You do?"

"You're the lady who makes television, right?"

"I guess. But there are a lot more people involved besides me. I could never do it alone without them."

"Can I be on your show?" Her pleading eyes looked up at Alison. How could she say no to any of these children?

"Of course. We'll find a place for you. Give me your full name and I'll call my assistant, Henry. He's doing all the casting."

"Do you want me to show you around? I'm an excellent guide. I do it all the time when people visit."

"Yes, I would love a tour. Lead the way!"

Jolene took Alison's hand and proceeded to tell her about each room as they walked around. Alison guessed she must have been about nine or ten years old. She was cute as a button with long, curly brown hair tied up with a ribbon, and a small frame holding her fearless little self. Alison wondered what her story was and how much pain she had endured.

When they went into the kitchen Alison was aware many of the older children were there, helping to prep for the next meal. Classical music was playing and Catherine, the head chef, was busy directing her young staff. Jolene pulled at Alison. "Come on. I want you to meet my sister, Mary Beth." Alison followed Jolene to an area near the stove set up for prepping vegetables. A tall, slender girl was attentively engaged in chopping carrots. As they approached, she looked up and Alison noticed she had sad, but beautiful blue eyes.

"Hey, Jojo. What are you doing back here?" She cautiously glanced at Alison.

"I'm giving a tour to Miss Rockwell. She's the television lady." Jolene was jovial, feeling very proud of herself. Quite the opposite of Mary Beth.

"Oh. Nice to meet you." Then she put her head down and went back to work. She obviously was not into conversing with Alison like her younger sister was.

Alison decided to leave it alone. "Yes, nice to meet you. Smells good in here."

Mary Beth kept chopping. "Always does."

Jolene tugged at Alison again. "Come on. I have more to show you."

Alison turned to follow her, but couldn't help but feel a forlornness surrounding Jolene's sister. She was curious but didn't want to pry.

Jolene intuitively picked up on her thoughts. "Don't mind her. She doesn't talk much. Not since the accident."

"Accident?"

"Our parents were killed four years ago in a car crash."

"I'm sorry." Alison couldn't imagine losing her parents at such a young age.

"And she's turning eighteen in June. I think she's worried about what will happen next. I know she doesn't want to separate from me, but she won't be able to stay here any longer."

"Right." Alison was quiet as the realization of what happened to older orphaned and foster children hit her. "Does she have any plans at all?"

"I think she would like to stay here and get a job as a cottage mentor for the older kids, but there may not be any openings."

"I see." Alison silently reflected on the predicament, understanding why Karen Thompson was working so hard. Developing a successful after-foster care program was sorely needed.

"I don't want to be separated either, but I try not to think about it." Jolene's concern was evident even though she tried to hide it.

Alison put her arm around Jolene. "It's six months away until June. I'm sure Mrs. Thompson is working on solutions for her. And you. I don't think you should worry about it. I always believe things will work out. You'll see." Alison hoped they would—and now she was determined more than ever to make sure they did.

Alison looked at her watch. "I think I better get back to work with the others. You've been a fantastic guide. I can see you have many talents."

Jolene beamed at her. "Thank you. Let me take you back. And don't forget to call your assistant about me."

"I definitely won't." Alison had an idea, but she wanted to run it by Karen first. She had to ensure they got the exposure and the funds to start a successful program.

When Alison entered the office, Karen looked up. "Alison. Come see what Liza has done. It's brilliant!"

Alison joined them and was equally impressed with Liza's skills. She would thank Jake later for loaning her to the cause. "Hopefully the show will drive the audience to donate on the website, and Fairside Manor will have the funds to start the program you want, Karen. I can't see how it wouldn't work."

"Yes, I agree. Fingers crossed!"

"It will," Liza said, with confidence. Then she picked up her camera. "I'm going to get some more shots. Is it okay if I take pictures of some of the children? I will get your permission before printing."

"Fine. Let me call for someone to take you around."

"I'd suggest Jolene," said Alison. "She was quite the guide."

"I agree. Let me get her."

Jolene came skipping into the office and took Liza's hand, eager to be of service. Alison shifted in her seat. "I have another idea I want to run by you."

"What is it?" Karen knew most of Alison's ideas were creative and unique.

"Jolene introduced me to her sister in the kitchen and told me their story. I was thinking. If Jolene was open to it, they could tell their story on camera. Like a private interview. And we could use it in our campaign. Do you think she would be agreeable? I could tell she has suffered, so I don't want to upset her. Or maybe we could just interview Jolene and talk about Mary Beth. What do you think?"

"Let me talk to the girls later and feel it out. Mary Beth is a kind, sweet girl, but has been shut down ever since the accident. She was just thirteen years old and was in the car. She survived, but her parents didn't. I think she feels some guilt, but I'm not sure. She wouldn't open up to our psychologist, so I just let her find her way around here over the years. She's done well and is successful in school, too."

"I don't want to do anything to hurt or worsen Mary Beth's emotional well-being."

"Don't worry. I'll feel it out when I talk to them. Perhaps if I can make her see this might help hundreds of other foster care and orphaned children, she might do it. If not, we'll think of something else. I think your idea is a good one, and we should pursue it."

"Let me know tomorrow what happens."

"I will. Your heart is in the right place, Alison. I know you get how dire this situation can be for the older kids. They often rotate in and out of foster care but inevitably end up back here." Karen stood up and put her arm around Alison. "Let's go find Liza."

***

Alison snuggled up in front of the fire with a steaming cup of tea after Liza went home. The afternoon had left her somewhat emotionally drained. The stories she heard had convinced her this program was more important than ever. Lost in her thoughts, she didn't hear the door slowly open until she glanced up.

Jake stood tall in the entrance, handsome as ever, cloaked in a red flannel shirt and blue jeans. His regular attire. "Didn't want to disturb you, but I was curious how it went at Fairside."

"Please. Sit. I want to tell you all about it. How about a cup of tea? I have a whole pot here. Sara keeps me stocked with caffeine." She laughed.

"I would love some."

Jake joined her in the plush, oversized armchairs as she proceeded to tell him about the day's events. Jake could see a new kind of intensity stirring in Alison's heart, and he understood it. An identical sentiment had hit him when he got involved with Fairside.

And now, they shared the same passion.

Staring into the flames, Jake made a decision. "Would you like to join Annie and me for dinner tonight? At our place?"

Butterflies rippled across Alison's stomach. This felt personal not business. "I would love to join you for dinner. What should I bring?"

"Just yourself. Annie and I have it covered."

Loud, rapid footsteps indicated Annie was about to enter the room from the corridor. She ran over to them, and Jake wrapped her up in his arms. "I've invited Miss Rockwell to dinner tonight and she has graciously accepted."

"Oh, goodie! You can sit next to me."

"I would love to." She gazed up at Jake. "What time?"

"Six-thirty?"

"I'll be there. It will give me time for a shower. I'm looking rather ragged these days. And it will only get worse, you'll see." Alison grinned as she knew what was in store for her.

Jake looked at her and was direct with his compliment. "You always look beautiful, Miss Rockwell. I wouldn't worry about it."

Surprised by the flattery, Alison said, "Thank you, Jake. Very kind of you."

"It's the truth." No more delays expressing himself.

Annie walked over to a side table where *The Brightest Star* was laid out. Alison had been putting the final touches on it earlier. "Can you read this to me tonight? Please?"

"It's still in the rough stage, but I will bring it."

Annie leaped to hug Alison. "I can't wait."

"You can critique, but don't be too hard on me." Alison grinned.

"Never."

As Jake watched the two of them together, he embraced the oncoming motion of an openness in his heart. Clara would have wanted him to find happiness again, and this woman seemed like a natural fit into his family. Annie adored her, and she was one of the kindest women he had known. And beautiful. Even if she lived in another city. Suddenly, the muscles in his stomach constricted. How could it work? Maybe he hadn't calculated this through enough. Menacing thoughts of doubt were resurfacing but Jake nudged them away.

Alison's cellphone went off. Carolyn. "I have to take this, sorry."

Jake stood up and directed Annie to the door. "See you tonight."

"Yes!" Alison picked up her phone. "Hi, Carolyn. How are you feeling?"

"I'm fine. Getting stronger every day. What's this I hear about a fundraising campaign on my show? When were you going to tell me?" Carolyn was determined to get to Maple Ridge. She needed to step in and remind everyone who was the real boss of this show.

"I'm working out the details now. I will have something to show you by tomorrow evening or Monday morning. Liza will have the mock-up of the website with information, pictures and possibly an interview."

"Liza? Who's Liza? I don't remember seeing her on the budget." Maybe this was her loophole with Alison. She could be getting in over her head with the budget. "Did you clear this with George?" she smirked to herself.

"Yes, but no need to worry. It's not costing us a thing. Liza's on loan from Jake Sanders for the next couple of weeks. It's his gift to Fairside." Alison could feel her stress level starting to rise. Carolyn was immensely bothered not to be involved with details on a daily basis. She suspected she was going to show up in Maple Ridge sooner rather than later.

Jim Anderson's nephew. She needed to contact him again.

Carolyn's brain began formulating a possible angle to disrupt Alison's place in the company. She knew if she did a good job, Carolyn's position could be in jeopardy. "Send me everything as soon as you have it. I want to be included in the email to George, understand?" Even though she had temporarily been taken off production for this particular episode, she was not going quietly. She knew Alison would do anything she asked of her.

"You've got it. Take care of yourself." Alison wanted nothing more than to get off the phone as soon as possible.

"I will." And hung up.

Alison let out a long sigh, knowing she could never go back to work for Carolyn. Too much stress. And she wasn't a nice person on top of it all. Perhaps fear or even loneliness were underlying reasons for her coldness. Alison knew she didn't have a family and this job was the most important thing to her. It kept her self-esteem afloat and gave her purpose. Alison decided she could be compassionate with her by thinking about her like this. After all, she was just human like the rest of us. She straightened up her desk and went upstairs. Now was the time to put on one of her dresses. She wanted to look attractive for Jake, as a woman, not just a colleague. Nothing could replace Clara, but she hoped to win a special place in his heart.

***

Carolyn hobbled around her apartment, pacing back and forth on her crutches. Pausing to look out the window at the Manhattan streets below, an idea came to her. Next week she would have a chat with Jake Sanders. She had some pertinent information about Alison he needed to know.

Chapter Fourteen

Darting around the kitchen, Jake and Annie were on duty making a delicious roasted chicken with assorted vegetables, a tossed salad and warm bread still in the oven. Sara had graciously given them an apple pie when she heard they'd invited Alison to dinner. Cooking was a productive outlet for Jake's nerves as he anticipated the possibilities of a relationship. In his heart, he knew Alison could be the one.

When the doorbell rang, Annie ran to open it. "Welcome to the Sanders! Let me take your coat."

As Alison walked in, she noticed the fire was blazing, the table was set by candlelight, and Jake was bent over the oven in the kitchen. The Christmas tree they had decorated looked magical with its shimmering lights and a glowing aura. As she walked into the living room, Jake appeared from the kitchen. His jaw dropped at the sight of her. She was dressed in a flowing, green dress made of silk with velvet trim around the sleeves and collar, and had changed into a pair of high heels from her boots at the door. She was stunning, and Jake was unable to speak for a moment.

Alison came closer and handed him a bottle of wine. "Here's my contribution. Well, Sara handed it to me on the way out. I think it might be from your uncle's collection in the cellar. Hope he doesn't mind." She could tell Jake liked what he saw.

"I'm sure he doesn't. He won't miss it." Jake brought himself back to reality. "You look gorgeous. I mean it. I think I'm underdressed." He laughed as he glanced down at his regular jeans and flannel shirt attire.

"No problem. I needed a change and a chance to dress up. I've been in work mode nonstop and couldn't resist getting into the holiday groove. After all, tis the season! And besides, I like the way you look in jeans and flannel. Very handsome." There. She had told him what she thought, even if she was blushing.

"Thank you, Miss Rockwell. Kind of you to say so." Jake's grin widened as he fell into a playful mode of flirting.

"Do you need some help? It smells heavenly." Alison couldn't take her eyes away from Jake's intense stare.

"We've got it covered. After all, my sous chef is outstanding." Jake placed his hand on Annie's shoulder. "Would you like a glass of wine while you wait for dinner? It will be about fifteen minutes."

"If you are."

Annie interrupted. "Why don't you guys go talk by the fire? I'll finish the salad, Dad. Then can I change my clothes and put on a dress, too?"

Jake lovingly touched his daughter's face. "You are the best daughter any father could want. Of course, you can wear a dress. You two are going to make me feel unfitting for such formal company!"

Alison added, "But the chef must keep to his attire, in case there are emergencies in the kitchen."

"Let's hope there are none of those. We'll finish the salad, Annie. Why don't you go upstairs and change? Right, Miss Rockwell?"

"Of course." Alison didn't care what she did as long as she was close to Jake.

Annie gleefully went upstairs, while Jake and Alison put the finishing touches on the salad. Jake poured their glasses of wine and suggested they sit on the couch in front of the fire.

As they sat down, Jake was close to Alison. She could smell his faint cologne mixed with the delectable aroma of food cooking in the kitchen. She liked it. She liked everything about this moment. The fire. The man. The possibilities.

Jake looked at her. "What are you thinking?"

He caught Alison off guard, but she wanted to be completely honest with him. "I'm thinking, how lucky I am to be spending an evening with you and your daughter. And I'm even getting fed!"

"Funny. I'm thinking the same thing. How lucky I am such a beautiful, radiant woman has walked into my home to share this evening with me." He held up his glass. "A toast. Here's to new acquaintances, a successful show, and creating future memories with those new friends."

Alison raised her glass. "Yes, to a promising future." She looked Jake squarely in the eyes, hoping he felt her intention. She wanted him to know the door was open.

Jake sank back into the couch. "Tell me more about yourself, Alison Rockwell. What is your family like? Why New York?" Jake was interested to hear about her personal life and what led her to this point.

"Where do you want me to start?"

"Anywhere."

Alison proceeded to tell him about her family, growing up in Connecticut, going to college and landing on *Hands-On Kids*. It had been quite a journey—but nothing like these last two weeks. This period had been memorable and overwhelmingly life-altering. Alison's shoulders relaxed, and her eyes sparkled as she moved from talking about her past to revealing personal hopes and dreams to come. "Enough about me! I've been gabbing incessantly. What about you? What's the real story of how you landed at Anderson Estates?"

Jake wanted to share more of himself with Alison. About the accident, his childhood with Uncle Jim, boarding school, college, even Clara. Since they didn't have much time, he briefly highlighted the main events of his life. As he spoke, Alison slowly began to understand him better. What he must have gone through with such loss at a young age. The immense caring and love he had received from his uncle. And the journey bringing him to settle in Maple Ridge. Listening to him only confirmed what Alison had been thinking all along. This was an extraordinary man. He was kind-hearted, thoughtful and willing to sacrifice his own dreams for those he loved. But now, with the launch of his new imprint, it looked like his creativity and business skills were going to have the perfect platform to merge and flourish. A surge of pride filled her heart.

Jake put his glass down on the table and reached out, gently touching Alison's hand. "Now you know pretty much everything about me. At least the important stuff."

Alison placed her hand over his. "Thank you. I appreciate you being so sincere with me. And genuinely honest." The warmth of his fingers was radiating up her arm.

Jake reached up and softly brushed a loose hair away from her face. "You're welcome. And thank you for doing the same." Jake wanted to lean over and kiss her but heard the tread of little feet coming down the stairs.

Alison thought he might kiss her, but she heard Annie approaching as well.

Vibrant as a shiny candy cane, Annie twirled in front of them, decked in a red dress with her hair tied up in a white bow. "I'm ready for dinner."

"You look beautiful," Alison exclaimed.

"Yes, you do, darling. Now, I'm truly underdressed," said Jake.

"It's okay, Dad. We'll still eat with you." All three of them laughed.

"You better or the chef may not serve you." Jake stood up and offered his hand to Alison to help her off the couch. "Let's eat."

The three gathered around the table, as holiday music played in the background. Her hopes for something more happening with Jake were strong as ever and she could even feel self-doubt melting away. After saying grace, everyone began eating and Alison looked up with total pleasure in her eyes. "This may be the best chicken I've ever had. How did you learn to cook like this?"

Annie spoke up first. "He watched a lot of cooking shows after Mom died. I think he was afraid I would starve." Everyone laughed.

"It paid off. Your culinary skills are far superior to mine, just saying."

"Good to know." Jake grinned.

As they continued to eat, Annie noticed Jake and Alison were periodically sending glances to each other indicating they were definitely interested in each other—even if they didn't admit it. Annie was sensitive for her age and very much aware of their attraction for each other. She was hopeful they would do something about it. Adults are so silly sometimes, she thought.

After dinner, they relaxed while drinking peppermint eggnog and talking around the fire. No denying the room overflowed with holiday spirit. Jake glanced at his watch, aware it was getting late. "Annie, I think it's time to get ready for bed. What do you say?"

"Miss Rockwell, did you bring your book?"

"Yes, I did. I left it in a bag by the door. I'll be up in ten minutes."

"Thank you. And thanks, Dad, for the dinner. I love you!" Annie threw her arms around Jake, squeezing him hard.

Jake held his daughter close. "I love you too, sweetheart. I'll be up to say goodnight after your story." He paused to watch her as she released her grip and trotted up the steps.

Alison noticed the big mess in the kitchen. "Let me help you clean up a bit before I read to Annie."

"If you insist. But I can handle it myself, just saying." He grinned at her.

"Good to know," she said, grinning back at him.

Alison quickly fell into the rhythm of working with Jake in the kitchen as if they had been doing it for years. Until a voice at the top of the stairs interrupted them.

"I'm ready." Annie, dressed in her pajamas, was sitting on the top step, anxiously awaiting Alison.

Alison put down her dish towel. "Wish me luck!"

Jake reached out and gently touched her arm. "Don't worry. She's an easy audience. She's going to love your book. I did."

Alison squeezed his hand. "Thank you."

Annie jumped into her bed, pulled up the covers, and pointed to the spot next to her. "You can sit here. Then I can look at the pictures. What's the name of your story?"

"The Brightest Star," replied Alison.

"Oh, I like it already." Stars always made her think of her mom.

Alison slowly opened her book. She felt a tingling inside, as if receiving a sign that she was on the right path of fulfilling her destiny. It was just a simple reading, but it held a more relevant meaning for her. "Once upon a time, there was a very, very bright star named Alina. Her light was the brightest of all the stars. She had always been very bright, even as a child." Alison continued through the story while Annie listened intently.

When Jake had finished his kitchen duty, he headed upstairs to Annie's room. Hearing Alison read, he decided to wait outside the door and listen.

Nearing the end of the book, Alison looked over at Annie. She was still wide awake. "As Alina looked down at earth, she felt another wish coming her way. She smiled and knew someone, somewhere believed in the magic of wishing upon a star. And surely, when the time was right, happy surprises would come their way. The end."

"Read it again!"

Alison laughed, and on cue, Jake walked into the bedroom. "I think once is enough tonight, darling. Miss Rockwell has had a long day. Let's allow her to get home at a decent hour."

Annie looked at her dad and knew when not to argue. "Another time?"

"Yes, another time." Alison rose to her feet. "I'll be downstairs when you're done."

"Be right down," Jake replied.

Alison walked into the kitchen thinking she would help clean it up, only to find Jake had finished everything. My, he certainly is efficient. She walked around the living room, looking at the art and photographs of his family. She picked up one of Clara, taken in her art studio in Manhattan—a beautiful woman with striking facial features. Thoroughly absorbed in the image, Alison didn't notice Jake descending the stairs. He came up behind her.

"She was an extraordinary woman," he said, his voice filled with emotion.

Startled, Alison jumped. Embarrassed for snooping around, she was quick to respond. "I'm so sorry. I couldn't help but look at your pictures. I hope you don't mind."

"I don't mind. It's time I'm more open about my past. Especially with you." He moved closer to Alison. "She would have wanted me to be happy. Move on if the right person came along and not feel guilty about it. I think I've been trying to for quite a while but just couldn't. I guess the right person never came along—until now." He slowly approached and reached his hand up to gently brush a hair from her face.

Alison was quivering inside. She could hear Jake's breathing and feel the heat of his body drawing nearer. The magnetism between them was palpable as her knees grew weak. She could only whisper, "Yes?"

"Yes. Until I met you." Jake slowly leaned down towards Alison, softly bringing his lips to hers.

Alison met his kiss with a passion of her own. It was a gentle kiss, but their desire bonded them in the moment. Afterwards, Alison could only look into his eyes, searching for what she hoped was there. The same feeling exploding inside of her.

Jake kept his body close to hers, gazing into her eyes. "I hope you don't mind I kissed you." He wanted to make sure he wasn't stepping over a boundary they both had tried hard to keep.

Alison stammered, "No. Not at all."

"I've wanted to for some time, but our work situation prevented me from doing so. I guess I decided work or no work, I didn't want to hold it in anymore."

Alison could hardly catch her breath. A little light-headed, she was trying to get the words out. "Yes. I know. I've been feeling the same way. But I'm glad you did. We'll just have to keep our personal life separate from work."

Jake laughed. "If we can. But yes, I will make a gallant effort to do so." He touched her face again. "You are a beautiful woman, Alison Rockwell."

Alison blushed. "I'm glad you think so." She didn't want the magic to end, but knew it was getting late and she had to get up early to finish some work before church. She also needed some time to process what had just happened. "Thank you for a lovely evening, Jake. And dinner. And everything."

"The pleasure was mine, Miss Rockwell." Jake felt a sense of relief. Like a heavy burden had been lifted off his chest. "I'll walk you home if you like."

"Thank you, but it's such a short distance, I'll walk on my own. You stay here in case Annie needs you."

"Are you riding with us to church tomorrow?" Jake didn't want to let her go, but he knew this had been a big step and enough for now.

"I would love to. Same time?"

"Yes. I'll see you in the kitchen for breakfast."

"I'll be there."

Jake helped put her coat on, handed her the bag with her book in it, and stared into her eyes once more. "I think your book was a success, don't you?"

"Annie may be a little prejudiced towards liking it, but I enjoyed the compliments. The real test will be when I read it to someone who doesn't have any connection with me."

"I have a feeling this book will be well received." Jake opened the door for her.

"Goodnight, Jake."

"Goodnight, Alison. Sweet dreams."

Alison tip-toed into the winter's night as feathery flakes of snow drifted in the air in front of her. *What just happened?* She glided towards the house in an enchanted, dream-like state, determined to take the magic of this night into the depths of her heart and hold it there for safe-keeping.

Chapter Fifteen

Alison's body stretched under the silky sheets of her bed, basking in luscious memories of the previous evening. Still, on cloud nine, she wanted to stay there forever. She pulled the covers up to her chin, fending off any pesky questions disturbing her bliss. If doubt reared its ugly head, she would ignore it. Of course, she had a thousand questions racing through her mind wondering what came next? She took a deep breath and told herself to relax. *Enjoy this moment and whatever may come your way. You can handle it.*

But what if he regrets the kiss? Alison gently shook her head and jumped out of bed. *Get a grip! Nothing of the sort will happen.* But she knew she would drive herself crazy if she didn't practice living in the moment. And thank god, Jenny was arriving today along with Henry and the director. Just the distraction she needed. She quickly got dressed for church and went downstairs for breakfast. She was looking forward to seeing Jake again. Yes, all would work out.

As she followed the scent of bacon sizzling, she could hear Annie's voice chattering away. She took one last look in the hallway mirror, ran her fingers through her hair and entered the kitchen. Annie chirped, "Good morning Miss Rockwell. How are you? Did you have fun last night?"

Everyone laughed, and Alison caught Jake's inviting eyes riveted on her. The same feeling of shared chemistry was still there. "Yes, I had a wonderful time with you last night." Then she made sure to send a glance of acknowledgment to Jake. "Your father is quite the chef."

"You were quite the perfect guest, I must say."

Sara immediately noticed something different between the two of them. She knew they liked each other, but something must have happened to take it to a different level. She hoped so. They both deserved each other. Sara responded, "How so?"

"Alison read me her new book. Have you seen it?"

"No, I haven't. But I would love to."

A rosy hue spread across Alison's cheeks. "Annie is a good audience."

Jake wanted her to know his feelings hadn't changed since the night before. "I think it's wonderful, too. You are a budding, new author, waiting to explode. You'll see. I'm usually right about these things."

Sara agreed. "Yes, he usually is, if it involves business of any kind. I'm a first-hand witness over the years."

Alison's eyes looked away for a moment as all the praise hit her with a feeling of awkwardness . "Thank you, to all of you. I guess we'll have to wait and see what the future brings." Avoiding any further conversation of herself, she turned to Sara. "Do you have everything you need for the guests arriving today? Is there anything I can help you with?"

"No, dear. Everything is set. Jenny's room is next to yours, and I put Mr. Hastings on the first floor down the hall. The rest of your crew are staying at the inn, correct?"

"Yes. I didn't want to overwhelm you. Sam Hastings has been the director for five seasons. As a producer, I want him easily accessible. We'll have notes to go over every night."

"When do they arrive?"

"Later this afternoon. They each have a car and Henry is coming into town as well."

"I'll make a nice supper for us tonight. Say, around six?"

"What about us?" Annie asked. "Are we invited?"

Alison looked at Jake before he could protest Annie's request. "Of course. You both are part of the innermost undertakings of this show."

Sara added, "Yes, and part of the Anderson family. Don't forget! Remember, you are the real host and hostess."

Jake laughed. "I guess we are." He glanced intently at Alison. "At your service, Miss Rockwell."

Their eyes locked, and Alison felt like the previous evening was still happening. Nothing had changed. She could relax. "Be careful what you ask for, Mr. Sanders."

"Oh, I'm very clear on what I'm asking for," replied Jake, not backing down.

Alison blushed, and Sara was most definitely assured something had happened between them. Sara hoped their feelings would work out. She knew Jake would never move back to New York, and she didn't know how Alison felt about Maple Ridge and small-town living. But from her interactions with the community, Sara could see it might be a perfect fit for her as long as she didn't have big city aspirations for her future. Then there could be a problem.

Alison looked at her watch. "I need to make a couple of quick calls before we go. Meet you at the car in fifteen?"

"Yep," Jake replied. He and Annie went back to his house to freshen up and get the car.

Alison checked in with her staff to ensure everything was going as planned. She was getting excited for the upcoming week, even with a romantic diversion brewing in the background. She was ready for both. Bring it on! She grabbed her coat and walked outside. Winding along the path to the car, Alison was looking forward to some peace, quiet, and prayer time.

Arriving at the church, Jake said, "I'm going to drop Annie off at Sunday school. I'll meet you inside."

Annie piped up. "Can Alison come too?"

Alison didn't hesitate. "Yes, I'd love to escort you. Let's go."

Jake decided not to argue. He was getting used to the three of them spending time together. It seemed so natural. He realized he didn't want it to end. How it was going to work out, he had no idea. But after last night, he was feeling more confident Alison felt the same way. He had always done what was best for his daughter and now, perhaps, the time had come to do the same for himself. For both of them. It seemed they both wanted the same thing. The same person. Alison Rockwell.

As the minister spoke about the spirit of Christmas and giving, Alison sensed she was undoubtedly sinking into her authentic self. She was comfortable in her own skin and content with life as it was. She couldn't be happier and knew Jake was part of the reason.

Unknown to Alison, Jake was sitting next to her, dwelling on a similar introspection. He hoped his plan worked. He didn't want to get his hopes up too high, but there was a good chance it would.

As Alison finished her conversation with Christine after the service, Jake approached them. "Excuse me, ladies, but can I have a word with Alison?"

Christine gave him her brightest smile. "Of course. You two must have much to do."

Alison laughed. "I think we all do." She nodded to Christine. "I'll see you tomorrow."

Jake gently touched her arm as they moved away from the crowd. "I hope you don't mind, but I have to spend some time at the bookstore today. And take Annie to her friend's house so they can go sledding and play together. I'll drop you off at the house, let Annie change her clothes, and then I'm going to be busy the rest of the day." His voice was gentle, resisting the urge to pull her into his arms again. He wanted her to know he cared.

A warm sensation wrapped around Alison's heart. Jake's priority for considering others inspired her. "Of course. I don't expect you to be at my beck and call every day, or every minute." She grinned at him. "You have a life to live and a business to run. I actually need the afternoon in my office to prepare for all the chaos about to descend upon Maple Ridge."

"I'm sure you can handle it, Miss Rockwell."

"Hopefully so, Mr. Sanders."

Jake wanted to say something about last night, and he didn't know when he would get another private moment with her. "I meant what I said about finding the right person last night. I'm glad I kissed you." He waited for her response.

Alison blushed, but tenderly touched his arm. "I am, too."

With braids flying, Annie came skipping into their private bubble. "Let's go so I can go over to Katie's house, Dad."

Jake put his arm around her. "Ready when you are."

"You've gotten very good at this chauffeur thing, Mr. Sanders." Alison liked teasing him.

"I think so." Jake couldn't be happier. "Let's go, girls."

The three of them left the church and headed home. As they left, Reverend Michael took notice and reflected on how closely Jake and Alison had interacted when they spoke to each other. He smiled. Perhaps a Christmas miracle was in store for them both.

***

Alison massaged her hands, taking a break from organizing, double-checking details, and trying to stay calm. Engaged in her work was the best way she knew to distract herself. But Jake had made a bold move. But how would it work? She knew Jake would never leave Maple Ridge. She hadn't even thought about what it would look like if she left New York. But to give up her career for a man? She gently placed her hand by her heart, trying to soothe the nerves tightening in her chest. *Get a grip, girl. It was just one kiss. Nothing else. But still, a beginning.*

Looking out at the snow-covered hills, she saw Jenny drive up. Just what the doctor ordered. She jumped up, grabbed her coat, and ran out the door into the frigid air. As soon as Jenny got out of the car, Alison gave her the biggest hug. "I'm so glad to see you! You don't even know!"

Jenny was still in shock, witnessing the magnitude of Anderson Estates. She returned Alison's hug with equal enthusiasm. "Me too! And I can't believe we are staying here. This place is mammoth! Much bigger than I ever imagined."

"I know, right? Come inside. It's cold out here." With arms around each other, the two friends went inside. Sara was at the door.

"Welcome! Marty will take your bags upstairs and you two can get catch up. I'll bring tea and snacks to your office in a bit." Sara knew Alison needed her girlfriend and was very aware of the dance she had been doing with Jake. As a woman, she knew those kinds of emotions could wreak havoc on any sane person.

"Our office is in the main library on the first floor," said Alison. "Very cozy and relaxing. Probably the best we've ever had as a workspace."

"Can't wait to see it." Even with Mike in her life, Jenny missed Alison. Nothing could replace a best girlfriend. As Jenny walked through the hallway, her eyes were soaking in the beauty of the Anderson home. She was even more impressed by the craftsmanship and architectural design as an artist. Alison followed her into the guest bedroom, and Jenny collapsed on the soft, velvety quilt covering the bed. "Why didn't you tell me how incredible this place was? I was expecting some little inn in the country!"

"I guess I've been so busy, I didn't think to mention it."

Jenny had also noticed there was something different about Alison. And she didn't think it was the excitement of being producer for *Hands-On Kids*. "I think there's other personal matters going on."

Alison knew her friend could read her like a book without any words. She paused, then spoke. "I've been getting closer to Jake, my host."

"And what does 'closer' mean?" Jenny's intuition had told her there might be some romantic involvement with this man. She could tell by Alison's voice over the phone whenever she mentioned him.

Alison knew she couldn't keep any secrets from Jenny. Nor did she want to. "Jake and I have spent a lot of hours together. He's been more than gracious with his support and assistance in all the preparation work for the show. But as time has passed, I feel we both are exploring in our own heads what it could be like to be together. Romantically speaking."

"And how do you know?"

"A kiss happened. Last night."

"And?"

"He told me this morning he was glad he had kissed me."

"And?" Jenny wanted more.

"Nothing else. All very new. And I don't know how it could even work long-distance. And he has a daughter, Annie. She's wonderful as well. The three of us have been hanging out together."

"This sounds more serious than you've been letting on. We have to assess this situation. When do I meet Jake?" Even though romance was in the air, Jenny felt protective of her friend.

"You'll meet him tonight at dinner. Sara is making a feast for us, Jake and Annie, Henry and Sam. It should be fun. Before all the commotion begins." She laughed.

"The apartment has been lonely without you there. But I've been spending more time with Mike, and I think we may have a future together."

"I knew it!" Alison had always liked Mike. They were a perfect fit. "Do you think he'll be able to come up for the last day or two of shooting? There's plenty of room here if you want to invite him."

Jenny eyes widened. "Really? This place is so romantic. I'll ask him later in case he can get away from work. They're starting to wind down for the holidays."

"Settled. Now freshen up and meet me in the library. At the bottom of the stairs turn right, down the hall and you'll find me. I'll leave the door open."

"Be right there."

***

Carolyn promptly delivered her daily check-in by phone. As always. Alison picked up. "Hi, Carolyn. How are you?"

"I'm fine. More importantly, what's going on there? Are the staff starting to arrive? Is Sam there yet? What are your plans for tomorrow in prep?"

Alison knew Carolyn would be calling for these ongoing updates and would most likely appear soon. As long as things ran smoothly, she had nothing to fear from Miss Parks. Alison gently rubbed her temples, trying to prevent a headache from coming on. Although she was more confident, worry had a way of creeping in and playing havoc with her mind.

When Carolyn hung up, she knew she had to get to Maple Ridge. Another week of rest and she was hiring a driver to take her there. She decided to book a room at the inn under a pseudo name, so no one knew she was coming. Her visit would be a surprise and not expected. Better, since Alison couldn't prepare beforehand. Carolyn snickered to herself. And she was putting a call into Jake tomorrow. She was getting her show back!

*****

When Jenny entered the large library converted to the production office, she gasped. "How did you ever set up everything by yourself? And a fireplace? I could live in here. I love it!"

"Jake helped me by bringing in furniture and arranging it with me. He wasn't afraid to jump in and help me these last couple weeks, whenever and wherever I needed it. Quite gallant in a selfless way."

"I'm liking him already. Now, show me what you have to start prepping set designs. I'm so grateful to you for this opportunity." Alison had given her additional duties as set decorator.

"How could I not hire you? It was easy since you're doing two jobs at once." She laughed. "George has been approving almost everything I ask. And besides, you brought my budget down."

"You know I'm ready." Jenny flung her arms in the air and twirled around in a little happy dance.

"And I have plenty of volunteers ready to help with anything you need. You will meet them tomorrow at the community center."

"Perfect!"

Alison's hands spread over the visual plans and sketches on the table, pointing out responsibilities for Jenny. A reflection out the window caught her attention. "Jenny, Sam is here. I'm going to help him get situated. Back in a bit."

"No problem. I want to expand on some of these ideas and show you both tonight."

Alison gave her a thumbs up. Jenny's arrival calmed the pestering thoughts swirling around her brain. Navigating emotions was easier with her friend by her side.

***

Sam was a handsome fellow, tall and fit. His hair was brown and wavy, slightly longer, just touching his collar. He had alluring, dark eyes and a benevolent smile with a knack for making others on a set feel comfortable. He was single, in his mid-thirties and had found financial success with his steady gig on *Hands-On Kids*. Alison knew he dated but she didn't think he had a girlfriend. But she wasn't sure. He never invited a woman to the set when filming or attending any of the wrap parties.

As Alison opened the door, Marty was right behind her, ready to take his bags. "Hi, Sam. Welcome to Anderson Estates. How was your trip?"

"Fine. Quite the set-up you've arranged, Miss Rockwell. Very impressive." Sam had always liked Alison. He had seen the way Carolyn treated her and it had bothered him. But it wasn't his place to say anything. It would be a welcome relief to work with her as his boss, even if she was younger. He knew she was committed and well capable of producing. He was happy for her and this new opportunity.

"I think we have Mr. Anderson to thank for everything. Come in." Alison gave him a quick hug and then let Marty take over. "After you've settled in your room, come join us in the library." She pointed in the direction down the hall. "It's our office while we're here. Dinner is at six."

"I'm looking forward to working with you, Alison. I hear you've been doing an impressive job in the preparations."

"I'm giving it my best shot! Just follow Marty. He'll take great care of you."

Sam was happy to be in Maple Ridge. His parents and younger sister were back in Ohio and he would most likely fly out there on Christmas Day. *Hands-On Kids* had become his family and doing a Christmas show helped to fill the void he sometimes felt at the holidays since he was usually working.

Alison joined Jenny back in the library, and the two freely chatted about personal things as they went over details. Jenny loved working even though she would prefer sitting in front of the fire with her cup of tea while hearing details of every encounter Alison had experienced with Jake. But bits and pieces of their developing relationship came out in the conversation. At least until Sam showed up at the door.

"Welcome to your new office. Come sit at the conference table and catch up on our plans. I gave you a desk over there in the corner. The production truck will arrive on Tuesday, so I know you'll probably move back and forth between the two. But I thought staying here would give you a quiet respite when you needed it. I think we have everything you might need. Tell me if we don't and I'll get it for you."

"I have to say, I've never worked in such a homey environment. Perfect for the holidays. I think the Christmas spirit is with us, ladies."

Jenny added, "I agree. How could we not be successful?"

Alison clapped her hands together. "Thank you both for coming early and for being so positive. I think we have a great team, don't you?"

"Most definitely!" Jenny raised her tea cup in the air. "To sharing the Christmas spirit with the world through the lens of *Hands-On Kids*!"

Alison joined her toast. "And bringing hearts and minds together in this time of giving and celebration!"

Alison gave Sam a mug and he raised it with theirs. "And giving parents new ideas of how to spread the Christmas spirit with their families and others!"

The three co-workers erupted into laughter as a voice resonated by the door. "Hey, what's all the noise in here?" Jake's broad shoulders spread across the entranceway as he stood watching them with an unconcealable grin on his face.

Alison turned and caught his eyes directly looking at her, even with others in the room. Jenny caught the look they were giving each other. *Oh my, she's sunk. He's gorgeous and obviously into her.* And Jenny could see she was totally smitten with him. One look expressed a thousand words.

Alison raised her hand towards Jake. "And here is our gracious host, Jake Sanders. Come in and meet everyone."

Jake was eager to meet Alison's core team. He walked in, shook Sam's hand and greeted him, then turned to Jenny. "And you must be Alison's best friend, Jenny. Nice to meet you."

"And you as well. I've heard you've been taking very good care of our producer."

"I've tried." Jake looked fondly at Alison.

"He's done an awesome job of doing so." Distracted by a text on her phone, she added, "It looks like Henry is here and is on his way over."

Jake said, "I almost forgot. I was sent in here to tell you dinner will be ready in about fifteen minutes if you want to freshen up."

"Thanks, Jake. Let me tidy up the office and everyone can meet in the dining room."

Sam eased himself into one of the plushy armchairs and let his head fall back, taking in the change of scenery. "I feel like I'm on a retreat rather than a job. Hope I can hold on to this feeling all week." He laughed.

Alison laughed with him. "Better hold on to it because it might get a little bumpy from here."

Jake was staring at Alison. His heart was rapidly beating, spellbound by her loveliness and bubbly personality. Jenny picked up on his adoring vibe and was hopeful he could be the kind of man Alison deserved. Someone who cared about her rather than just himself.

***

Alison stood in front of the mirror in her bedroom and decided to put on a dress. After all, this might be the last relaxing dinner she would have for a while. Henry arrived on time, pleased to be with his veteran crew, especially Alison. He had missed the daily interactions they usually had. Working remotely was adequate, but together was much better.

Sara was cruising around the kitchen, humming a Christmas tune, ecstatic to be entertaining. She loved the holidays, and the Anderson house was often full of guests. But this year was special, and she knew it.

As they sat down at the large dining room table, Annie came barging in, eager to meet everyone. She immediately went up to Alison. "Can I sit next to you?"

"Sure!" Alison placed her hand on her shoulder. "I want you all to meet an essential part of our team and hands-on consultant to the production. This is Annie Sanders. Jake's daughter. She's been invaluable to me these last two weeks and will also have a main part in the shooting with Sean and Melissa."

Annie graciously greeted all of the guests and Jake stood proudly by her side. He looked over at Alison and silently mouthed, "thank you." He appreciated how Alison could make anyone feel comfortable and welcome. It was another gift of hers.

After sitting down, Alison gave a prayer of thanks before they dug into the feast Sara had prepared. Within moments, laughing, and upbeat conversations floating back and forth. Sam and Jake seemed to hit it off, talking about art, directing, and New York. Alison was glad he had some male company for a change. It seemed most of her key people in Maple Ridge were women, which she loved, but guys need companionship, too.

After dinner, they all helped clean up, in spite of Sara's resistance. No one listened to her, so she surrendered. Might as well let everyone enjoy the giving spirit of the holidays.

Getting their tea or coffee, they gathered back in the library for one last meeting. As Alison walked away, she felt a light touch on her shoulder, and she knew it was Jake.

"I have to get Annie to bed, but I wanted you to know I can chauffer you all around tomorrow. It will probably be the last day, since I have to do some things at the bookstore and with Annie's school before they're out for holiday break. Since I have a large vehicle, it might be easier until your staff get physically acquainted with the town and surrounding area."

Alison placed her hand on his arm. "Yes, thank you. It will be a busy day, and I want to start right after breakfast. We'll hit the community center and bakery in the morning, and then Fairside Manor in the afternoon, ending at the bookstore."

"You can use my office upstairs if you need to go over anything from the day and meet with Liza. She should be there in the afternoon. I know she's busy with move plans in the morning."

"Jake, I'm happy you're here."

Jake wanted to kiss her again but knew there wasn't enough privacy. "And I'm glad you're here, Alison Rockwell." He held her gaze for a moment longer.

Was she crazy, Alison wondered, as Annie came running around the corner, announcing she was ready to go home, or had Jake almost kiss her again? She shook her head and retreated to the library for a quick production meeting with the others before bed.

Alison took a long, hot shower and afterward sat on the edge of her bed, brushing her hair. Looking down at her phone, she noticed she had gotten two voicemails during dinner. One from Carolyn and one from Steve. She texted Carolyn back and told her everyone had safely arrived and would send the day's schedule to her in the morning. She was exhausted from the day and couldn't deal with her now in more ways than one. Steve's message said he missed her and wanted to speak to her. She saw him in a much clearer light these days for the man he truly was. Sweet and kind at times, but primarily selfish and self-centered. She was grateful she had been given this opportunity to get away from New York and gain a new perspective. She liked the way her life was evolving in Maple Ridge and didn't know if she wanted to leave after the holidays. She wondered what Jake would think if she stayed. She put her brush on the dresser and climbed into bed. Closing her eyes and breathing deeply, she listened to an inner voice speaking to her. *Don't get ahead of yourself, girl.* This is where trust comes in—trusting in a higher power that all will be taken care of in her life. It was how she wanted to live her life and rolled over to turn out the light.

Chapter Sixteen

Jumping into a busy day came second nature to all of them, and Alison was confident in all of her colleague's skills. Everyone piled into Jake's car carrying computer bags and juggling production materials. As they descended upon the community center, Marilyn watched as the team seamlessly executed their preparations with precision. Her body pulsed with energy as she joined them, grateful to be part of such a marvelous event happening in Maple Ridge.

The next stop was Sweet Ridge bakery, where Christine welcomed them with coffee and snacks. She had set up a table in the back to have some privacy and get a feel for the place. Jenny could see she had a close relationship with Jake, but Christine's face lit up when introduced to Sam. Sam was an open, charismatic guy and the smile on his face seemed glued in place after he met her. The two strolled around the kitchen together while discussing where the best shots might be, how to set up the cameras in the back, and how much space he would need. Jenny whispered in Alison's ear. "I think our director may have found a new friend."

Alison smiled. She could see Sam was enjoying Christine's company and perhaps there might be a spark between the two of them. She hoped so.

Close to lunch time, Jake suggested they pick up sandwiches and drinks and take them out to Fairside for themselves and the manor staff. "He is thoughtful, isn't he?" Jenny whispered to Alison.

"Yes, he is." Alison knew Jake had won over her heart, partly by his loving and generous ways. Yes, he was handsome and sexy as ever, but the inside of him made him most attractive. Little did Alison know Jake often had the same thoughts about her.

Liza joined them at Fairside, and after the production meeting, Karen called on Jolene to give a tour. Before she got to the office, Karen spoke to the others. "I've talked to Mary Beth and Jolene about doing an interview together, and they have agreed. Although, Mary Beth was hesitant. She has been very withdrawn since the accident, and she needs to be handled gently." With raised eyebrows, she eyed Sam. "And I trust you will, right?"

Sam understood. "Yes, you have my word."

"And Alison and I will both be with you."

"I will do everything I can to make her feel comfortable. I'll try to do it with only one camera. And I suggest we do it in a location she selects. Let her feel she is more in control of the situation."

"Good idea," agreed Alison. She wanted the story to be truthful and engaging but not at the expense of upsetting Mary Beth.

As Jolene came knocking at the door, Karen opened it, and there she was, the bright, bubbly nine-year old enthused to be their tour guide. Sam, Jenny, Henry and Alison went with her and Jake and Liza stayed behind to work on last-minute details for Karen's website and fundraising campaign.

As the production crew filed out, Jake said, "We'll be right here if you need us." He spoke to the whole group, but his focus was only on Alison. Karen and Jenny both noticed the magnetism between the two but did not say anything.

The five of them meandered through the manor and grounds, discussing the best places for shooting. Most of the children were at school except for the older ones who had been released after mid-terms for holiday break. Some were helping in the kitchen, where Jolene knew her sister would be working.

Mary Beth was in the back, as usual, prepping vegetables. When the head chef saw them come in, she said to her, "Why don't you join your sister and these nice people in the cafeteria. Take them some cookies. I put a plate out over there."

Mary Beth looked up at Miss Waters and then saw Jolene. "Okay."

Jolene ran up to her before she grabbed the cookies. "Hi, sis." Mary Beth hugged her and said, "Hi, little one." It was the only time Alison had seen her smile—whenever Jolene was around. "Let's sit out there. Do you want to take the cookies out?"

Jolene was eager to help. "Yes!"

As all of them sat down, Alison greeted Mary Beth. "It's nice to see you again. And thank you for meeting with us. We appreciate your willingness to do this interview." She introduced her crew. Sam gently explained how logistics would work and gave her a copy of the questions, so she could prepare or delete any that made her feel uncomfortable. He wanted to film in a day or two, so they could be airing it during the earlier episodes as part of the fundraising campaign.

Mary Beth looked over the questions. "Do you have a pen?"

"Yes," said Sam.

She proceeded to cross off a few of the questions. Most of them dealing with the accident. "There. I deleted some. Let me think about where a good place would be to do it. Probably the library since it is quiet there."

"Wherever you want."

Alison scanned the sheet of questions and knew she'd have to work on them in order to get the story she needed and still be sensitive. "Do you mind if I look these over? I may want to change some. I'll stop by tomorrow to show you and see if you agree to any changes I make. What do you say?"

Mary Beth's mouth twitched for a second but then she nodded

her head in agreement. "You know where to find me."

After the tour, they gathered back in Karen's office. Alison faced the group. "Last stop. We saved the best for last." Her gaze was meant for Jake who caught it. "Starlight Books!"

Jake laughed. "I don't know if you'll agree, but I'll lead the way on this one." Jenny and Sam couldn't stop talking about how well Alison had done so far on the pre-production tasks.

"I couldn't have done it all without Jake Sanders."

Jake laughed. "Yeah. Best chauffeur ever."

"You were more, and you know it, Jake."

Jenny and Henry smiled at each other in the back seat. They knew exactly what was going on between the two of them, and Sam was beginning to catch on, too.

"If you say so, Miss Rockwell."

Still blushing, Alison proceeded with her vision for the show's finale. She had secured a well-known children's author who lived in New York and was willing to come on the show for the Christmas Eve shooting. She would arrive on the morning of the twenty-fourth and probably head back to New York after the episode. The episode was being filmed in the afternoon so the whole crew would have time to get back to their families for Christmas Eve.

Entering the bookstore was like stepping into a magical wonderland. Lucy and her new assistant, Cindy, couldn't stop embellishing the picturesque surroundings, and Annie and Tim had helped as the ideas kept flowing. Sam slowly shook his head back and forth, pleasure written all over his face. "This store is the best set we've ever had for the reading segment, Alison. You were right about this place."

"I know. Let me give you the grand tour." She led her crew around the store while Jake and Liza went upstairs. Annie and Tim were stationed at a large table in the back of the store, wrapping orders. Alison pointed to them. "Our best elves."

Annie put down her scissors and moved closer to introduce Tim to the others. He stood tall as he reached out his hand. "Nice to meet you. Welcome to Starlight Books."

Sam clasped his grip. "And I hear you're going to be one of our main actors."

"That's right, sir." Tim was well-trained in manners, being raised by a military father. "I'm looking forward to it."

"You know the most important thing, don't you?" asked Sam.

"To do a good job?"

"Yes, but the most important is to have fun!" exclaimed Sam. "Think you can?"

Tim looked relieved. "Yes, sir, I can!"

"And you can call me Mr. Sam as well."

"Okay!" The biggest grin spread across Tim's face.

Lucy put her arm around her son. "Tim, our video call is soon. Let's go upstairs where the room is quieter."

Tim turned to the rest of them. "My dad is calling in a few minutes. Got to go." Leaping two steps at a time, he followed his mom up the stairs.

Annie said, "I feel for him. He's missing his dad. I wish he could be here for Christmas, but he's deployed somewhere. I guess, he'll get to see Tim on television at some point."

As Annie's big, brown eyes looked up at Alison, her heart ached. She wished there was some way she could create a Christmas miracle and bring Tim's dad home. But she didn't have that kind of clout anywhere, and she knew it. She decided the next best thing would be to pray for him. "Yes, with film you always have it."

Upstairs, Jake made some space at one of the empty desks with a computer for Lucy and Tim. "Here you go. Say hi to John for me." Jake knew how hard being apart was for the both of them. He wished there were something he could do.

Tim could hardly contain himself when John Barnes came on the video screen. He had told his dad about *Hands-On Kids,* but now since the time for shooting episodes was drawing nearer, he couldn't sit still. "And guess what, Dad? I met the director! And the film crew is coming tomorrow."

"Sounds terrific, Timmy. I'm sure you'll be amazing. Just remember to have fun!"

"Mister Sam said the same thing. And you'll be able to see it all since they're recording it."

John wished he could be there with all of his heart, but duty called. "Can't wait to see it! I'll try and call next week, and you can tell me more."

"Okay, Dad. I love you!"

"I love you, too, son. Now let mom and me talk a bit, alright?"

"Alright." Tim left his mom alone with his dad and went back downstairs to find Annie and the rest of the gang.

"How are you holding up, Lucy?" Even though Lucy was one of the strongest women he knew, John was always concerned she worked too hard being a single parent and holding down a full-time job. Jake was often there to fill the male role when his son needed it, and John appreciated Jake and the financial opportunity he had provided for his family. They had known each other since they were kids, and he was glad they had reconnected when Jake moved back to Maple Ridge. And the fact that Annie and Tim had become best friends made it even better.

"I'm fine, darling. I don't want you worrying about me. The whole town is aflutter in Christmas festivities, and I'm busy as ever.

We're going to be fine." Lucy tried to give him her biggest smile, reassuring him his family was safe and well. But in her heart, she was missing him terribly. Nothing could fill her heart like the love of her husband. This holiday was tough without him, even though Jake tried his best to keep her occupied and include her in the day-to-day affairs of business. She prayed for his safety and hoped he would return soon. But the military sometimes changed his schedule, which drove her crazy, but she honored her husband's commitment and dedication to his country.

"Remember how much I love you, dear. Always and forever."

Lucy fought back tears but managed to respond. "Remember how much I love you, John. Always and forever." She blew kisses to him and he gestured back with the same display of adoration. "Stay safe and we'll see you when we see you."

"Have to go, Lucy, my love. See you when I see you." They said the same phrase when they were both trying to hold it together.

And with the click of the screen, he was gone. A tear rolled down Lucy's face. Now she could let her emotions release without reservation. She didn't want her husband or Tim to see her upset. No matter what anyone said or did, being separated was difficult. She took a breath, blew her nose, wiped her face and stood up. Being busy was the best way she could ride the wave of these emotions. As she walked past Jake, she said, "Thanks, Jake. Appreciate the privacy. I'll be downstairs if you need me."

"Anytime, Lucy." He said a silent prayer for the Barnes family. "I'll be down in a bit." A New York number appeared on his phone, so he picked it up.

"Jake, Carolyn Parks here. I need to discuss something with you."

Why was she calling him again? "I only have a minute. What is it?"

"In reviewing Alison's background, I remembered she has a degree in Literature." Carolyn knew about the imprint. "I think she may have ulterior motives for developing her professional relationship with you to pursue her writing career, not the television show. Very inappropriate, I must say."

Jake chuckled. "Funny, she read her book with my daughter, and Annie loved it. I think she is quite capable of handling two careers if she wants. Is there anything else, Miss Parks?"

Frustrated, Carolyn had nothing more to say. "No, but if something else comes up, I'll let you know."

"You can be assured, Alison is doing her best job up here in Maple Ridge." Jake had no time for this nonsense. And neither did Alison.

As Carolyn hung up, she was fuming. She needed a new plan.

***

The store was bustling with activity. Jake found Alison and motioned to speak to her. He watched her walking towards him and could feel his heart beating faster. The spark between them was getting stronger, no denying it.

"Everything alright?"

"Yes, couldn't be better." He had decided to keep Carolyn's prying phone call to himself. Alison didn't need the stress. "I have to take Annie to a rehearsal for the holiday show tomorrow. Are you guys ready?"

"Yes, we were just wrapping up. I'll gather the troops." As she spoke, she gently touched his arm.

Jake reached over and placed his hand on hers. "Thank you." Their eyes locked for a moment until Annie came running up.

"Come see how many presents we wrapped. We're almost done with your orders."

"You are amazing! We have to go home now. You have rehearsal tonight and I want to make sure you eat something healthy."

"Okay, Dad. I hear you. Let me get my backpack and I'll be ready."

***

As the crew entered the house, Sara served tea and her announcement for dinner time. Alison looked at Sam and Jenny. "Why don't you two take a little break and we'll meet for dinner? I think we had a productive day, don't you?"

"The best." Jenny hugged her friend. "This is going to be so much fun. I can feel it."

Sam nodded his head. "I agree. I think I'm going to work on a few things in the office before dinner, if you don't mind."

"Me too," said Jenny.

Alison shook her head. "I might as well join the party. I just didn't want to be a slave driver." Then she glanced at Henry. "Are you in?"

"All yours, boss." Henry was enjoying this new way of working in a more relaxed environment.

Alison glanced at her phone and saw Carolyn had called earlier. She'd better return her call, and Steve had left another voicemail. She would listen later. And her mom had called as well. Carolyn first, then her mom.

Carolyn picked up right away. "Where were you? You should have your phone on at all times!"

Another scolding. "Sorry, Carolyn. I was in the middle of an important conversation." Carolyn's persistent nagging wasn't going to get her down or sway her from focusing on the production quality. She ended the call as soon as possible.

When Mrs. Rockwell heard Alison's energetic words, she could sense a lilt in her voice and attributed it to her new job. But she wondered about Jake Sanders. Alison frequently talked about him, and as a mother she knew when there might be something brewing in the relationship arena. She was looking forward to meeting him. Then she would know. A mother's instinct was never wrong.

Plans were made after dinner since more staff would be arriving the next day. Alison would accompany Sam and one cameraman to Fairside to interview Jolene and Mary Beth. Two more days until the real show began. Alison had millions of ideas swirling in her mind as she tried to fall asleep, but her thoughts kept drifting to Jake. Maybe they could work something out when *Hands-On Kids* was finished shooting. Was there really a chance for a relationship with him? As her head lowered onto her pillow, she could see the stars shining brightly out the window. She closed her eyes, remembering her wish had been sent to the stars and was in safe keeping until the time was right.

Chapter Seventeen

Alison and Jenny filled their mugs with coffee as they chatted with Sara. Sam walked in with his jacket on, carrying all his gear. "I think I'll stop by the bakery for coffee and breakfast, if you don't mind."

Behind Sam's back, Jenny's lifted eyebrows signaled a subtle message. Alison said, "Sure, you can chat with Christine about any last details. They have wonderful croissants. Enjoy!"

"Meet you back here around one." He grabbed his briefcase and took off out the kitchen door.

Jenny said, "There is definitely some interest on his part—more than baked goods!" They both laughed.

"I know. I think Christine might be interested in him as well. Wouldn't it be lovely?" Alison let herself daydream for a moment about the possibilities of love. Including her own.

Her thoughts were interrupted by the backdoor opening. Shaking the snow off his boots, Jake rubbed his hands together, trying to get warm. "Good morning, ladies. How are you?" He looked down at his boots. "Sorry, Sara. I'm trying my best not to get dirt on your floor."

Sara waved her hand. "Don't bother. I'm used to people traipsing in and out all day. Besides, I have extra staff this week to take care of the cleaning." She laughed. "Coffee?"

"No thanks, I've got Annie in the car waiting and have to get her to school. I wanted to check in with you, Alison, to remind you I'll be tied up all day. Call me on my cell if you need anything." He knew he could have texted her, but he was getting used to seeing her every day. And he didn't want it to stop.

"No worries. Everyone has a car. Jenny or Henry can take me

places if needed. Thank you for telling me."

Jake nodded, soaking in his vision of Alison, then returned to his truck.

Sara looked at Alison. "I haven't seen his spirits so high in a very long time. I think you're a part of the reason. Hope you know."

Alison knew her spirits were lifted by his presence as well, and she didn't want it to end. To avoid giving any response, she picked up her phone. "Henry should be here any minute."

"Right behind you." Jenny raised an eyebrow, looked at Sara and then followed Alison to the office.

***

Alison and her camera crew arrived at the manor after lunch. Entering the large hallway, Karen motioned them to her office. "Mary Beth almost backed out, but I talked her into doing it. I emphasized that by telling her compelling story, audiences who had business connections, or financial means may be inspired to help more foster care youth and orphans turning eighteen. And between you and me, I know this would be the most healing thing she could do for herself. It's been four years! She doesn't need to carry this weight on her shoulders anymore. I hope I'm right."

Alison's facial expression grew serious. "What can I do?"

"I told her you would come to get her when you arrived. She's in bungalow five. Perhaps you could give her a few words of encouragement. Jolene, on the other hand has been ready all week." She laughed.

Alison motioned to Sam. "Why don't you get set up in the library and I'll go talk to Mary Beth. I shouldn't be very long."

"Sure thing. I understand." Sam's volunteer work with teenagers in New York had taught him how delicate situations could be.

As Alison approached the small bungalow, she could feel a quiver of trepidation in her gut. Not quite sure of what to say, she silently prayed to be guided, then gently knocked on the door.

Mary Beth slowly opened it. "Come in." She was dressed in a lovely, blue cotton dress that hugged her delicate figure, and understated make-up profiled her face. She was stunning.

"You look beautiful! Can I sit down?"

Mary Beth pointed to a small table and chairs by the window. "We can talk over here."

"I want you to know all of us are appreciative you've agreed to do this interview. I think you know what our goals are, but I wanted to know if you have any questions or concerns before we get started."

Mary Beth looked down at the table and then up at Alison. "I'm scared. I don't like to talk in front of people, and I don't like to talk about my past." Her hands were visibly shaking, twisted tightly together over her lap.

"I understand. I don't like talking in front of people either, if you can believe it. I like working behind the cameras."

The corners of Mary Beth's mouth lifted as she raised her head.

"Listen. You know most of the questions. We won't ask the ones you crossed off our list. And it will just be you and me and Sam, the director. And of course, Jerry, the guy holding the camera. But we can pretend you're just talking to me."

"Instead of this Sam?"

"Yes, I'll do it with you. He won't mind. He loves being behind the camera anyway."

Mary Beth was quiet for a second. "And you really think this will help? To fund after-foster care programs?"

"Most definitely. Donors need to see real people coming to a crossroads and facing a scary situation without the support they need. They have to hear a personal story, so they can relate to helping out with a cause."

"All I have to do is just talk with you?"

"Yes. I won't ask you to do anything else unless you want to do it."

Mary Beth shifted in her chair, smoothing out the skirt of her dress with her hands. "Do I look okay?"

"Gorgeous. Your make-up is flawless. I won't even have to touch it up." Alison laughed, and Mary Beth cracked a smile.

"Let's go then."

Mary Beth grabbed her coat, and the two of them walked towards the main house. When they got inside, Alison put her arm around Mary Beth and whispered into her ear. "You're going to do great. No worries. And we can always stop the camera. Remember." Alison wanted her to feel secure and know she was in control of the situation. "And you might even have fun." Mary Beth looked at her and smiled for a second time.

When they entered the library, Jolene came running over to her sister, giving her a big hug. "You'll see. This interview will help us stay together, like a Christmas miracle." Mary Beth hugged her little sister and kissed the crown of her head. She wondered just who was the wisest of the two of them.

Sam introduced Jerry and pointed to the couch by the fireplace. "We'll chat over here."

Alison spoke up. "I'm going to do the interview if you don't mind, Sam." She looked at him and he understood immediately.

"Of course. I like behind the camera anyway."

A quirky smile rose on Alison's face. "See, I told you." She laughed, and Mary Beth appeared somewhat amused.

Jolene and her sister sat next to each other and Alison sat in an oversized, cushioned chair next to them, so they were very close together. Alison slowly began the interview with the history of how they both had arrived at Fairside Manor. Mary Beth let Jolene do most of the talking, but honestly answered Alison's questions without much detail. Alison knew she had to get some emotion from Mary Beth, but also felt protective of her. They each described their daily life as residents in the orphanage, and Mary Beth seemed to relax more as time passed. Then the interview steered towards Mary Beth and what would happen when she turned eighteen, which was only six months away.

At first, Mary Beth put her head down and fidgeted with her hands in her lap. Alison reached out and placed her hand on hers. "It's okay. We can stop if you like."

But Mary Beth seemed to gather herself. She straightened her posture, looking straight into the camera. and grabbed her sister's hand. "No, I need to talk about it." Her voice rang out strong and clear. "I'm scared. I don't know what is going to happen to me. I don't want to leave my sister even though I know she's in good hands. I need to be close by, to keep an eye on her and perhaps someday bring her home to live with me. But I need a place to live and a good job. My grades are excellent, and I would like to attend college someday. But I have to first think of where am I going to sleep? How am I going to feed myself? Will I be homeless? What's going to happen to me?"

Alison could see tears were welling up in Mary Beth's eyes. But she knew she had to keep going. She gently lowered her voice. "What do you think would help you? What would help you make this very tough transition into living on your own?"

Mary Beth regained her poise. "We need money. Karen

Thompson our director has created a small after-foster care program here, but she can only afford to place one or two of us each year. We need a community support team who will care for this cause and establish a fund to keep it growing. Most of us are healthy, strong young women and men who have dreams and desires just like any other eighteen-year-old. We got dealt a crummy hand in life preventing us from having a normal family life. Most of us have experienced trauma and loss, which made us stronger, but also more vulnerable. I'm not too proud to say we need help." She stopped and bent over to hug her sister. "I don't want to lose Jolene in my life. I just can't."

Alison knew when to take over. "And you won't. *Hands-On Kids* is committed to getting the word out there. With this interview and our website, we will simultaneously be running a fundraising campaign for our new foundation and its program, *Hands-On Beyond*. Please visit our regular website and give generously. But remember, we need the community to step up and think about housing and jobs as well as finances for this program. This is our Christmas wish for these brave young people, and we hope you will join us in our efforts. After all, tis the season for giving! Merry Christmas everyone!"

Jolene and Mary Beth released their hold on each other and faced the camera. "Merry Christmas!"

"Cut!" Sam took over and ended the session. "Wonderful, ladies. I have everything I need. Thank you!" He knew he had amazing footage to work with in the editing booth. He looked over at Alison and she knew it, too.

"How'd we do, Miss Rockwell?" Jolene was grinning from ear to ear. She'd been a natural with the camera, just as Alison had predicted.

"You both were fantastic. You have done a great service for your friends and others facing the same challenge. And Mary Beth, I know how difficult it was, but your willingness and bravery to be honest and forthcoming clearly communicated the needs for this program. Now, we get to see what happens."

"Thank you. I don't know what came over me, but I suddenly felt freed up enough to speak my mind. And thanks to you, Miss Rockwell, I think something has shifted inside of me. I'm feeling unusually happy." A slow smile emerged, and she even started to giggle.

"I guess Christmas miracles never cease!" They all laughed together. "I think Mrs. Thompson has some goodies for you both in her office. We'll meet you there."

"Sure thing. And thank you again." Mary Beth stood up and hugged Alison. "Let me know if there's anything else I can do."

"Believe me, I will. I may need you for something else in the next week. Probably in pre-production."

"Count me in." Mary Beth grabbed her sister's hand and left.

Sam looked at Alison. "I think we just witnessed a major transformation and healing. Good job, Alison."

"A blessing for sure. Thanks guys. I have to get back to the office and then we better leave for the bookstore."

"Right behind you, boss." Sam teased her.

"Ha, ha. Very funny." Alison shook her head at his joke, but inside, her heart was about to explode.

She couldn't wait to tell Jake about the interview. The filming had exceeded her wildest expectations. A chill ran down her spine as she wondered what the future might bring if she were to continue this kind of work.

***

Henry, his assistant, Tameka, and Jenny arrived at the bookstore at the same time Alison, Sam, and Jerry did. Henry came up to Alison and whispered, "Can I talk to you for a minute? In private?"

Alison took off her wool hat and unwrapped her cashmere scarf. "In the back it's quiet. I'll let the others check out the store." She glanced around and didn't see Jake. He must be upstairs. Finding a corner without browsing customers, Alison turned to him. "What's up?"

"I looked at the so-called conference room at the inn and talked to the manager. Two things. I don't think it's big enough for a planning space. And two, the pipes leaked last night, and it flooded. They're working on it now, but it may take up to five days to repair. Do you think Jake would be open to letting us move in upstairs? His space would be perfect—plenty of room for us to set up workstations. The film truck could even park in the back. The parking lot is plenty big enough, and I assume Jake owns the property."

Alison pondered for a moment. "I don't see why not. I'll talk to him. Thanks, Henry. You're thinking like a producer!"

Alison knew Jake had been more than generous during this entire process, but she also recognized his space would be perfect. Luckily, she didn't feel apprehensive about asking him. She assumed he was upstairs, so she ventured out to find him.

The door was ajar, so she walked into the hallway. His office was on the left, and she could hear him on the phone. She could tell he was becoming busier and hoped her request wouldn't interrupt his flow. He saw her standing outside and motioned for her to come in.

As soon as he got off the call, he stood up, coming closer to Alison. He was glad to see her. He liked having her in his life and had been contemplating how to make it more permanent. "How'd it go at Fairside? Success?"

Alison lit up. "Unbelievable! I think you'll be blown away when you see the footage. Mary Beth suddenly opened up and became this courageous, articulate young woman. Sam is anxious to start editing."

"Terrific! And very surprising. I can't wait to see it."

Alison brushed a hair from her face gathering her composure, then fixated on Jake's eyes. "I have another favor to ask. I know you're busy and you've done so much already, but we have a little snafu."

"What?" Jake found himself mesmerized just staring at Alison.

"Henry just told me the conference room at the inn is rather small and it had a flood last night. Repairs may take up to five days."

Jake was already ahead of her. "And you want to use my space as a production office?"

Alison laughed. "You are psychic. Yes. What do you think? It will only be for a week and then we'll be out of your hair."

A week. Only a week. Was that all Jake had left with this woman? "Of course, Alison. No problem. I don't know if I have enough tables and desks, but I can get some."

"Don't bother. I'll have the crew bring everything from New York tomorrow in the truck. They'll set it up and you won't have to do a thing except see us all the time."

"I can deal with that."

"And one more thing."

"Yes?" Jake was amused at her fierce innocence about business arranging.

"Can we park our truck in the back?"

"Of course. My staff is minimal right now, but this will give me a chance to see how a thriving, active company will operate up here.

The space is yours."

Alison leaped up, throwing her arms around Jake, and gave him a big hug. Suddenly their faces were inches apart. "Thank you." She lingered there for a second, wondering if he would kiss her again, but Liza interrupted them.

"Sorry to disturb you but I heard Alison. I was curious to see how the filming went. Is Sam downstairs?" She wasn't sure if she had intruded upon an intimate moment, but she was starting to see the chemistry between the two of them. And she was relinquishing her desires for Jake as she could see they were perfect for each other. Although, what would happen when Alison returned to New York was unclear.

"Wait until you see the footage! I'll get the others and bring them upstairs."

Jake added, "I've just given permission for the *Hands-On Kids* production office to be set up here temporarily. Don't worry. You will be immersed in the action. It will probably make your job easier, too."

"Can't wait." Liza knew she was at the forefront of something fresh and exciting emerging. And she felt like she would be helping others, not to mention she was closer to her sister. Yes, Maple Ridge was beginning to feel like home.

Alison said, "I'll be right back. Let me get the others." Descending the staircase to the bookstore, a fluttering in her heart from another intimate moment with Jake energized her. Another close moment that might have ended in a kiss. What was she going to do when it ended in a week? She moved quickly and rounded up the staff to tell them the good news. The catastrophe had been diverted.

***

Carolyn gleefully dialed George's number. One of her loyal staff had informed her about the minor flood. Perfect. Alison would never find another space in time to house the staffing office. She had pulled some strings and found another site. Her lips were pursed in a sneer as she tapped her fingernails on her desk, waiting for George to pick up.

"Miss Parks, how are you feeling?"

"Couldn't be better, but I have some disturbing news." As she relayed her message, her stomach quivered in anticipation of saving the production. But her wishful expectations were instantly squashed.

"That's funny. I just got off the phone with Miss Rockwell, and everything is under control. Jake Sanders offered his space, and they moved in this afternoon. But thank you for looking out for her." Leaning back in his chair, George rolled his head from side to side and chuckled.

A squeezing in Carolyn's chest unsettled her. "Oh. I didn't know. I'll give her a call."

"Yes, do. No need to worry, Miss Parks. Have a good night." And he hung up.

Carolyn's fingers tightened around the pen she was holding. She raised her arm and threw it across the room. She wasn't going to let some young, inexperienced wannabe take over her livelihood. No, not on her watch. She was going to Maple Ridge, and she had a new plan.

***

Snuggling up to the fire, Alison plopped down with her notebook and scores of to-do lists. Jenny and Sam were at their desks going over their pre-production details. Alison's ringtone broke the silence. "Guess who?" They all laughed.

"What's going on up there? I heard about the flood. You do know you start filming in two days."

Alison shook her head and explained what had happened. "I will send you a report in the morning. Thanks, Carolyn. Goodnight."

Alison looked at Jenny and Sam. "I have a feeling she's going to make an appearance soon. I don't know if I'm ready."

Sam looked her point-blank in the eye. "You are doing an exceptional job, and the crew loves you. The network will know what a gem you are and keep you in some producing role. I know it. Take it from experience. I've been in this business longer."

"Thank you. I appreciate your confidence." The crease in Alison's forehead softened.

"I agree. You have nothing to worry about, even if she surprises us," added Jenny.

Alison sunk far down into the cushioned headrest of her chair, trying to let the stress melt away. She stared into the flames, hypnotized by her thoughts for her future and what may come. Deep inside, she knew change was coming. And she was okay with it.

Chapter Eighteen

Alison's arms stretched up, taking a movement break, then she reached for her coffee on her desk. Letting the warm liquid slide down her throat, she calculated her to-do list in her head. Interview edits done, check. Website ready, check. Film crew arriving, check. The New York cast would appear by early afternoon, and everyone would meet in the conference room at Starlight Books around four. Hopefully all on the same page and working like a well-oiled machine.

Alison's eyes were glued to her computer, perusing the website Liza had done, and a sense of satisfaction settled in her chest. Jake was lucky to have her as an employee. She reminded herself, as much as she might like him, nothing had been said about what would happen after the production. And she certainly wasn't going to bring it up. Alison knew she had job security if all went well with *Hands-On Kids*. Would that be enough? But in her heart, she knew it wasn't.

Liza and Alison stayed behind at the manor to do the final launch. Liza turned to Alison. "Are you ready?"

"I want to call George and let him know it's coming. I promised him I would."

Alison scrolled to his number. Picking up, he asked, "How's it going, Miss Rockwell?"

"We're ready to launch and I wanted you to be the first to know. I think you will like it. I'll text you when it's finished."

"I'll be right here waiting. Good luck!" George had confidence the website would be a success. Everything else Alison had achieved thus far had been outstanding, and he knew the network executives were watching her closely. George liked her and wished only the best for her.

"Here we go. May all your devoted and hard work achieve the best outcome!" Alison raised her coffee cup.

"You mean, our hard work. Don't be so modest. This website is as much you as me. And Sam." Liza couldn't remember when she'd had so much fun working on a project. She was going to miss Alison when she left. She had a feeling Jake was, too.

After a few minutes of technological tweaking, Liza looked up at Alison. "Go try and open it on your desk computer. Let's see what happens!"

Before Alison could get to her desk, her ringtone went off. George was calling.

"Unbelievable! Beyond my wildest dreams! Alison Rockwell, you are a genius! The network is going to love this. The kids are going to love this. Are we linking the live segments to the website each day?"

"Yes. Liza is overseeing everything from Jake Sanders' office. Taking over his business space for production needs has been a lifesaver. He's been most gracious with everything."

"Yes, yes, I know. We made the right decision in hiring you. I've got to go. My phones are ringing off the hook. We'll catch up later. Good work."

"Thank you, Mr. Stevens." Alison's face lit up, glowing with pride.

"Sounds like it worked!" Liza let out a long sigh as the jitters in her belly subsided. The interview had caught the essence of the *Hands-On Beyond* program. "I think I'll stay here for a while if you don't mind. In case we have any glitches. It's quieter."

"I agree." Alison checked her phone. It was going nuts with texts and calls were coming in simultaneously. She looked up at Liza. "Oh, my. I think we need more staff to handle this. I didn't think it would explode so fast!" She was excited, but concerned.

"Don't worry. I'll call Karen. She has some volunteers ready and waiting. We might have to get to the bookstore sooner than later. I'll call her and tell her to send over some troops. We have to set up the hotline there. Agreed?"

"Agreed. Thank you, Liza. You thought of everything. So much for quiet, I guess." They both laughed. "You leave now, and I'll meet you there. I want to answer a few phone calls." Alison knew she had to call Carolyn. There were texts and several messages. She couldn't ignore her any longer.

***

Back in New York, Carolyn was irritated. The website looked amazing and she was determined to prevent Alison Rockwell from stealing her production. She had to devise a way to tarnish her reputation without completely tanking the show. After all, she knew the ratings had been dropping. She had one loyal staff member, Thea Caston, who would arrive in Maple Ridge later in the day, and then she would get a better idea of what was going on behind the scenes with her onsite reports. There had to be something she could use in her scheme. Suddenly her phone rang. It was Alison. Carolyn sat up and collected herself. "It's about time. What's going on with the website? Do you have the budget to run it? It better not distract you away from your producing responsibilities."

Alison expanded her lungs with a deep breath. "We have staff and volunteers all set up, Carolyn. What did you think of the website?"

"Fine. Like any other website."

"And the interview?"

"Adequate." Carolyn certainly wasn't going to give her the

gratification of praise.

There was no pleasing this woman, but Alison wasn't going to let her sour attitude affect her. "Another call is coming in and I have to take it. I'll send you a report later tonight."

"I just hope you're ready for tomorrow. Don't let this new idea interfere with the success of our holiday special, Alison."

"I won't. Take care of yourself, Carolyn. Talk to you later." Alison hung up before Carolyn could make any snide remarks. Wow. This woman was either jealous or just negative about the world in general. She wasn't sure what it was, but Alison suddenly felt sympathetic towards her. It must be exhausting to be so negative. But Alison found it easier to let it go each time she hung up with Carolyn. Too much to do.

***

Entering the bookstore, Alison saw Lucy ringing up customers at the register with Annie by her side, bagging books and gifts. She waved to them and proceeded up the staircase, but gasped as she entered the space. Henry and Tameka had utterly transformed the back area into an open, gigantic conference room. Staff feverously worked at multiple workstations surrounding a large, rectangular table. Henry came running over. "What do you think?"

"I think you're a genius! I never thought we could get something up and running like this in such a short time." Alison placed her hand over her heart, looking at him. "Thank you."

"Come on. Let me show you."

Alison glanced over at Jake's office first, but noticed the door was closed. Most likely due to all the noise and commotion taking over his building. She knew she would see him eventually.

As they walked back, Henry stopped at one of the open office spaces. "Here's your office in case you need privacy. Jake suggested it. He doesn't need it yet. And you're right next door to Liza to keep up to date on the website."

"You thought of everything." She was touched that Jake had been a part of the set-up. His generosity never ceased to amaze her.

"Glad you like it." Alison pivoted around and saw Jake standing behind her. She hadn't even heard him approach.

"It's beyond my wildest imagination of how things could so easily come together. But not without the hard work of all of you, of course."

"We aim to please at Starlight Books and Publishing," Jake jested.

Alison giggled. "Did you see the website yet?"

"Yes, and all I can say is, *Hand-On Beyond* is lucky to have you. Bravo!"

"And thanks to you and Liza as well. And Sam. And everyone. It was a total team effort." A crimson hue edged across Alison's cheeks soaking in Jake's praise. But it also pleased her he took notice and was involved in the daily action. "We better get back to work."

As Jake watched her go, he knew she was on the road to accomplishment in her television career. Would she give up her dream of writing children's books? He was beginning to doubt she would even want to move to a small town like Maple Ridge, even if they felt something for each other. He would have to see what happened after the production. But he did know part of his plan would work—no matter if she was in New York or Maple Ridge.

***

As Henry left for the inn to meet the cast, he ruminated on his career. He loved working in television, and with Alison at the helm, he could demonstrate his creative skills without restriction. His head bobbed up and down to a tune on the radio. Yes, he had bigger dreams for himself and was looking forward to Nathan arriving next week so that he could share his good fortune and success with him. Staff cars from New York pulled in simultaneously, so Henry hopped out and helped with the luggage.

Tina and Justin were delighted to get out of the city for the Christmas special. They embraced Henry and were as pleasant as always. They were perfect as the hosts for a children's show and always exuded a positive attitude—even outside of Carolyn's stern nature—which they often ignored. Must have been from their years of experience working with difficult kids in school, Henry laughed to himself. And Carolyn could be difficult.

"What a beautiful town!" exclaimed Tina. "We're so stoked to be here."

Justin patted Henry on the back. "Thanks for setting everything up. Appreciate it."

"No problem." Then he faced Sean. "Welcome to Maple Ridge. I think you guys are going to have fun here."

Sean high-fived Henry. His adventurous spirit brought a fresh element of surprise to the cast, and he was game for anything new.

Melissa and her mother were last to get out of the car. Melissa's mother was the chaperone for the two since they were still young. She could be overbearing but was gracious when things were going her way. Or at least Melissa's way. They were similar in nature.

"Let's get you checked in and I'll give you an itinerary for today and tomorrow. At our meeting today, you'll get the entire schedule. You have a couple hours to rest, eat and then I'll have the car bring you all to the bookstore, where we have a conference room set up. Tameka will stay with you in case you need anything, but I've got to get back to the office." He looked at Melissa. "The kids we selected for the guest spots can't wait to meet you. You can show them the ropes, right?" Henry knew if he acknowledged Melissa's skills and stroked her ego slightly, she was easier to work with on the set.

Melissa smiled. She liked feeling important. "Will do."

"And Sean, you'll be staying in Jerry's room. I thought since you guys know each other, it was a good fit." Luckily, Jerry had agreed to be his evening chaperone. He knew he might have some work to do in the edit truck at night, but Henry offered to fill in when he was needed.

"Awesome! Maybe I can watch him edit."

"Ask him. You never know." Henry knew Sean had other aspirations in the television field as well. Even at ten years old.

Making sure everyone got settled and checked in, Henry texted Alison to update her. Feeling satisfied all was in order, he headed back to Starlight Books.

***

Alison found herself walking back and forth between her office, Liza's and the rear conference area. She wanted to spend more time on the launch of *Hands-On Beyond,* so her face perked up when Henry reappeared. Something inside was calling, and she wanted to follow her intuition, wherever it took her.

Amidst the craziness of production planning, Alison's thoughts often drifted to Jake. His door had been closed most of the afternoon, but she was comforted knowing he was there. As the staff meeting approached, she went downstairs to find Annie and Tim. Before they entered the meeting, she wanted to talk to them and found them in the back, wrapping presents for the store.

"Hey, you two. Are you ready for your first production meeting?"

They both lit up as bright as the twinkling lights in the window. "Yes!" they exclaimed.

"Are Melissa and Sean here?" asked Annie.

"Not yet but should be any minute."

"Can we wait for them and greet them?" Annie was fearless about any encounter it seemed.

"Why don't all three of us greet them?" She felt protective of Annie and Tim and didn't want them to feel overwhelmed in any way. But her fear might be a needless one, as she would soon see.

The bells on the front door jingled as the large *Hands-On* crew entered the store. Lucy called out to Alison to let her know they had arrived. But before she got there, Annie swooped in front of her and was the first to make introductions.

"Welcome to Starlight Books! We're so excited you're here! I'm Annie."

Sean was in front and, being the most social, reached out to shake her hand. "I'm Sean. Are you going to be in the show?"

Standing tall and lifting her chest, Annie answered, "Yes!" Then she turned to Melissa. "And you must be Melissa. I can't wait to work with you!"

Melissa was slightly taken aback by Annie's kindness. Very different from extras in New York. "Nice to meet you." Perhaps this onsite special would be more fun than she thought.

Alison shook her head. She should have known Annie would break the ice before she even got there. "Welcome. I hope you found the accommodations adequate and are happy as I am to have you here."

"Love this town!" said Tina. She had grown up in a small town in upstate New York and had always yearned to go back someday. But then she met Justin, got married and couldn't imagine going anywhere without him. She was still in love with him as much as on their wedding day ten years ago. They couldn't have children, so landing the gig at *Hands-On Kids* had nurtured their parenting desires. They both thought they would adopt one day, but the timing had never been right.

Being an avid reader and amateur writer himself, Justin was exhilarated perusing the store. "This place is awesome! Who owns it again?"

"My dad, Jake Sanders. He's upstairs. You'll meet him." Annie's pride was clearly evident. "Let me give you a tour before the production meeting."

Grinning, Alison exchanged glances with Justin and Tina. They all knew when a precocious child was invaluable to a show like theirs.

As they walked around the store, Melissa's mother stopped in front of Clara's painting. She was fascinated by its beauty and felt a sense of pain hitting her by surprise. It had been a long time since she had known the inner meaning of the joy of being an artist herself. She had studied art in college and even painted for a few years afterward. But when her marriage fell apart, she found herself as a single mom, struggling at times, and the paintbrushes and canvas were abandoned to the attic, never to be touched again. Something stirred inside of her, wondering if it was time to pick up the brushes again. She pondered if she had closed herself up too much over the years to ever find that blissful gratification again.

She quickly relinquished her thoughts upon hearing Melissa's voice. "Come on, Mom. We're going upstairs."

"Right behind you, honey." Mrs. Cavanaugh looked at her

daughter and speculated if her hardness had rubbed off on Melissa. She knew her daughter's ego could be inflated at times, but suddenly she was hoping the people Melissa would meet and work with during this Christmas special may positively influence her. Mrs. Cavanaugh knew she had let Melissa's success dominate her child's life these last few years, and lately, it seemed to have gotten out of hand. She had fewer friends and didn't smile enough, except in front of a camera. As a mother, she realized she had made some mistakes and hoped it wasn't too late to turn things around. She wanted her daughter to experience the freedom and joys of a childhood, even when she was consumed with the busyness of an acting career.

***

Alison flitted around the conference room, chatting with newcomers and staff. Jake stood against the wall in the back with his arms crossed in front of his chest, where he could see her in action. Yes, Alison was a very special woman. And a woman he wanted.

Alison saw him standing in the back and motioned for him to come closer. Jake had to concede, as everyone was staring at him. "I want us all to give a round of applause to the man who helped make all of this possible. Thank you, Jake!"

The staff gave him a standing ovation, and Jake's face grew red as he put his hands up, signaling them to stop. "I've been happy to help. Besides, what else could I do? Miss Rockwell is very persuasive." Laughter rang out. "Enjoy your week at Maple Ridge and don't hesitate to ask if you need something. Now, if you'll excuse me, I have my own business to run." Getting out of the limelight, he whisked himself back to his office.

The eye contact between Alison and Jake did not go unnoticed by Thea Caston, Carolyn's little spy. She wondered if anything was going on between the two of them. If so, it could be an interesting tidbit for her boss.

Alison let them know most of the meals would be catered buffet style at the community center, within walking distance of the inn and bookstore. Tameka and Thea were in charge of meals, but Marilyn had everything organized and managed with the budget she was given. Center activities had been rearranged or put on hold for the week as *Hands-On Kids* needed the facility. Everyone in town respected the schedule and there had been no problems, thus far.

Alison looked at the clock as her stomach rumbled. Hopefully, Sara had saved something for Jenny and her in the kitchen. She gathered up her things, said goodnight to the last few staff who were lingering, and told them to go get dinner and some rest. She walked downstairs, looking for Jenny, but was curious if Jake had left. He was in the back talking to Lucy and saw her coming down.

"I was just about to leave. Do you need a ride home?" He had missed hanging out with her since they were both so busy now.

"I was looking for Jenny. I can probably ride with her."

"She left for the community center and asked if I could give you a lift. She wanted to go over something with Marilyn before tomorrow."

Of course, she did, Alison mused to herself. "Sure, if you're ready. Where's Annie?"

She's at the center eating dinner with Tim. Lucy is going to drop her off when they're done. You know, since she's part of the crew now."

"Yes, she might as well get the whole experience." They both laughed.

"Sara texted me, and she saved some dinner for any of us coming home now."

Home. Alison liked the sound of that. They were going home together. Then she shook her head. *Don't get ahead of yourself.* "Meet you outside." She welcomed the crisp, fresh air filling her lungs. As they rode together, Alison rattled on about the progress made, and Jake rested his body against the seat as he listened. Ease came over him like the two of them had known each other for years. He knew he would soon have to make a move beyond their friendship before she slipped away from him.

When they got to the estate, Sara had dinner ready and had set up in the dining room, since she didn't know how many would return for an evening meal. Sam mentioned he would meet Christine at the community center, so he wasn't coming. It was just Jake and Alison. Alone.

Alison remarked, "We could eat in the kitchen, Sara. No need for the fancy table setting."

"I wouldn't think of it. Besides, Cecilia will take care of you. I've got something I have to do. No bother. You two enjoy. And not another word." Sara was adamant.

"I guess the boss has spoken." Jake pulled out a chair for Alison. "Here you go, mademoiselle."

Alison blushed as she sat down. She felt Jake lightly touch her shoulders. "There. Now try and relax for a bit while we eat. You deserve it."

As Jake sat down next to her, Alison sent a fleeting glance in his direction. She had never met a man anything like him back in New York, and Steve certainly fared poorly in comparison. *How can I leave this man?*

Jake picked up his fork to eat but hesitated for a moment. He was curious as to what her thoughts were for her future. He was going to inquire but then decided it was too early. The production hadn't even begun, and he didn't want her to feel like he was prying too much into her private life. Before he could say anything, Alison directed the conversation.

"Tell me the latest on your publishing company. What are your next steps after Christmas?" Alison would rather he talk about himself than ask her any questions. Her clarity seemed murky these days.

The corners of his mouth widened. She beat him to it with the future inquiry. He easily explained the details including his chief editor's arrival, the website and social media brand Liza would be building, and the kinds of books he was hoping to attract and promote.

Alison couldn't take her eyes off of him while he spoke. He described a unique publishing home like the one she had always envisioned herself settling into as a successful writer. Her deepest desire was being illustrated right before her very eyes. "Any writer would be fortunate to land at Starlight Publishing. I can't wait to see what you do."

Jake took a chance and reached out to touch her hand. "Yes, I wish you were going to be here to see it all unfold."

Before Alison could say anything, they heard Annie's voice yelling in the kitchen. "Dad! Where are you? I'm back!"

Jake reluctantly pulled his hand away, grinning at Alison. "In here. In the dining room."

Two seconds later, Annie came bursting through the doors. "We had so much fun at dinner! Tim and I ate with Sean. Melissa was with her mother. She didn't talk much, but I don't mind." She turned to Alison. "Don't worry. It doesn't bother me. I don't think she has many friends. I'll reach out to her. Everyone needs a friend, right?"

Alison leaned over, touching Annie's arm. "How did you get so smart?"

Jake put his empty cup down on the table. "Better get this young actress to bed early. She has a big day tomorrow."

"Get some rest and I'll see you tomorrow."

"Goodnight, Miss Rockwell." Annie hugged Alison. "Thank you again for coming to Maple Ridge. I'm glad you did." She smiled, looking up at her dad, whose eyes communicated the same feeling.

Jake held Alison's glance with intensity, needing no words. "Goodnight, Miss Rockwell."

"Goodnight, Mr. Sanders."

***

After Alison checked in with Carolyn, who had called and texted throughout the day, she went to bed. Jenny had come in earlier and was fast asleep. She was really doing two jobs, but Alison had made sure she had a skilled assistant to help her. She was hoping the assistant could take over her hair and make-up job, so Jenny would be free to be artistic director on the show—if it was picked up again for another season. Alison tried hard not to think about ratings. It only stressed her out and she didn't need to worry.

As her head hit the pillow, her thoughts drifted to Jake. Earlier, at the dinner table, was he going to say something? Was he going to ask her to stay? Or was that just a fantasy she had? It felt like he was going to talk about their relationship before getting interrupted. But she would never know. She rolled her head towards the window where she could see the stars shining brightly. In the stars, Alison saw hope and let that feeling wash over her as she fell asleep.

Chapter Nineteen

Jenny, Sam and Alison grabbed coffee from Sara's kitchen, rushing out the door to the community center bright and early. The camera crew was setting up, and Tameka was corralling kids. The recording would take place over an hour or two, then be edited in the truck by Sam. The final cut would usually be aired in the afternoon in their regular spot. But the Christmas special was different, since it was seen on television over five days. Four days which were cut, prepared and aired later in the day, while the last show, on Christmas Eve day, was live. It was more expensive than their regular one-hour weekly slot, but families had looked forward to it for the last five years and made it part of their holiday tradition.

Alison looked around for Jake, but didn't see him. He must have dropped off Annie and gone back to the bookstore. She wondered if they would ever have time alone again. It was going to be insanely busy from now until Christmas. George's number flashed on her phone, interrupting her thoughts.

"George, how are you?"

"Better yet, how are you? Excited? I just called to wish everyone good luck. The website looks amazing, and I have confidence the show will be a hit. Just wanted you to know." George liked Alison and was hoping she would secure the producer role full-time.

"Thank you. All systems go here. We start filming the arts and crafts segment in about an hour. Do you want to see the cut before it's aired?"

"No, I trust you. I'll watch it like everyone else. It will give me a better idea of how the world is seeing it. Talk to you later."

Alison hung up the phone. She was glad she had George in her corner. She would never get a pep talk from Carolyn.

The next couple of hours flew by. Thanks to Sean and Annie, the kids were engaged, saying funny things, and they had filled up several tables so more kids could be involved. Justin and Tina announced they would wrap the crafts and take them to places in the community during the week. Sean and Melissa closed out the show by talking to the audience about the importance of giving during the holidays. Alison would have Annie and Tim do the same in the next episode, and hopefully, Melissa would graciously agree to take turns with them. Alison knew how territorial or sensitive she could be. There must be some underlying pain causing her to put up walls and be so abrasive at times. Kind of reminded her of someone else she knew. And like clockwork, her phone rang. Carolyn.

"We just wrapped up the first segment."

"Send it to me. I want to make notes before you air." Carolyn was still holding onto the show with a vice grip.

"I'll let Sam know. Give him a couple hours." Alison wasn't going to let her interfere with her production flow.

Before Alison could fret about the call, everyone was scampering around her. Henry and Tameka were directing kids to the crafts table and many were helping Tina and Justin clean up. Marilyn had so many volunteers, they didn't need to do too much. Alison stepped forward and grabbed a microphone.

"Great job everyone! A reminder, our staff meeting is at two o'clock, so we can all watch the show at four. Sam and crew excluded of course. They'll be too busy!" She laughed, and applause rang out for the first successful day.

***

Thea Caston had been watching Alison closely. She was impressed with how easily Alison directed the series of events and kept a calm disposition in the thick of organized chaos. Thea knew she would have to find some personal dirt on Alison if she was to help Carolyn discredit her reputation. She wasn't quite sure what it was yet, but she would keep digging.

When Alison was reassured everything was under control, she grabbed a sandwich and coffee and went to the production office. Liza had already left, and she wanted to make sure the website was getting some live teasers of the show's upcoming episode. She hadn't seen Jake, so she figured he was in his office. After all, he had his own life to lead. He couldn't be there to hold her hand every day. Unbelievable how these thoughts crept into her brain on a regular basis.

As she walked into the bookstore, Lucy called out to her. "By the way, I'm supposed to tell you Jake had to go to New York on business rather suddenly. He'll be back tomorrow, and Annie is staying with us. He wanted you to know."

Alison's heart sank. He wasn't there. "Is everything okay?" She wondered why the sudden exit.

"Yes, just some publishing issues and he'll probably stay with his uncle. No need to worry. He'll be back in the morning."

"Oh." Her heart dropped to her stomach, regretting he wouldn't be there for the first episode—to celebrate all of their hard work.

Lucy could see she was visibly disappointed. "Don't worry. He said to tell you he'll be back to help tomorrow with the trees at Fairside Manor. This is just a quick trip."

Trying to ignore the letdown sitting in her gut, Alison put on her best cheerful face. "I'm sure he has plenty to do himself. We have more than enough staff now. I want him to realize, if the show is successful, he was a big reason for it. I couldn't have done it without him."

"I'm sure he knows, and he will be watching the first episode from New York. Annie most likely reminded him a million times before he left."

Alison smiled. "She probably did. Thanks, Lucy. I'll be upstairs if anyone needs me."

***

Alison closed the door and sat down at her desk. She couldn't believe how disappointment had rushed over her like a tidal wave when she learned Jake was in New York. Such a silly reaction to a normal turn of events. After all, she had done the same thing a week ago. But before the kiss. And the personal talks. She was starting to get attached to Jake without any acknowledgement of a secure future with him. *What am I doing?* She'd better get a grip on her unbridled emotions. Refocusing, she opened her computer to check on the website.

Liza had seen her come in and knocked at her door a few minutes later, anxious to get her feedback.

"Come in," Alison said.

"What do you think?"

"I can't believe you've done all this in such a short time." Alison was blown away at how great it actually looked and easily functioned. "I want to launch the interview and information on *Hands-On Beyond* tomorrow. Are we ready?"

"Yes!"

They had decided to reveal the first segment exclusively about the show and upcoming episodes for the Christmas special. But

Alison didn't want to waste any more time before kicking off the fundraising campaign. Since they were going to Fairside tomorrow, it would be the perfect spot to begin. It would give them five days before Christmas to keep the momentum in gear and, hopefully, be successful.

Lively chatter floated around the conference room as staff watched the first episode. Alison had checked in a few times with Sam in the editing truck behind the building and was confident the final cut was exactly what she envisioned.

She noticed Annie, Tim and Sean were bonding together. Melissa sat next to Sean, but kept to herself. She looked over at the three a few times, but she did not say anything. Alison imagined Melissa struggled between wanting to be a kid and have fun and staying safe in her protective cocoon as a successful actor. Her ego and fear were winning the battle. Alison made a mental note to reach out to her more.

As the credits rolled for the first episode, the whole room broke out into resounding applause and boisterous cheering. They had successfully launched the Christmas special. Alison exhaled a sigh of relief and announced she would be around for any questions for tomorrow's episode. She looked over at her youngest stars and motioned for them to follow her into her office.

Jake had made sure that Alison's office was furnished with plenty of comfortable chairs for private meetings. He thought of everything. "I wanted to congratulate you on a great first shoot. I felt the four of you were in sync and handled yourself like true, seasoned actors. How do you all feel?"

Annie spoke up first. "Great! I had so much fun working with you guys. Feel free to give me any advice you may have for the rest of the show. Or as we go along." She smiled directly at Melissa. She was determined to make her a friend.

Sean and Tim both agreed, but Melissa paused as she gathered her thoughts. "It seemed to flow without difficulty. Any notes for tomorrow?" Right back to work—where she was most comfortable.

"No. Just keep doing what you're doing. We already went over everything at the staff meeting. Get some rest after dinner. And I would like Tim and Annie to do the closing out statements tomorrow."

Melissa looked up, obviously agitated. "But Sean and I always close out the show. The guest actors have never done it before."

"I know, but I want to change it up and give you two a break. Then we'll alternate, and you and Sean will sign off on the next shoot. Agreed?" Alison didn't realize how much the change would ruffle Melissa's feathers.

Melissa was a professional, so she nodded. "Agreed."

Alison focused on Annie and Tim. "Why don't you two write out some ideas for your closing comments and run them by me tomorrow when you come to set. I'll have time to check them out. Deal?"

Annie and Tim smiled at each other. They were ready for more responsibility. Tim was pumped his dad would get to see him speak in the show. "Deal!"

The four of them left and headed towards the community center. Mrs. Cavanaugh had been waiting downstairs for Melissa and Sean. Lucy trusted Annie and Tim to have dinner alone and return to the store afterwards.

After dinner Melissa's mother joined some of the other staff she knew while Sean and Melissa hung out together. Thea had come in late and was sitting behind them at another table and overheard their conversation.

Melissa was still irritated about losing her speaking role for the next shoot. She said to Sean, "I think Annie is some kind of personal favorite of Miss Rockwell's, don't you?"

Sean didn't like to get involved with personal drama and Melissa always seemed to dwell on it. He shrugged his shoulders. "I don't know. I like her. She's got spunk. Good for the show."

Which bothered Melissa even more. "Remember, Alison was just a glorified assistant, and may now have a thing going on with Jake Sanders, the bookstore owner."

Sean shook his head. Here we go. Needless gossip. "How do you know?"

"My mother told me. And you know who Jake Sanders is, right?"

Sean could care less. "Who?"

"Jim Anderson's nephew! Probably the reason she's getting everything she wants and changing the show."

"I think the show is changing for the better. Alison's not as uptight as Carolyn. What if Alison and Jake have a thing? Why do you care so much?" Sean took a last sip of water and put his napkin on the tray.

Melissa let out a loud sigh and tossed her hair back. She wasn't going to get anywhere winning Sean as an ally. "I don't like change, I guess. Let's go."

Sean was already getting up. He'd had enough for the evening. He was ready to head back to the inn.

After they left, Thea smiled to herself. She had the information she needed and couldn't wait to get back to her room and call Carolyn. Their plan for exposing Alison's secret was developing. Thea was sure she would get a promotion from Carolyn for revealing Alison's secret. If Alison was getting special attention and had manipulated a relationship with Jake Sanders to do so, it could taint her reputation—and put Carolyn back in charge without a hitch. Thea made a mental note to investigate her suspicion further.

***

Jake had several successful meetings in New York and met his uncle for dinner. No matter how much success Jim achieved, he always remained a passionate, loving man, especially with his family. As Jake looked at the wine list, Jim strode into the restaurant, greeting people as he made his way to the table. Jake stood up to hug his uncle.

"Isn't this a treat? My nephew visiting me!"

Jake laughed. "Visiting you is like an early Christmas present. I know you'll be home in a couple of days, but I wanted to finish some business before the holidays really started. I figured you're doing the same."

"You know me so well. Let's order and you can tell me all about Starlight Publishing. Can't wait to hear about it."

Jake was eager to explain all the details of his day to day operations and his plans for the upcoming year. Jim's heart overflowed to see his nephew so vibrant and alive again. He made a few comments, but then changed the subject to the other project in Jake's life.

"Tell me everything, and I mean everything, about your experience with *Hands-On Kids*. Did you catch the first part today? Annie was adorable!"

Jake smiled. Right to the heart of the matters. Jim Anderson's superpower. "I admit I had reservations about being some producer's lackey for a few weeks, but it turned out to be very healing for both me and Annie. And fun, if you can believe it." He laughed.

"I've been in touch with George Stevens quite a bit, and from what I've heard, Alison Rockwell is turning out to be a major rock star. It appears the show has never been so creative, and the staff love working with her. She definitely deserves the executive producer promotion on a more permanent basis. I'm waiting to see the rest of the episodes, but management is pleased with her. What's your experience been?"

Jake looked down. A wave of fear engulfed his heart. Of course, the network would keep Alison and give her a promotion. How could he be so oblivious? Or rather, he just didn't want to think about her leaving. Instinctively he knew big things were on her horizon, and he knew he couldn't stand in her way. Nor, did he want to.

Jim could see the hesitation in Jake but didn't pry. Jake snapped out of his thoughts and said, "Everyone loves her. She's very organized and professional yet open and easygoing. Different from what I expected for sure. She deserves any promotion she gets." Jake smiled and went back to eating, or rather picking at his food.

"Good to know." Jim could tell Jake was hiding something but decided not to push him further. He'd be home in a couple of days and could observe for himself. But he suspected something was going on between Jake and Alison. Sensing from Jake's optimistic attitude lately, he thought Alison might be partially responsible. Whatever the case, he would know soon enough. "What do you say we go home? I have phone calls to make and I know you're leaving early."

Jake was relieved to end the conversation regarding Alison. Too many feelings, and he wasn't ready to share them with his uncle. He felt he needed to sort them out on his own first. But the realization of her immanent departure hit him harder than he expected. How could he ask her to give up a lustrous, booming career to stay in Maple Ridge? Jake looked up at his uncle and smiled. "Are you going to let me get the tab? I think it's my turn."

"Not a chance." Jim laughed. "Nice try, though." He stood up and put his arm around Jake. "Have I told you lately how proud I am of you?" He squeezed him and said, "Let's go. My car is out front."

"Thanks, Uncle Jim. There's one other thing I'd like to talk to you about, but we can chat in the car."

"Of course."

Jake's uncle had always been a guiding light in his everchanging world and the steady foundation supporting him through thick and thin. Yes, Jake Sanders was a blessed man and would eventually find his way in making the right decision for himself.

Chapter Twenty

Alison paced around her bedroom, getting dressed. She knew she had to integrate *Hands-On Beyond* carefully into the episode. The field trip would culminate in tree decorating at the orphanage, and she planned to show Mary Beth and Jolene's interview at the end. Alison glanced over at Jake's house as they drove out of the driveway. It didn't look like he was home yet, but Sara had reminded her he would be home in time to help with the tree delivery.

Alison paused in front of Starlight Books, soaking in the beauty of the shimmering lights bordering the front window before entering. Lucy called out to her. "Jake called, and he told me to tell you he'll be here in about fifteen minutes. He's checked in with the tree farm and they're ready for you."

"Thanks, Lucy." Relieved he was coming, Alison went to her office. She had a prep meeting with Justin and Tina and the four young stars to discuss the integration of the after-foster care program they were supporting. She wanted to hear Annie and Tim's closing remarks and make sure they were personal in some way.

Liza was in her office and was prepared to link the website with some footage as it came in. Alison was impressed by Liza's tenacity and knew her skillful dedication would be a cornerstone to the show's success. After all, it did take a village.

As suspected, Annie and Tim had written something genuine and personal. Annie and Jolene had been friends for a while, and Annie was able to capture the essence of what it must be like to live in fear knowing her only sister, and only family, would be in a dire state come eighteen years of age.

As they finished rehearsing, there was a knock on the door.

Alison barely looked up. "Come in."

The door opened, and Annie jumped up. "Dad! You're back." She ran over to hug him.

"I told you I'd be back early." As he hugged Annie, he looked over at Alison. Her beauty stirred a longing in him, and he could feel his heart pounding. He wanted to pull away from her but knew it would be difficult. But he couldn't stand in the way of her career. This he had thought about profusely on the drive back to Maple Ridge.

Glancing at Alison, he said, "Sorry I left so abruptly. I didn't want to bother you. Just wanted to let you know we'll be ready at the tree farm for you. The vans are out back for the kids. Henry gave me his cell, so I think we're good. Let me know if there's anything else you need." He circled around to leave. He needed to get out of the office. The less time he spent with her the better.

Alison called out, "Thanks Jake. I'm glad you're back."

He smiled, but his eyes darted away sooner than expected.

A puzzled look covered Alison's face, and a tautness in her stomach told her something was different about him. She could feel it. She wondered what had happened in New York.

She shook her head, trying to release those thoughts and refocus on the task at hand. She excused Annie and Tim, picked up her clipboard, and walked to the community center. Henry and Tameka had efficiently paired the community children with residents of Fairside Manor. Each pair of buddies would pick out trees with each other, before their delivery to the manor. Alison had personally selected some of the pairings hoping for friendships to be solidified. Melissa would be with Jolene, Annie with Nancy, Jolene's best friend, Tim with a shy boy Alison had noticed, and Mary Beth would be with Nikki, Christine's niece. Sean, though younger, would be with Eddie, a vibrant soon-to-be eighteen, young man. In Eddie's interview he had mentioned his keen interest in film making and Alison knew he might enjoy getting to hang out with Sean and learn more about the entertainment industry. The rest of the matching had been completed by Henry and Tameka.

As the vans unloaded at the farm, Alison caught a glimpse of Jake. He was with the owners, who were all prepared for an onslaught of children, but they were used to it during the Christmas season. Alison noticed other community volunteers pitching in, and Sam's crew was ready to go. Before she could walk over to him, she was swarmed by production staff who needed guidance or questions answered.

Jake had seen Alison but kept busy with the tree farm staff. He didn't know what he was going to do at this point, but he was clearly wrestling with internal confusion. Leaving New York, he had decided to pull away. But seeing her, brought up feelings of confusion and doubt. No denying he was falling in love with her, but was detaching himself the best way to handle things? How could he ask her to leave the city, her new job and imminent success?

After much laughter and sprightly shenanigans, the trees were loaded on the trucks and all headed to the manor. Alison kept her eye on Melissa and Mary Beth. Still, to her delight, she saw Mary Beth engaged and smiling with Nikki, and Melissa was unable to ignore Jolene's chatter and charm. They both appeared to be opening up on some level. Satisfied, Alison jumped into a car with the film crew to arrive before the vans. Sam had already sent another cameraman there.

At Fairside, Justin and Tim skillfully kept everyone in order, and with Christmas music playing in the background, the tree decorating became a party as more residents joined in. Alison had planned to show the personal interview of Jolene and Mary Beth at the end of the segment. She had shown it to Annie and Tim privately, hoping they could integrate the importance of what was at stake for the *Hands-On Beyond* program.

At the end, Sam took them to the library for more privacy. Annie did not disappoint in delivering a heartfelt speech about the significance of the new program and the need for funds and support. "Jolene became one of my best friends when I moved here from New York. After my mom died, I was very sad. Jolene had gone through something similar when she lost both of her parents in a car accident. She and Mary Beth gave me hope that I wouldn't feel so bad someday. Now Jolene is facing another problem. In June, her sister turns eighteen, and Jolene doesn't want to lose her either. Mary Beth needs a job and a home close enough to Jolene, so they can visit often. Please help us help her and others facing life after foster care or living in orphanages. They all deserve to lead productive, healthy lives."

Tim added, "Even though my dad is deployed months at a time, I am lucky to have both of my parents. When I finish high school, I know they will both be here to help me make a plan for my future and guide me through it. Let's all remember the message of this holiday season. Give someone else a chance to follow their dreams."

"Job offers, financial gifts or any other ideas you may have, go to our website and give freely," said Annie.

"And tomorrow, be sure and join us for cookies! Cookie making at its best! See you then!" exclaimed Tim.

And waving to the camera together, "Happy Holidays!"

"Cut!" yelled Sam. "Outstanding. Both of you." Sam couldn't wait to get to the editing truck and put this segment together. He hadn't felt this excited about his filmmaking in years.

Alison had stood in the back and watched. Her heart swelled with pride as she felt the possibilities of something magical brewing.

Clapping, she added, "Great job, you two! Now join the others in the cafeteria. I think there are cookies and hot cocoa."

"Thanks, Miss Rockwell. I hope we did a good job for you," said Tim. Always the soldier's son, wanting to serve.

"You certainly did." Alison smiled and left to find Karen. She was in the cafeteria with all of the kids. "Looks like you're busy. I'll catch up with you later. I think it went well so far. How about you?"

"I can't thank you enough, Alison. Both you and Jake have made this happen. Now we'll see what comes to pass from here. Fingers crossed!"

"Speaking of Jake, have you seen him?"

"He had to leave and go back to his office. But he was here for most of the filming."

Alison felt a twinge of fear as she contemplated his actions. Something was wrong. She expected him to at least stay until they saw each other. Before New York he would have offered her a ride back to her office. What had changed?

"Thanks, Karen. Talk to you later." She checked in with Henry to make sure he didn't need her and then hitched a ride with one of the film crew guys.

Tameka and Thea were in charge of getting the kids back to town in the vans when they were finished with their festivities. Tameka was counting heads to make sure she had everyone when Thea approached her. "Seems to be going well, don't you think?" Thea asked.

"Everyone loves working with Alison. Makes production easier."

"I noticed she looked happier these days. and Jake Sanders seems to really care about her. Don't you think?" Thea prodded.

Tameka was taken aback by the personal comment. She knew how close Thea was to Carolyn and suddenly became suspicious of her inquiry. "He's just one of those good guys. He's friendly with everyone."

"Do you think they have something going on?" Thea wasn't backing down.

Tameka's radar was keen, and she wasn't feeding into gossip about her boss. She liked Alison too much. "I doubt it. She's been swamped and he's just helping out."

"You know, he is Jim Anderson's nephew. It could be they have a personal relationship brewing. It seems Alison has gotten everything she wanted from the network without any resistance. Just an observation."

Tameka was done. "Enough gossip, Thea. Let's get back to work."

Thea had pushed as hard as she could but could see Tameka was not going to give her any helpful information. She knew she was on the right track and was determined to get Carolyn the facts she needed to oust Alison from her position.

***

On the other end of the cafeteria, Jolene had been hanging out with her friends and Melissa. Melissa couldn't seem to get away from her but was trying to less and less. She was warming up to this girl who was insistent on developing their friendship. At first, Melissa had been her typical cold self, but Jolene didn't even blink an eye at her attitude. She just persevered getting to know her.

Jolene turned to Melissa. "Do you want to see my room before you leave?"

"I guess so. I think the van's leaving in about five minutes. You're staying here, right?"

"Yep, but I'll see you tonight at the tree lighting ceremony."

"Hmm." Melissa was reflective, yet still hesitant.

Jolene persisted. "Come on!" She grabbed Melissa's hand before she could say anything.

Melissa's mother watched from the back and smiled at the two of them. Perhaps Maple Ridge was healing her daughter in a way she wasn't able to.

Jolene guided her up the long mahogany staircase to the second floor, where most of the bedrooms were for the younger children. She opened the door to her room, spreading her hand in a sweeping motion and said, "Here we are!"

Melissa looked inside and saw two sets of bunk beds and several dressers. There were two desks which they might all share as needed. The room was painted a soft yellow, and lace curtains hung from the window with dainty, pink flowers on them. It was cheery but minimal. Melissa noticed Jolene didn't seem to mind sharing it with so many girls, but it took Melissa by surprise. She had always had her own room. She couldn't imagine not having a place for her books, toys, and a closet for her clothes. "Nice," was all she could say.

"I know it's small, but it's homey. We're all friends and everyone gets along. Some day when Mary Beth gets a job and makes money, I'm going to move into a bigger home with her and have a room of my own again!"

Melissa could see the hope in Jolene's eyes and it touched her. She suddenly realized how lucky she was to have the life she did. And a mother who was still alive. "I bet you will."

"We better go back downstairs. Don't want to miss your ride. Come on." Jolene motioned to the door and the girls quickly returned to the foyer where everyone was gathering. As Melissa silently followed, she ruminated on her new friend and her very different life.

***

Alison noticed Jake's office door was closed as she returned to her own office. She decided to invite him to watch today's segment air later with the crew. No harm in asking. After all, they had kissed. But it seemed so long since they had spoken intimately and felt the undeniable attraction between them. A threatening sense of doubt was seeping into her brain and she needed to do something to stop it. She was a brave woman and would just go knock on the door and get the truth. She wasn't crazy.

Pushing through her fear, Alison raised her hand to the door. Jake yelled out to come in, but his head was buried in a spreadsheet when she entered. He looked up and saw her. "Hey, sorry I had to leave after the shoot, but I've got to finish this before the holidays take over. How'd it go?" He put his head down and pretended to keep working. Looking at her was too hard.

"Great. Annie's a natural in front of the camera. I wanted to invite you to watch with us at four. In the conference room."

"If I'm done. Thanks." Jake's cell rang. He briefly glanced up at her. "Have to take this."

"Sure. See you later." Alison left. A twinge of fear squeezed her heart. Maybe he was just stressed from work and didn't realize helping her would take away so much time from his priorities. Whatever it was, she didn't like it.

***

Later in the day, as everyone gathered in the conference room, Alison felt herself somewhat preoccupied, looking around for Jake. She had noticed his door was closed and didn't really know if he was in the building or not. She walked over to Liza and gently whispered in her ear. "Have you seen Jake?"

"I saw him leave about thirty minutes ago, but he didn't say where he was going. I've been too busy with the website."

Alison smiled at her. "Of course, you have. Which keeps looking more amazing each day, by the way."

"He said he'd see me at the tree lighting tonight, so you could probably catch him then." Liza knew they had been developing a relationship, but something seemed off. She couldn't quite put her finger on it, though. Whatever it was, she hoped they worked it out.

Alison decided to drop her silly concerns and went to sit with her young actors. They always had such a fresh perspective on things, which she hoped would take her mind off Jake. But the episode flipped her around. Her eyes filled with tears at the interview and she realized her real work might be in launching the *Beyond* program for orphans and foster care kids. She could always write, but something bigger than herself was pulling her. She didn't understand the message yet, but some intuitive clarity was bubbling up, trying to permeate its way through her muddy thoughts.

Afterwards, Alison caught a ride back to Anderson Estates with Jenny. As she slid into the passenger seat, she was quiet, looking out the window. Jenny looked over at Alison. "What's wrong? I've known you too long. You can't hide anything from me."

Alison laughed. "Yes, true. My interactions with Jake have changed. He seems distant since returning from New York."

"He could just be having a crazy, busy day. I say we give him the benefit of the doubt. But I'll pay extra attention to the matter. I'm on it, so don't worry."

"Thanks. I need another viewpoint. Maybe I'm letting old patterns of insecurity get the best of me."

"Just focus on what you've accomplished so far, Alison Rockwell. You've been incredible in this new role and I know the success of the show is mostly due to you."

"And Jake. I couldn't have done this without him. I just want to share each successful moment with him." Alison wrung her hands together. "Jenny, I'm falling in love with him, and it scares me. I thought he felt the same way, but now I'm not so sure. The spark between us seemed dim today."

"Not to worry. You have no idea what's going on and all this speculation will get you nowhere. Trust me. Been there."

"You're right. Being afraid is stupid. Thanks, Jen." Alison knew her excessive worry was unnecessary, but the truth was, her feelings for Jake were real. In the kitchen, Cecilia had prepared a light dinner before they went back to town. Alison eased herself into a dining chair, grateful for the quiet interlude of activities.

***

The streets were crowded as the entire community gathered around the town square. The lamp posts were adorned with evergreen swag holding large, red bows and golden, metallic bells woven with white lights and glittering stars. Alison waved to people she knew but didn't see Jake anywhere. The kids stood close to the tree, waiting for the special moment. Alison hung back, content to be out of the spotlight. Then she saw him—hugging a beautiful woman similar in age. She had long, wavy blond hair, was tall, and impeccably dressed. She had a presence about her that definitely screamed "big city" girl. Alison was crushed. This woman must be from New York and the reason he had suddenly pulled away. She watched as they laughed, hugged again and lovingly gazed at each other. How could she have been so naïve? To think he was really interested in her. Alison couldn't take any more. She turned and walked away.

As she wandered away from the festivities, Alison found herself in front of the church and decided to go in. No one was there, and she silently slipped into one of the pews. She needed guidance and her faith had always gotten her through difficult times. Why was this happening? Was it over with Jake before it even had a chance to begin?

"Is everything alright, Miss Rockwell?" Surprised, Alison turned around to see Reverend Michael standing behind her. "I didn't mean to startle you, but I thought you would be at the tree lighting."

"Oh, hi. Guess I needed a meditative moment."

"Do you want to talk about it?" Reverend Michael had a sixth sense about people and could easily see Alison was troubled.

"Maybe."

Michael took that as a yes and sat down next to her. "Is this about the production?"

"No. Partly. It's more personal."

Michael knew right away it was about Jake. "What's going on with the special person we discussed some days ago?"

Without going too much into detail, Alison proceeded to describe ambiguous situations between Jake and her. Not mentioning his name, she poured out her feelings and thoughts. Reverend Michael patiently listened. Then he spoke.

"You know, I've found nothing gets resolved when there's a one-sided conversation going on in your head. Yes, you make observations, hear things, and think you know, but when it involves another person, we never truly know what they think unless we ask. Very simple. Just ask."

"But what if it looks and feels so clear? Isn't it better to walk away?"

"Depends on what you have to lose. Is it something or someone who matters to you? Does the person make you a better person? Inspire you and fill you with joy? Then it might be worth the risk of making a fool of yourself. And these days, there is so much room for miscommunication, I believe it's worth the risk. Don't let your pride stand in the way of possible true happiness, Alison." He gently patted her shoulder and lovingly smiled at her. He hated to see her so tormented, especially since, in his heart, he had faith the two belonged to each other.

Alison considered the Reverend's words for a moment. Was Jake worth the risk of revealing herself, even if he had moved on? What was the worst thing that could happen? After all, if he had a new girlfriend, she would be leaving in a few days and never have to see him again. "Maybe you're right. We've been friends first, so I shouldn't be afraid to talk to him about it. Am I being silly?" she asked, searching for an answer in Michael's eyes.

"No, dear. Not silly. Just human. And remember, there is a divine plan for us all. Have faith."

Alison smiled. "Yes, I guess all this fear and self-torment could be resolved with a little more faith." Then she laughed. "Thank you."

"You're most welcome. I like having these little chats with you." He looked at his watch. "If we leave now, we can catch the tree lighting. What do you say?"

"After you." Alison rose from the pews and followed him out.

***

Alison strode towards the center of town, and luckily caught the moment the giant Christmas tree lit up. Sounds of oohing and ahhing resonated from the community, and Alison felt more at peace than she had all day. She scanned the crowd, didn't see Jake anymore, but saw Jenny. He must have taken his new girlfriend somewhere for a bite to eat or drink. She reassured herself she would talk to him soon. When the time was right.

She waved to Jenny who came right over. "Ready to go home?" Alison wanted to keep this feeling of tranquility, get some work done in her office, and go to bed soon.

"Whenever you are."

Alison noticed the lights weren't on at Jake's when they drove up to the estate. As they walked into the kitchen, Alison asked, "Tea?"

"Yes, and I'll get a fire started in our office if Cecilia hasn't already done so."

Waiting for the water to boil, Alison heard a car drive up. She peeked out the window. Jake! He was here. But, oh no! The woman was with him. And he was carrying her suitcase. Alison didn't have time to hide before they barged into the kitchen.

Jake looked up and saw Alison. His heart was pounding. He had been trying to pull away from her, and he was beginning to suspect she felt it. And he was feeling guilty. He put on a smile anyway. "Hi there."

"Hi. I was just getting tea." She looked over at the beautiful woman. "I'll leave you two alone."

"No, no, no!" she exclaimed and went over to Alison. "I don't know where Jake's manners are, but I'm Maggy Anderson. His favorite cousin." She laughed as she teased him.

"I've heard so much about you! My dad thinks you're doing an outstanding job. I'm here to help in any way I can."

Tension began releasing in Alison's shoulders. Not a girlfriend from New York but his cousin. The powerful television executive from Los Angeles. Alison got a hold of herself and reached out her hand. "So happy to meet you. Your dad is a most generous man. I hope we're not interfering with your holiday vacation."

"Are you kidding? I live for this stuff. This is the most upbeat I've seen my hometown in years. And all thanks to you." Maggy's large green eyes danced with an inviting honesty and her natural beauty emanated a kind spirit like her father.

"I had a lot of help from your cousin." She looked over at Jake, who still felt distant. He smiled but put his head down, attending to a text on his phone.

"Good. He's a competent man." Maggy put her hand on his arm. "Thanks, coz, for picking me up at the train station."

"Any time. I'll let you two get acquainted. Annie is getting dropped off in a few minutes. I'll see you tomorrow."

And before Alison could say anything else, he was out the door. She turned to Maggy. "Can I get you some tea?"

"I'd love some. I need a hot bath and bed. I hope you don't mind, but I'll catch up with you tomorrow. I'm kind of beat from traveling."

"I understand. I'm going to do a little work in the library and do the same. Jake set us up in the library with an office space."

"Smart move." Maggy looked around, grabbed a cookie Sara had left out on a plate and sighed. "It's good to be home." Then she took her cup of tea and said, "Goodnight. Nice to meet you. I'll see you in the morning."

"Sleep well." As she watched Maggy leave, Jenny walked in.

"Who was that?"

"You're never going to believe it. Come on, let's go sit in front of the fire."

"Right behind you."

Chapter Twenty-One

The rays of the morning sun shone in through the curtains of Alison's room. She momentarily lolled in bed, reflecting on the previous evening's events. She was somewhat irritated with herself for jumping to conclusions about Jake, but relieved her fears about Maggy had no merit. She had been ridiculous. Reverend Michael was right. She needed to talk to Jake. And soon.

Today was cookie day, and after arriving at the bakery, she glimpsed at her phone and saw George was calling. She stepped outside for some privacy.

"Hi, George. How are you?" Alison was hoping he was satisfied with the show so far.

"My phone's been ringing off the hook this morning. And on a Saturday. Our advertisers want more space on both the website and television ads. It seems last night's airing struck a chord of generous giving and a premonition of how successfully this show is evolving. They want to make sure they have spots in the new year as well. It's unbelievable! Well done, Miss Rockwell!"

Goosebumps poured over her body like a waterfall. Alison was stunned. She had hoped the show would be successful and *Hands-On Beyond* would have a chance, but this response was the best news ever. "Fantastic, George. Thank you for letting me know."

"Believe me, the network is thrilled, and you may have saved this show. Have to go but can't wait to see the rest. Keep it up, Alison. And happy holidays!"

"Yes, happy holidays to you, too."

The biting, frigid air did not affect her. Alison only felt shocked. Of course, she had dreamed of a favorable outcome, but the reality was sinking in. She just hoped the money and opportunities for the after-foster care kids and orphanage graduates flooded in as well.

The door opened, and Henry popped his head out. "There you are. What are you doing out here in the freezing cold?"

"Had an important call. Too noisy in there. I'll tell you about it." Suddenly her body started to shiver. "I'm coming in now."

Glancing around the room, she saw Annie and the kids, but not Jake. She walked over, and Annie jumped up to greet her. "Morning Alison, I mean Miss Rockwell." She tried to keep professional when they were on set.

"Hi, Annie. Is your dad here?"

"He said he would be here soon. Had to go to his office first, but dropped me off. Are you making cookies?" Annie's questioning eyes danced with child-like wonder.

"No, but I'll eat some." They laughed. "Go on and listen to your instructions and I'll see you after the shoot."

"Okay." And she ran back to be with the other kids.

Alison was anxious to talk to Jake but knew during active production wasn't the best time. Maybe she could pin him down later this afternoon in his office, behind closed doors where he couldn't walk away.

Satisfied everything looked in place, Alison took a spot near the back. She noticed Sean and Eddie had been spending a lot of time together and had become fast friends. She also noticed Justin and Sam had been sharing their love for the entertainment industry and answering all of their questions. She hoped the boys were inspired.

As the cameras rolled, Alison looked down and saw a text from Carolyn. "Call Me!" Always demanding. Alison texted back. "Filming. Will in a bit." Then she decided to put her phone in her pocket and ignore the next abusive comment.

As filming wrapped up, the kids were fidgeting around, restless to eat some of the cookies. Christine reminded them most would go into the refrigerator to be saved, wrapped and delivered on Monday as part of their community service project. Still, she had made plenty two days before, so they could celebrate after the shoot. Alison could see the spark was still there between Sam and her. She hoped they could keep it going after Sam left. Satisfied, she left for the office.

As Henry reviewed his notes, Thea approached him. "The production is going well, don't you think?"

Henry was surprised Thea was being so nice. He knew she had been irritated when Alison gave him his position. She had worked for Carolyn longer and thought she deserved the job. "Yes." Henry lifted his eyebrow. "Do you need something?"

"No, I'm good." Thea glanced around. "I haven't seen Jake Sanders around much these last couple of days. Did he and Alison have a falling out?" She decided to go straight to the point. Time was ticking.

Henry knew there was something she was digging for. "What are you talking about?"

"I heard some rumors the two of them were becoming a 'thing'. You know." Thea smiled at Henry.

"Thea, keep your gossip to yourself. Jake and Alison worked hard to set up this production and have become friends, no more. Now go help Tameka. It looks like she needs it." Henry couldn't be bothered with Thea's hearsay, but his instinct told him he should tell Alison to watch her back. He didn't trust Thea.

***

Alison's stomach was in knots as she approached Jake's closed door. She had raised her fist to knock when Liza saw her.

"You're here. You've got to see this. Our website is flooded with donations and the network keeps sending me advertisers who want to get in on the act. Come see as soon as you put your things down."

Alison couldn't refuse Liza. She walked past Jake's office to her own and then joined Liza. "George called me this morning to let me know. But seeing it in person with you, I'm overwhelmed." She placed her hand on Liza's arm. "Thank you so much. We couldn't have done it without you."

"I'm so into it! Perfect project for the holidays. It's made me feel like I'm really part of the Maple Ridge community."

Alison's heart was torn. She was beginning to regret going back to New York. She had fallen in love with the people here, and she didn't want to stop working for the after-foster care program. She wondered if her destiny was indeed television.

Liza noticed the change on her expression. "What's wrong? You made this happen."

"Me and Jake. I couldn't have done it without him. Have you seen him?"

Liza knew they both had feelings for each other, but it appeared they were both being stubborn about making any decisions to bring themselves together permanently. But Liza understood a woman's dilemma. She'd had her share of unrequited love in Boston. Alison was probably waiting for Jake to make a move. "He's in his office."

"Thanks." No doubts. She was going in.

***

Jake's vision was fixed on the mountains outside his window as he twiddled a pencil in his hand and stared into space. He knew he was avoiding Alison, but he didn't know what else to do. Maybe he should talk to her. A rap on the door interrupted his daydream. As Alison walked in, Jake knew he couldn't get away this time and had to face a discussion he had been dreading. Discussing his odd behavior was only fair to her. When he looked up, his heart throbbed. "Hi. How'd it go this morning?"

Alison had decided to just ignore the angst gripping her heart for the last couple of days. Act like everything was normal, just as it had been before his trip to New York. But she couldn't. And she knew it.

"Fantastic! The kids had a blast; Annie and Tim were pros, and we got some great footage. You should watch with us later in the conference room." She was trying.

Jake looked down, pretending to shuffle some papers. "Yeah, maybe I will. Sorry, I've been busy. Trying to put everything in order before Christmas."

"Jake?"

He looked up at her. He had to tell her how he felt. From his heart. But he could feel himself shutting down. It was safer, and he had spent the last several years cultivating his avoidance mechanism after Clara's death. He felt himself slipping into the abyss again. He didn't want to, but he felt helpless. Alison deserved more.

"Yes?"

Before Alison could speak, Lucy's voice sounded behind the door. Alison opened it and found Lucy standing there with a bouquet of red roses in a vase. Seeing Alison, she exclaimed, "There you are. Look what was delivered for you. Aren't they beautiful? Shall I put them on your desk?" Lucy didn't notice Jake and Alison were in the middle of a potentially intense conversation.

"Oh my! Who are they from?" Alison had no clue who could be sending her flowers.

Lucy handed her the card. As Alison read it, her eyebrows lifted.

Jake noticed her expression. "Secret admirer?"

"I guess so. Steve, my ex." Alison pursed her lips with a furrowed brow.

"Maybe he doesn't want to be an 'ex' any longer. Seems to me you've got someone back home wanting you." Jake was short and to the point.

Lucy could see they needed some privacy. "I've got to get back to the store. I'll put them on your desk." And she left.

Alison inhaled and focused her eyes on Jake for a moment. The connection was still there, only now clouded by fear and apprehension, on both of their parts. She didn't know why his mood had changed, but hers was a direct reaction to his pulling away. "Honestly, Jake, I'm not sure where my home is any more."

Jake's curiosity was piqued. "What do you mean?"

"This whole experience has transformed me on some deeper level. I feel I may be ready for some big changes in my life. And it scares me." Alison knew she wasn't directly expressing her concerns about their relationship, but she wanted to share with him anyway. She had missed talking with him these last few days.

Sensing her openness with him, Jake couldn't ignore her. After all, they had been friends first. Maybe he should just go back to the relationship before the kiss. But in his heart, he knew he couldn't forget about the kiss. Or the fact he had been—and was still—falling in love with this woman. But he would try. She deserved at least his friendship. "What kind of changes?"

"Maple Ridge is growing on me. New York seems so far away." She looked down at her phone ringing. "Never mind. I've got to take this. Maybe see you later?"

"I'll try." Jake was going to say more but Alison left quickly. He had to make a decision. He knew it was an unreal expectation, but he wanted Alison to decide to stay on her own accord. But maybe he was missing the point. He shook his head. Jake couldn't make any commitments. He needed to talk to someone. He had never felt so confused.

***

As Alison sat at her desk, she reflected on her conversation with Jake. She certainly hadn't been explicit with him, but dropping a hint was enough for now. Steve had called twice, so she decided to call him back. The flowers were definitely a surprise.

He picked up right away. "Hi! Did you get the flowers?" Steve was determined to win her back.

"Yes, they're lovely. Thank you."

"I wanted you to know I'm thinking about you. I'm so proud of you, Ali. You are becoming a successful producer. Very exciting. How are you doing?"

"Busy, but things are flowing without many hitches. I've got wonderful staff." Alison didn't feel like giving him any details.

"Terrific! I'm hoping I can see you soon. I've changed, Alison. I've realized how much you mean to me in our time apart. And I want us to try again." He paused for a moment. "What do you say?"

"I'm not sure, Steve, but I don't think it would work. I can't discuss it now, but I wanted to thank you for the flowers. Very thoughtful." Alison couldn't remember ever getting flowers from him in the two years they had dated, except for some wimpy bouquet on Valentine's Day he probably had picked up at the corner market on his way to her apartment.

"I know you're busy but hopefully after the holidays we can get together." Steve was a on a mission.

"Maybe. Listen Steve, I've got to go."

"I understand. We'll talk soon."

"Goodbye, Steve. Merry Christmas." Alison hung up, pressing her lips together, and pondered on Steve's actions. A little too late.

***

After the staff viewing in the afternoon, Alison looked around the room for Jake. She saw him standing in the back talking to Maggy. He saw her look at him, smiled and gave her a thumbs up sign before walking out. Alison bit her bottom lip as she watched him leave, not knowing when she would see him again.

Jenny stepped closer to her. "Okay, friend. Let's you and I have dinner tonight. What do you say? Mike is coming tomorrow, your parents are coming Monday, and we may not have much girl time together before the holidays. We can relax at the estate and have a glass of wine in our library suite."

Alison put her arm around her. "Probably just what I need. Sam told me he's going to have dinner with Christine tonight, and the kids seem well cared for by Henry and Tameka. Even Melissa is getting along with the girls, especially Annie and Jolene. I'll call Sara and let her know."

"Excellent! I've got a couple hours of work left and then I'm free."

"Same here. Thanks, Jen. You always know what I need." Resolution with Jake would have to wait. Again.

Chapter Twenty-Two

Maggy had insisted Jake let her take him out to dinner. Annie was spending the night at a friend's house and she wanted some privacy with her cousin. Ever since Jake lost his parents, he had become more like a brother than a cousin. Living on the opposite coast wasn't always easy for Maggy. Yes, she was incredibly successful, but her family was more important to her. She hoped she could move back to New York one day and be closer to them.

Sitting across from Jake at their favorite Italian restaurant, Maggy lifted her glass of wine. "Here's to the successful launch of Starlight Publishing." Her radiant smile beamed at Jake, and he could feel the love she had for him. He felt the same way about her.

"And here's to my most beautiful cousin who never ceases to amaze me with her talent and love." Jake toasted his glass, then took a large sip. He needed it.

Maggy set down her glass, and with laser-focused intensity, she asked, "What's going on, Jake? I know you, and there's something not right. Does it have to do with the business? Or is it Alison? You were so happy a week ago when I talked to you. I thought, maybe, this woman was finding a way into your heart. Am I right? What happened?"

Jake grinned and shook his head. "You know me so well. I'm stoked about the imprint launch and satisfied with the capable and creative people I hired. No glitches or regrets there. But Alison..." Suddenly a gloomy shadow obscured his mood, and he seemed to drift far away in thought.

Maggy pulled him back. "What the heck happened? What are you afraid of?" She wasn't going to let him off the hook until they had resolved the issue. She couldn't stand to see him this way. Again. Distraught and receding into his shell.

Jake knew he couldn't hide anything from Maggy. And he didn't want to. "When I was in New York, your dad informed me how happy the network was with Alison's work. They will be offering her a promotion and permanent position as a producer, possibly executive producer in the near future. She's so young and bright and certainly deserves this."

"What's the problem?" Maggy wasn't going to let this slide.

"The problem is, I can't do a long-distance relationship. I don't want to spend time away from Annie, and I can't ask her to give up her job and move to Maple Ridge. It wouldn't be fair. And I'm worried I've let Annie become attached to her, and she'll be gone in a few days. Our relationship became closer as we spent time together, and I think Annie was hoping she would stay. Permanently."

"What does Alison want?"

"I imagine the dream job in New York."

"Have you asked her?"

"Not really. She doesn't know about the promotion yet."

"Silly man. You have to talk to her. Make it a 'what if' question—like a hypothesis—without giving her details. To see what she is actually wanting and thinking. Unless you get dad to talk to her first. Then you could ask her how she feels about the offer."

Jake pondered Maggy's words. "Maybe you're right. I could talk to him tomorrow when he arrives."

"You have to do something, Jake Sanders. And before the finale of the show. I don't like to see you tortured like this and, you know, Annie picks up on all of your emotions. Do it for her if not yourself. Ask yourself, what is best for Annie? I think Alison would make an exquisite addition to our family. Just saying." Maggy reached her hand out to touch Jake. "You deserve love again, Jake. So, does Annie. I think you could both have love with Alison. Open back up to her again and see what happens. And for gosh sakes, don't shut her out. Women hate that!" She laughed, pulled her hand back, and took a sip of wine.

Jake ran his fingers along the stem of the wine glass. He would talk to his uncle. Maybe the news could be delivered sooner, and Jake could find out how she felt about staying in New York and pursuing a television career. He took a large sip of wine. "You're right."

"I know." She grinned.

"The weird thing is, she's also a writer. And a good one too. Children's books of all things. I think I'm going to offer her a publishing deal before she leaves."

"Smart move. Keeps you connected. And who knows what may happen?" Maggy wanted to reassure him. "Now, let's eat."

"Yeah, I'm starved all of a sudden. You're the best, Mag. I needed this."

"I love you, Jake."

"I love you, too."

***

Sitting at her desk in the library before church, Alison's head was bent over her notebook when Annie skipped through the door. "Breakfast is ready. Sara told me to get you and Jenny. Is she around?"

Alison put down her pen, allowing Annie's cheerfulness to lift her mood. "Good morning to you! She'll be right down, and I'll be there in a minute." Alison wondered if Jake was in the kitchen.

"Okay!" Annie said and skipped back to the kitchen.

Alison stopped outside the entrance for a moment and listened to Jake's inflection while expressing himself. His booming voice resonated in the room and he was even laughing. Maybe he was back to his normal self. She adjusted her sweater and ran her fingers through her hair before stepping into the kitchen. "Good morning, everyone."

"Good morning," they all chimed.

Jenny waltzed in behind her. "Smells good in here."

"Sara left us quite a spread," said Maggy. "She went to choir practice early."

Alison lifted her head, catching Jake's eyes zeroing in on her. The corners of her mouth raised effortlessly, the chemistry still there.

After Jake's chat with Maggy, he decided to be friends with Alison and not let there be any weird vibes between them. "Come on, sit down and dig in." He grinned and gestured to a chair for her.

The knot in Alison's stomach began to unwind as she witnessed Jake's seemingly changed behavior. She still wanted to chat with him alone and hoped whatever happened may be resolved. She hopped onto the chair, grabbed some toast, and joined in on the conversation.

***

After the service, Henry took off, excited that Nathan was arriving at the inn for the remainder of the shoot. He knew Carolyn would never have allowed personal partners to do so, and he was grateful. Sean and Melissa were headed to Fairside Manor to hang out with their new buddies. Melissa had become much more pleasant and her mother was thrilled. Alison mused that Sam spent time with Christine whenever he could get away and would most likely be found at the bakery later.

As she looked around for Jake, she saw him talking intimately with Reverend Michael. She noticed him glance over in her direction once and wondered what he was saying. Was it about her?

Before she could stew on it any more, Maggy patted her on the shoulder. "Annie and I are going Christmas shopping this afternoon, and you're coming with us. No buts about it."

Alison turned around to see Maggy, arms crossed, intently willing her to come. Shopping. Maybe just what she needed. She hadn't had a chance to buy hardly anything and her parents were coming tomorrow. "No buts, eh? How could I refuse? Can we go home first to change?"

"Absolutely. Let me catch Jake. He's our ride. And by the way, we're having a big Christmas celebratory dinner at the estate tonight. My dad will be here, and he wants to meet all of your closest crew before they disperse after the shoot on Christmas Eve. Can you send out a text to them? Sara said be generous with your invites. She lives for these dinner parties!"

Alison's pulse was racing. Jim Anderson. She was finally going to meet him in person. Her nerves jolted her for a second but dissipated quickly at the thought of meeting the generous man who had made everything possible and who had raised Jake from a young boy.

***

Jake dropped the girls off and then headed back to his office. He needed to check on Lucy and get some paperwork done before his uncle arrived. Being just a friend with Alison was difficult. He wanted to reach out, touch her hand, pull her close and kiss her again. Unrestrained desire seemed to surge inside of him, and he felt like he was going to explode if he didn't share it with her. Tonight, he would talk to her. He would present the 'what if' question to her as the businessman. Maybe her answer would surprise him.

Liza rubbed her temples and let out a sigh. The *Hands-On Beyond* program was surging on the internet and their website's mailbox had been filling up with multiple inquiries and interest from all over the country. She rose from her desk in search of Jake. Standing in his doorway, she asked, "Can I talk to you a minute?"

"Sure." Jake couldn't be happier with his hire of Liza. She had fit in with the community immediately and had worked way more hours than he was paying her. He would have to give her a nice Christmas bonus. "What's up?"

"Our *Beyond* program is bursting at the seams. It needs an excellent manager, and I know Karen will be too proud to ask you. I think you will want to hire someone full-time to oversee it after the holidays. I can volunteer some hours, but when our launch happens, I'm sure I'll be too busy. Either we have to budget in a salary or you take a bigger role in sponsoring. Just being straight with you."

"Good to know. I had a feeling this might happen when I saw the aired episodes. Alison really did a spectacular job, didn't she?"

"She sure did. I'm going to miss her."

"Thanks for the input. I'll talk to my uncle, too. Maybe we can come up with something between the two of us." Jake paused. "Shouldn't you be out Christmas shopping or something? Spending time with your sister? Finish up whatever you're doing and get out of here. And by the way, you're invited to dinner at the Anderson estate tonight. My uncle wants to meet the key players before the holidays."

Liza smiled. "Alison already texted me."

"Of course, she did," mused Jake.

"See you later, Jake. Shouldn't you be out shopping, too?"

Jake put down his pen. "Yes, you're right. I'm leaving soon." Jake needed to get a couple of more things for Annie, and he wanted to get something for Alison, although he had no idea what to get her. Hopefully, he'd know when he saw it.

***

Maggy slipped her arm through Alison's as they strolled down the main street, peering in the decorated windows and chatting about gift possibilities. Annie ran ahead, leading the expedition, anxious to look at everything.

"Let's go in here," she exclaimed to them.

Alison glanced up and saw an old-fashioned country store filled with holiday ornaments, unique gifts and enchanting treasures festively organized like a Norman Rockwell painting in the window. "I'm game."

"This is a great boutique," said Maggy. "I always find unusual gifts and the prices aren't too expensive. You'll find something nice for your parents and maybe even Jake." She grinned at Alison. She knew what was going on, but she didn't want to be uncomfortably forward. Still, she did want to get some information which might help her cousin. After all, Jake was her family and deserved all the support he could get. Especially after witnessing his apprehensive turmoil the night before.

Alison wondered what Jake had told Maggy. She found her to be warm and inviting, not at all pretentious or stuck-up. Maybe she could talk to her about Jake. "Yes, I would like to find something special for Jake. He's been wonderful with me."

"He's a great guy. And not because he's my family, but he's always been that way. When we were kids, he helped me whenever I needed it, and we've always talked about everything since then. My heart broke when Clara died. I hated to see Annie and him go through such grief and tragedy. He had already experienced enough death in his life with the passing of his parents at a young age. But lately, I've seen a change in him. I wonder, does it have anything to do with you?" Maggy stopped, her eyes penetrating Alison dead-on. She could be intense that way. After all, she was a Leo with a bold spirit.

"With me?" Alison was taken by surprise by the assertive comment.

"Yes, you. I won't beat around the bush. Are you going to tell me how you feel? Because I can definitely see he has feelings for you."

Alison's heart was in her throat. "Do you think we could talk somewhere private? After shopping?" Alison welcomed Maggy's insight. After all, she only had three days until Christmas.

Maggy put her arm around Alison. "Whatever I can do to bring you two together—if it's what you want—I'm in. I care deeply about Jake, and I kind of like you too." She laughed. "Until later. And I'm not going to forget!"

Browsing around the store, Alison found most of her presents, including ones for Jake and Annie. Dangling in the window, a luminous star ornament caught her eye with the written message, *Wish Upon A Star for Dreams Do Come True.* She hoped the gift would be a personal reminder of their heartfelt times together and become a treasured addition to their tree. The clerk wrapped it in shimmering gold paper, adding a delicate bow with a reddish luster. Thanks to George, the staff was getting a nice bonus, and she got a few personal things for Jenny, Henry, Sara and Annie. Still browsing, she felt a tap on her shoulder.

"Find everything you want?"

Alison twisted her head around and came face to face with Jake poised next to her, close enough to touch. "What are you doing here?" Alison was surprised and couldn't think of anything else to say. Things still weren't normal between them.

"Same thing you are." Jake laughed with a gleam in his eyes. "Like you, I've been crazy busy lately. Needed to get a few things." He glanced down at her bags. "Looks like you've been successful." Jake found it harder and harder not to grab her and kiss her passionately.

"I think so. Almost finished. Maggy's back there with Annie if you want to say hello. The next stop is the bakery for coffee and gingerbread cookies. Want to come?" Alison decided to be bold.

"Sounds like fun, but I need to buy presents for those two, so if they're not in here, it would be helpful. Do you mind?" Jake wanted her to know he had a good excuse.

"Of course, not. I'll go get them." Alison wanted to touch him, kiss him on the cheek, and run off somewhere to be alone. Memories of their unforgettable night at his cottage were tempting her imagination. She longed for another intimate moment and was getting clearer about what she needed to do.

Collecting her thoughts, Alison slowly made her way to the back of the store, rounded up Maggy and Annie, and headed for the entrance. Passing Jake, she said, "See you tonight?"

"I'll be there." He held her eyes in a desirous stare but didn't say a thing. Then she was gone.

Chapter Twenty-Three

Combing her hair as she dressed for dinner, Alison caught her reflection in the mirror. "What are you doing?" she asked herself out loud. She had an idea, but she needed to talk to Jake about it. She never had her private talk with Jake's cousin. When they had entered the bakery earlier, friends of Maggy's flocked around her, anxious to catch up on the latest details of her life, and there was no other opportunity to chat afterward. Her parents had called to say they wouldn't arrive until the next day, which alleviated some pressure for her. She loved them but would feel responsible for entertaining them at dinner tonight. Selfishly, she wanted the time to converse with Jim Anderson. She had seen a car drive up earlier, so she knew he was in the house.

Dinner wouldn't be ready yet, so Alison decided to go to her office for some last-minute follow-up tasks. As she passed Jim Anderson's private office, the door opened, and he and Jake appeared.

"And here she is!" A tall man in his early sixty's stood behind Jake and walked forward.

Startled, Alison quickly regained her composure. "Hi. Mr. Anderson, I presume?"

"You presume correctly." Jim was an attractive man with distinguished grey hair, fit body and a commanding presence that immediately took over a room without effort. "And you must be the famous Alison Rockwell. I've heard wonderful things about you, but your work speaks for itself. I'm thrilled with the direction you've taken *Hands-On Kids*. And the philanthropical element you've added is stellar. We've never seen the ratings this high as I'm sure George told you. Congratulations!"

Alison's cheeks reddened. "Thank you, Mr. Anderson. But it has been a team effort. I couldn't have done any of it without Jake."

Jim lovingly put his arm around his nephew. "Yes, he is special, isn't he? Couldn't be prouder of this guy." Jim laughed. "Now, what do you say we head to the living room? I'm anxious to meet all of your staff."

"Yes, sir."

"And please, call me Jim. You're in my home tonight as my guest, not my employee. I love Christmas!" He gestured his hand towards the hall. "After you."

Alison obeyed and walked in front of him, feeling Jake's eyes following her.

***

As people arrived, they mingled in the living room, being served holiday cocktails and champagne. Alison made the rounds chatting with her staff and was happy to see Nathan with Henry. Mike would be joining Jenny tomorrow evening, so all the couples were coming together. Would Jake and she ever become a couple? He certainly had been more open in the last twenty-four hours, but would they ever get a chance to talk? For now, though, her next conversational priority was Jim Anderson. And she was going to approach him after dinner.

The meal was lively, and spirits were high. Alison had noticed Carolyn's calls were fewer, which was a relief. But her gut told her the harassment was not over. She was seated next to Jim and Maggy was on the other side of him. Jake was next to her and thank goodness, Jenny was next to Alison. Nearing the end of dinner, Jim's large frame rose from the chair, tapping his fork against his glass.

"I would like to propose a toast. To Alison Rockwell and all of you. You have truly changed the trajectory of *Hands-On Kids*—and for the better. I couldn't be prouder of this enterprise. Cheers to all of you!" In unison, everyone raised their glasses. "And there's one more thing I would like to announce. If she agrees, Alison Rockwell will continue to be your commander in chief for next season—in addition to the executive producing title. You certainly deserve it, Alison, and I'm happy to be the one to announce the network's decision before the holidays."

Alison froze as everyone in the room clapped and shouted. She certainly wasn't expecting this. Yes, she thought she would probably keep some kind of producing role under Carolyn, but to permanently get her position? And an executive producing credit as well? Which meant she would have creative license to explore and implement new ideas as she had done in Maple Ridge. But it also meant staying in New York—away from Jake—and possibly a whole other life.

Promptly she gathered her wits and said, "Thank you Mr. Anderson, for the generous offer, but I couldn't have done any of it without all of you." Her eyes scanned the room and fell on Jake's. He smiled at her, but she knew he had probably known about this promotion. She sensed he had pulled away to make room for her career. Before, she had been clear, but now her brain felt like mud. She didn't want to lose him but needed time to think. Redirecting the conversation, she said, "Now, let's eat!" Her discomfort was eased when everyone returned to filling their plates and eating.

Jim leaned over to Alison. "You don't have to make a decision today, Alison, but I wanted you to know. Think about it and let me know your decision, if you can, before you leave Maple Ridge. Now, enjoy your dinner."

Alison glanced at Jake, but he was wrapped up in a conversation with Maggy. Jenny whispered in her ear. "You're white as a sheet. Pull it together. I know what you're thinking. We'll talk about this later." Always the friend, she could read Alison without a word being said.

***

Everyone left soon after dinner, since they still had two more days of shooting and would be getting up early the next morning. Jake was the last to leave. When Alison was finished saying goodbye to her staff, he approached her. "Congratulations. You deserve the promotion." Searching her eyes, Jake wanted to see if there was any ambiguity lingering there for this big step in her career. He had no doubt she could handle it, but did she want it?

Alison returned the attention with her own questioning eyes. "Thanks. I was quite surprised, to be honest. I never dreamed they would give me Carolyn's job. She's going to be very upset."

"I'm sure the network will find another position for her. From what I heard, one without kids. Seems her personality isn't suited for it." Jake paused. "How do you feel about it?" There. He had asked her.

Alison stammered. "I don't know. I think I need some time to process. I actually had some other ideas."

"Really? Like what?"

Then like clockwork, an unexpected but familiar interruption occurred as the door swung open and Annie rushed into the room. "Dad, I'm back!" She ran over to Alison. "Did you have fun at dinner? We did. Melissa's mom took us all out."

"Sounds awesome," said Alison. Would she ever get a moment with Jake?

He looked at Alison and then Annie. "Why don't you say hello to Uncle Jim? He's in the living room, and then we'll go home."

"Okay." She skipped out and they were left alone.

"I do want to hear about your ideas, Alison, but it seems we can never find the right time." He laughed.

"Yes. I know. Maybe tomorrow? I can stop by after the shoot in the afternoon?"

"Sounds like a date." Jake shrugged his shoulders. "You know what I mean."

"Yes, Jake, I do." Alison's body yearned for his arms to embrace her, reassuring her of his desire for her. Was it still there?

Annie appeared, holding Jim's hand. "Looks like the party's over," Jim said. "I told Annie we would continue the festivities on Christmas Eve."

As Annie put on her coat, Jim whispered low in his nephew's ear. "The favor you asked of me? I'm working on it. I'll know more tomorrow." He patted Jake on the back.

"Thanks. I appreciate it." Jake picked up his coat and moved closer to Alison. "See you tomorrow."

Alison's heart was beating a hundred miles an hour. She couldn't control it if she wanted to. "Yes, see you tomorrow." And then he was gone.

***

The center buzzed with activity. The children were animated as they prepared for the community service episode. After wrapping ornaments and boxes of cookies, they would be taken by van to several nursing homes and the hospital. Alison was delighted to see Sam had recruited Eddie to help him with some behind-the-scenes work with the filming. Eddie was a natural and Alison saw a bond forming between them. She often saw him hanging out with Sean and Justin as well.

She didn't see Jake anywhere, but hadn't expected to. He was probably in his office. Immersed in her clipboard to-do list, she didn't hear Henry approach. "Alison!" His voice was frantic.

Alison flipped around. "You scared me. What's wrong?"

"You're never going to guess who I just saw get out of a car at the inn!"

Alison's heart sank. She knew. "Carolyn?"

"Yes! And I saw her talking to Thea. What do you want me to do?"

Alison thought about it for a second. "Nothing. Keep doing your job. I wondered why I hadn't heard from her in twenty-four hours. We just do our job and welcome her whenever she steps on to our set."

Henry looked baffled by Alison's response. "How can you be so calm?"

"We've done nothing wrong and the network's ratings are better than ever. By now Carolyn has heard about my promotion, and I'm sure she's worried. I'm not scared of her, Henry, and neither should you be."

Henry nodded his head. Alison inspired him.

Easy words—but harder to live by. She knew a confrontation was coming but kept her attention on the present. Henry, Tameka and Jenny had everything under control, so she could focus on the important announcement happening at the end of the day's episode. Working on *Hands-On Beyond* seemed to calm any angst she was feeling about Carolyn. Her passion for the program was growing more each day, satisfying an emerging purpose she unknowingly had yearned for.

Satisfied the production was under control, Alison drove out to Fairside Manor, where Sam and a few others met her for the special closing interview with Mary Beth and Jolene. She wanted to do it before the last Christmas Eve segment, since that would give an extra twenty-four hours to inspire people to donate and offer housing or jobs for the youth. She wasn't trying to dodge Carolyn's presence, but Henry could take care of her. Alison had a feeling she would be showing up at the sites, guided by Thea. She'd see her soon enough. She needed to focus her attention on this closing interview.

Karen was in her office on the phone and motioned for Alison to come in. She hung up and gleefully exclaimed, "It's unbelievable! I'm getting calls and emails left and right. Other directors from around the states are calling me, asking for advice on how to become a part of the program. It's a full-time job, Alison. I never dreamed we would become so successful, so fast."

Alison's heart was pounding. Her intuition had been right on. "Congratulations! Can we talk a minute?"

"Sure, close the door."

"I have an idea." Alison proceeded to tell her. It felt like the right decision.

***

As Alison's inevitable departure approached, Jake knew he had to make a move. Today. No more waiting. Whatever happened would be the for the best, as Clara had always said. And she was usually right. He smiled. She would have liked Alison.

Liza peeked her head in his office. "Got a minute?"

"Sure."

"*Hands-On Beyond* is an incredible success, Jake. Have you given any thought as to what your role will be in its continuation? We will need a director and a governing board. What do you think?"

"Yes, Jim and I talked about the situation last night. We're going to continue the conversation later."

"I just don't want to lose momentum after the holidays. I wish Alison would stay and take on the position."

Jake's heart rate accelerated like a rocket. The thought hadn't crossed his mind. Would she be interested? Enough to leave her very successful and rising career in New York? "She would be perfect, but you heard Uncle Jim announce her big promotion last night."

"But what does *she* want, Jake?" Men could be clueless thought Liza. Had he even thought to ask her?

Jake looked out the window and then back at Liza. "I'll talk to her. And Liza—"

"Yes?"

"Thank you for all of your hard work. You've gone way beyond your duties here. And you've only been here a week or two. I'm glad I hired you." A wide grin spread across his face.

Liza laughed. "Me too. It was the best move for me too in many ways." She pivoted to leave. "Back to my computer!"

Jake picked up the phone to call Jim. No time like the present.

***

Mary Beth's sweaty hands were fidgeting as she sat next to her sister on the small couch in the manor library. She had agreed to one more interview, but the cameras still made her jittery. She didn't think twice when Christine and Melissa walked in with Alison. She liked Christine and had enjoyed working in her kitchen throughout the week for the show. Melissa and Jolene had become friends, which made her happy.

Alison pulled up a chair while Christine and Melissa flanked them on either side.

"This interview will wrap up the week and the kick off for *Hands-On Beyond*. I appreciate you both agreeing to do this. The questions will be easy." Pointing to the other two, she said, "These ladies will be participating also, so not as much pressure." She looked directly at Mary Beth. "Ready?"

"Ready," they all replied.

Sam, Eddie and Sean walked in with the film crew. The three of them had become quite the team. Sam enjoyed mentoring kids, and clearly, Christine had become smitten with him over the last week. And the feeling was mutual.

Melissa took the lead on the overview and progress of the program. She was radiating more brightly on camera lately, and her essence was shining like a true star. Mary Beth was even smiling.

Christine turned to the camera. "I would like to make a special announcement today. As a small-business owner in Maple Ridge, I have been inspired by the work the *Hands-On Beyond* program is trying to do." She reached her hand out, placing it on Mary Beth's shoulder. "And I will be offering Mary Beth a full-time position at my Sweet Ridge Bakery after she graduates."

Mary Beth's eyes widened, and her mouth fell open. She froze for an instant in disbelief. Overcome with emotion, her voice was barely audible as she said, "Really?"

"Yes." Christine squeezed her hand.

Mary Beth's body was still in shock as the realization hit her. "Thank you," she whimpered. She could barely get any words out.

Melissa beamed, and her voice was filled with new animation as she added, "*And*—we have an apartment in town— given anonymously—you will share with another Fairside graduate at a reduced rate. You're staying in Maple Ridge!"

Hands over her mouth, Jolene screamed, then grabbed her sister. Squeezing each other, tears began pouring down both of their faces. Uncontrollable sobbing seemed to spring forth like a geyser erupting from the deepest part of their souls, washing away all the worries and fears they had carried inside them for too long. No other words were needed.

"And there you have our first Christmas miracle," Melissa said, directly into the camera. "Thanks to *Hands-On Beyond*. See you tomorrow for our finale, on location at Starlight Books. A special treat for Christmas Eve, so tune in and see. Happy holidays!"

As Sam panned the cameras out, Alison knew the joy filling the room would overflow to the television audience. As her heart expanded, her future became crystal clear.

***

Jake hung up the phone with Jim and understood the choice was Alison's. He wouldn't do anything to influence her, but he had to let her know how he felt. He would only regret it later if he didn't. How could he wait until she decided on her career path first? Congratulate her on New York and say goodbye? Or embrace her in his arms and welcome her to Maple Ridge? If he was truthful, he wanted to hold on to her tightly and never let go.

A knock at his door sounded and Henry appeared. "Hey Jake, got a minute?"

"Sure. What's up?"

"Alison wanted me to ask you if you would like a minute on the episode tomorrow to announce the launch of your imprint. She thought it would be a clever promotion of your new company."

Of course, she did. "If you have space. I actually have an announcement of my own I would like to make, if it's okay."

"I'm sure it is. I'll ask her. You've done so much already, Jake. I hope you know how much the staff appreciates you."

"Thank, Henry. But I think the credit goes to Alison. I just helped."

Henry rolled his eyes as he walked out the door. When were these two going to get together?

***

Alison grabbed two coffees at the bakery before heading to her office. An excuse to see Jake although she knew she didn't need one. Her stomach tightened, and her shoulders needed a massage. She wasn't sure how he felt anymore, and even if his feelings had changed, she was doing what was best for her. She knew it inside.

Walking down the hallway, her pulse sped up when she saw Jim Anderson's lofty figure coming towards her. "Hi. I didn't know you were coming."

"I wanted to see your operation here firsthand. Jake was right. It fit in quite nicely."

Alison couldn't think of what to say so she offered the second coffee to him. "Would you like a cappuccino? I have an extra."

"Don't mind if I do. Want to give me a tour? Then I thought we could meet in your office about my proposal."

"Sure. Follow me." Alison looked back and saw Jake's door closed. She wondered if they had been meeting. She escorted Jim around the space, introducing him to other staff, and eventually circled back to her office. "And here we are." She opened the door and invited him in. Her nerves were twisting inside and made breathing difficult. She slowly calmed herself. Thank goodness for the years of yoga.

Even though Jim was a very wealthy and influential person, his gentle, kind manner touched those who came in contact with him. "Tell me what you thought about the offer and if you've come to a decision."

Alison placed her coffee cup on the desk as she sat down and slowly began expressing her ideas and thoughts about everything. Jim listened intently, and soon they came to an understanding. When they were finished, Jim stood up and shook her hand. "As you asked, I will keep this conversation private until you've talked to some people. Remember, I support you."

"Thank you, Mr. Anderson." Alison was relieved.

As the door opened, they turned to walk out and nearly collided with Carolyn. She was quick to pounce, and with her hand outstretched, she introduced herself to Jim. "Hello. I'm Carolyn Parks, producer of *Hands-On Kids*. It's so nice to meet you."

"Ah, yes. George Stevens has told me about you. Are you feeling better?" He looked down at her leg and saw she was still on crutches.

"Yes, thank you. The doctor permitted me to travel, and I wouldn't miss the Christmas finale of the show. I haven't missed one in five years!" She smiled, putting on her best front, obviously sucking up to him.

Jim motioned to Alison. "Alison has done a spectacular job. You must be very proud of her." Jim knew Carolyn was only there to protect her job and cared nothing about her staff. He had been informed by George of the many complaints.

Carolyn put on a fake smile. "Yes, I am. Do you have a minute to chat? Privately?"

Jim looked at Alison.

Alison didn't want any conflict. "You can use my office. I'm going to check on Liza." She turned to Carolyn. "Come join us at four in the conference area. We watch the episodes together."

"How sweet," she smirked. Carolyn walked past her into Alison's office, and gestured for Jim to follow. "Shall we?"

Jim gave a reassuring look to Alison, then closed the door behind him. Alison didn't care what Carolyn had up her sleeve. She was free from her afflicting reign and moving forward with her life. She needed to have a conversation with George, then she could make announcements of her own tomorrow.

***

As Carolyn settled into her chair, she straightened her posture and eyed her boss. "Mr. Anderson, I want you to know I fully intend to resume my duties as full-time producer after the holidays. I apologize I haven't been able to work directly with the staff, but I've been monitoring Alison daily."

Jim nodded his head, knowing she had probably *harassed* Alison daily.

"I have one thing I would like to bring to your attention."

"Yes, what?"

"I know your nephew, Jake Sanders, has been assisting, but I think Alison may have used, shall I say, an emotional influence on him to get what she wanted. One of my staff has told me that her manipulation was very inappropriate and unprofessional. And I thought you should know the truth before any promotions were given. I felt it my duty as a veteran producer to inform you, since you are here in person."

Jim was quiet, then spoke. "I'm not sure who told you this gossip, Miss Parks, but George and I have received other information about Miss Rockwell. Thank you for your input, and I will discuss this with Jake." Jim was done with this conversation. "Now, if you'll excuse me, Miss Parks, I have a conference call." He stood up. "Try to enjoy the holidays and the success of the show. I know I will."

Carolyn wasn't satisfied with how the conversation had ended, but she could do nothing more. "Thank you, Mr. Anderson, for your time."

Jim was already at the door holding it open for Carolyn. "Merry Christmas."

As Carolyn walked out, she turned. "Perhaps we could talk again about the network's upcoming schedule before I leave."

"I'll let George know. He will contact you for a meeting."

"Okay. Thank you." Flushed with a crimson face, Carolyn felt defeat burning her body, and she didn't like it.

Jim Anderson was used to jealousy, manipulation, and power struggles, running multi-million-dollar businesses, especially those in the entertainment industry. And he knew Alison possessed none of those qualities.

Chapter Twenty-Four

A blissful state of mind settled over Alison like a calming after the storm. She was eager to share her new direction for the future and celebrate the holidays with her parents. After settling in at the inn, Alison took them to her office to view the day's episode. Passing Jake's open door, she paused. "Hi. I wanted to introduce you to my parents."

Jake stood up, walked closer, and held out his hand. "Nice to meet you. You must be very proud of your daughter. She's done an incredible job producing *Hands-On Kids* and establishing its outreach program."

The tender look between Jake and Alison did not go unnoticed by Alison's mother. She recognized an affectionate spark. "Yes, we are always proud of Alison. She's quite fearless with her career choices, but we're just happy to spend the holidays with her. I hear you were instrumental in helping her."

"She made it easy."

Alison blushed at his comment and decided to redirect the conversation. "Enough. Let's get you both a seat for the screening. Thanks, Jake. See you later?"

"Most definitely."

Alison felt her heart swell, but for the moment she had to concentrate on other things. She got her parents settled, then looked around for Carolyn. She didn't see either her or Thea and pulled Jenny aside to ask if she had seen them.

"Yes. And Carolyn didn't look pleased. She left the building and Thea followed. What happened?"

"I'm not sure. I left her with Jim Anderson when she requested a private meeting. Nothing to worry about, I guess." Alison smiled and put her arm around her friend. "Let's enjoy this. I can't wait to see everyone's reaction to the announcement at the end of the show."

Jenny grinned. "You're really in your element, Alison. Hope you know."

"I think I do, Jen. I think I do." Alison was ecstatic that all of her plans were coming together. Now, if the last piece with Jake would resolve, she would have everything she ever wanted.

***

Alison's face lit up, and her pace accelerated while explaining her future plans with her parents at dinner. Her parents had already witnessed an uplifting atmosphere during the staff screening. Hearts wide open, even some of the guys were tearing up at the end when Mary Beth was offered a job and housing.

Still on the clock, Alison picked up the phone when she saw it was Henry. "What's up?"

"We've got a problem. The author from New York is sick with the flu. She can't come. What are we going to do?"

Alison's heart sunk. Just when things were going so well. "Let me think a minute." Then she got an idea. "Give me an hour. I'll call you back."

"Let me know if there's anything I can do."

"Will do." Alison turned to her parents, but they could see she needed to go.

"Go on, sweetheart," said her dad. "Do your thing. We'll see you tomorrow. Call us if you need anything."

"We love you, Ali," added her mom. "And we're very proud of you."

Alison kissed them and hurried off. She needed to find Jake.

***

Alison didn't want to interrupt Jake at his family dinner, but she knew she had to. She could hear them laughing in the dining room when she entered the house. She tip-toed in, and Annie saw her immediately. "Alison! You're here."

Alison wrinkled her brow. "Yes, I'm sorry to interrupt your dinner, but I wondered if I could talk to Jake a minute. Something just came up for our last shoot."

Jim answered. "Don't worry about it. You're welcome here anytime."

Jake stood up. "Let's go to the library."

"Thanks. And sorry. It will only take a minute."

Jake was happy for a moment alone with her, which lately, seemed impossible. "What's going on?"

Alison explained her situation with the sick author, hoping Jake would know someone, perhaps one of his authors featured at his store. Or a local writer.

"I think I have the perfect person. Give me Henry's number and I'll take care of it."

Of course, he would. "Oh, Jake. Thank you. But let me know what I can do. I didn't mean to dump this problem on you. I want to help, too." Now Alison felt guilty.

"No problem. Very easy. Just a phone call." Jake reached out, touched her arm and searchingly looked into her eyes. "Alison, don't leave town until we can talk. I have something I want to share with you, and I want to wait until you are completely finished with your duties."

Alison placed her hand over his. "There's something I want to discuss with you as well. I won't leave. My parents are in no hurry."

Jake squeezed her hand. "I'm going to make some phone calls. See you tomorrow?"

Alison nodded her head as she watched him go. His lingering touch on her arm sent shivers through her body, and she knew in her heart she had made the right decision. No matter what.

***

Jenny was flitting around, arranging pillows and furniture while adding last-minute décor to the intimate yet spacious stage at Starlight Books. Jake had agreed to close the store until the afternoon. People would have plenty of time to purchase last-minute gifts and pick up their orders. Alison noticed Henry and Jake were earnestly discussing something and wondered when the new author would be arriving. As she walked closer to inquire, Jake got an important phone call and ran up to his office to take it. She turned to Henry. "Who's the new author? Everything okay?"

"Yes. It's a surprise. Jake didn't want me to tell you until he introduced her. Since he is the owner of the bookstore, I thought it would be advantageous for his business."

"Smart thinking. Jake certainly deserves any accolades coming his way."

Alison's chest swelled with pride as the children settled into their spots. She had faced an enormous challenge and succeeded beyond her wildest expectations. And most importantly, her heart had been forever touched, and her life altered in a unique and profound way.

As the show opened, Justin and Tina introduced a short video clip Sam had produced, featuring the kids and their week of holiday activities. When it finished, Tim took the microphone. "And now, here is the owner of Starlight Books and Publishing and our gracious host, Jake Sanders. He has a special surprise for all of us."

Watching Jake, Alison still got butterflies. She wondered who the author was.

Jake scanned the audience and saw Alison standing in the back. "Hello. My name is Jake Sanders, and this is my bookstore, Starlight Books. I am starting a new publishing company for children's writers and am proud to introduce my first author. She has been the steady force behind this show and *Hands-On Beyond*. Here to read *The Brightest Star*, I welcome our very own, Alison Rockwell."

Electrifying shockwaves hit Alison unexpectedly. She froze for an instant until Jenny came up behind her. "He called you, girl! Get up there!"

Everyone was clapping and cheering as she slowly approached the front. Annie walked onto the stage with the original manuscript and handed it to her. Alison saw the mischievous look in Jake's eyes as he motioned her to sit in the rocking chair, as all authors do when reading to a group of children. Or millions watching.

Alison cleared her throat. "Thank you. I don't know what to say."

Jake pointed to the cameras. "Just share with us your beautiful book."

Inhaling slowly into her jittering nerves, Alison looked out to the children. "Well, what a surprise!" The fact Jake had orchestrated this whole event blew her away. "Shall we begin?" She glanced one more time at Jake, whose adoration looked promising.

"Once upon a time, there was a very, very bright star named Alina. Her light was the brightest of all the stars." Alison became lost in her storytelling as a magical tranquility permeated the set for the entire story. The children were engaged, as all eyes were glued on her. Nearing the end of the tale, Alison concluded, "As Alina looked down at earth, she felt another wish coming her way. She smiled and knew someone, somewhere believed in the magic of wishing upon a star. And surely, when the time was right, happy surprises would come their way. The End."

As she closed the book to the roar of applause, Sean stepped on stage with her. "And we have another surprise." He looked over at Tim. "For Tim."

A tall, athletic man in uniform came forward from the back of the store. "Dad!" Tim ran to meet his father and was immediately wrapped in his arms. Sam turned the camera towards them and a shriek could be heard from Lucy as she rushed to their side. John pulled his wife close to his chest. She looked up at him as her voice choked with tears. "But how?"

"Our entire unit got a week pass for the holidays. Definitely a miracle!"

Alison glanced over at Jake, then noticed Jim Anderson standing in the back and wondered if they were responsible. Cameras were rolling, and she motioned for the hosts to come back on stage for the closing.

Justin, Tina and the younger hosts gathered together on the stage, and Tim brought his dad with him. After delivering inspiring closing remarks, they invited all the children to sing a rousing chorus of *We Wish You A Merry Christmas*. Then it was over.

The audience brought their hands together as whooping and hollering reverberated throughout the store. Alison still felt numb— but exhilarated after her astonishing surprise. She looked for Jake and saw him walk towards her.

"Congratulations! Great job, Miss Rockwell." Jake's eyes caressed her entire being with loving affection.

Alison couldn't contain her feelings and immediately grabbed him in a fierce hug. "Jake, thank you! Thank you." When she released him, she looked intently into his eyes. "Why didn't you tell me?"

Jake grinned. "And spoil the surprise? The look on your face was priceless!" He started to laugh.

"And Henry helped you?"

"Of course. It was a team effort. Come upstairs when you're finished here, and we'll chat more about it."

Alison paused for a second. Did he want to talk just about publishing her book or how he felt about her? "Yes, we can finally have a conversation we've been missing." She wasn't backing down.

As she watched him walk away, Alison heard a voice behind her.

"You were spectacular!"

Spinning around, she gasped, coming face to face with Steve.

"Steve! What are you doing here?"

"I thought I'd surprise you and watch your last shoot. I'm on vacation now and wanted to support you. I haven't given up on us, Alison. Here, these are for you." Steve handed her a Christmas bouquet.

Alison couldn't believe Steve was still in the picture. She thought she had been clear with him—but obviously, Steve did what Steve wanted. She slowly took the flowers so as not to be rude. "Thank you for the flowers, but you didn't have to drive all the way up here." She didn't know what else to say.

"But I did. I've had much time to think about us, and I can see how I wasn't attentive to your needs and desires when we were dating. I've changed, Ali, and I want to prove it to you. Please, give me another chance."

Alison observed him for a moment, seeing him as a man who realized his past mistakes. But was her success the reason? Or did he really have genuine feelings for her? One thing she knew for sure. She no longer had feelings for him. Her heart had opened to another. Gently, she spoke. "Steve, I appreciate the gallant effort you're making, but I've moved on. We weren't quite right for each other and I think you know it. And besides, I won't be living in New York much longer."

"Is it Jake? Have you fallen for him? I saw the way he looked at you," Steve said, a sinking sense of defeat overcoming him. He knew he had lost.

"I can't say yet, but I need to make my rounds with my staff." She smiled at him and said, "Merry Christmas, Steve. Take care of yourself." And she walked away.

***

Glancing back at Alison, Jake had seen Steve with the flowers before he left the room. Although tempted to observe their interaction, he decided against it and continued to his office. Regardless if she went back to him or not, Jake knew he would still have her in his life as her publisher. But in his heart, he knew that would never be enough.

***

As a euphoric sensation flowed through her veins like a river, Alison embraced a shared joy of satisfaction with her production staff. There was a Christmas lunch and an early showing of the episode in the afternoon. She had arranged Christmas gifts, and Henry was taking care of staff who needed to leave early. She spotted Karen and gave her the heads up to meet her in the office. Justin and Tina were waiting for her when she got there.

"Are you two ready?" Alison could feel their excitement in making this decision.

"Absolutely. We couldn't be happier." Tina was glowing.

A moment later, Karen entered with Eddie behind her. He had no clue what was happening but greeted everyone with a big smile. "Great job, everyone!"

Alison had placed all her chairs and couch in a circular formation. "Let's sit here." She looked at Eddie. "You must be wondering why we asked you to come."

Eddie cocked his head, still clueless.

Alison continued, "*Hands-On Beyond* had a successful launch, and we'd like to offer you one of the first spots. If you're interested."

Justin spoke up. "Tina and I would like to offer our home as your new residence in New York. After you graduate, of course. And Sam Hastings is offering you a job as his assistant for employment. He couldn't be here now, since he's editing in the truck, but he wanted you to know. We've all seen your hard work, persistence and good nature, and we want to help."

Eddie was speechless, his eyes wetting with pools of tears. Like Mary Beth, he had lost his parents in an accident at a young age. Luckily, the aftermath of his tragedy had been healed during his stay at Fairside Manor. He always had hoped one day he could pursue his own dreams, but never imagined it would be so easy.

Karen put her hand on his shoulder. "Take your time."

Eddie wiped the moistness off his face. "I don't know what to say. Yes! Of course, yes! I would love to come to New York!" He jumped up and walked over to Justin and Tina, hugging them in a grateful embrace. "Thank you. Thank you. You won't be sorry."

Justin and Tina laughed. "I don't think we have anything to worry about," added Justin.

An air of happiness infused the room. Karen continued, "They would like you to come visit for the second week of your Christmas break, and they'll make periodic visits here when they can before you graduate in June. Then, we will arrange your move."

"Sam's waiting for you in the truck," Alison added. "Why don't you go see him? He's pretty psyched too."

"You guys are the best. I can't believe this is happening to me."

"You deserve the best in life, Eddie. Now go find Sam." Eddie hastened out the door, anxious to find Sam. Alison leaned back in her chair and breathed a sigh of relief, delighted by the outcome. "Success, don't you agree?"

Everyone laughed. Justin put his arm around Tina. "This couldn't have come at a more perfect time for us. We've been thinking about adopting for a while and this gives us a chance to put our parenting desires to good use. We both realized the desperate need for helping these kids and look forward to staying connected with Maple Ridge. We're kind of fond of this place."

Tina agreed and stood up. "We're going to pack and will see you all at the last screening"

After they left, Alison turned to Karen. "I'm making my announcement today and we'll chat after the holidays."

"Perfect." Karen hugged her and went back to Fairside. Alone in her office, Alison's nerves fluttered, reflecting on what came next. But she was ready. The inevitable no longer scared her.

Chapter Twenty-Five

Jake's hands were folded against his chin with elbows on his desk as he surveyed the snow-covered hills out his window. Thinking of Alison, his thoughts were cut short when Annie ran in. "Dad! You have to come with me. We're all having lunch together and a gift exchange before Melissa and Sean go back to the city. Tim's dad is coming too."

As a single father, these last few years had taught Jake the importance of patience and willingness to put another human being's needs before his own. His plans to see Alison would have to wait. Again. "Sure. I just cleaned up. Let's go." Annie grabbed his hand and they bumped right into Alison outside the door.

Smiling, she said, "I see you two are off somewhere."

"We're going to the community center for lunch and a gift exchange. Want to come?" asked Annie.

Jake looked at Alison and shrugged. "Guess I'll see you later?"

Alison nodded Jake and turned to Annie. "Thanks Annie, but I'm going to find my parents and Jenny. I'll see you at the screening. By the way, thank you for doing such a marvelous job this week. You're a natural."

Annie let go of her dad's hand and hugged Alison with a tight grip. "I just wish you were staying in Maple Ridge."

Jake interrupted. "Don't worry. She'll come visit. After all, she is one of Starlight's first authors."

"Yes, true." Alison shifted her weight from one foot to another, not wanting to leave, and still wondering if Jake wanted more in their relationship.

He touched her arm. "Please don't leave before we have a chance to talk."

Alison placed her hand on his, gazing into his magnetic, blue eyes. "I promise."

And they left.

***

After lunch with her parents Alison went back to her office. Jenny and Mike had joined them, and she was finally able to discuss her future plans with Jenny. After watching the outcome of her work these last few weeks, none were surprised by her choices. Although the final episode had aired live earlier, the staff gathered to watch the taped segment for themselves. Some had left, but Alison had arranged a shuttle bus to take anyone who needed a ride back to the city when the viewing was over. She looked around the room and saw Jake sitting with Annie, Tim and his parents. Luckily her mom and dad were in no rush to get home and had told her they would stay another night in the inn if she needed to tie up loose ends.

After watching herself read her book aloud to a live television audience, Alison was teeming with emotion. Since the moment when Jake announced her as his first author, she felt she had been living in a dream. Her dream, now a reality. Gathering her composure, she slowly walked to the front.

"I wanted to thank all of you for working so diligently and earnestly during these past weeks. Words cannot express how grateful I am to each and every one of you. I have a few announcements to make before we leave." In her vision, she caught Jake's eyes riveted on her. "In the new year I will be leaving *Hands-On Kids* to become executive director of *Hands-On Beyond*. But I will leave you in good hands. Next year you will be shepherded by Henry Adams as producer and Jenny Marshall as creative director. I will act in a consulting role only." Jenny and Henry stood up. Some of the staff were stunned, but those close to Alison knew it was coming. "Henry and Jenny have special gifts for all of you, so be sure you see them now before heading out. My heart is full, and I want to wish you a very Merry Christmas and Happy New Year!" Clapping and cheering resounded in the room—and then it was all over.

Jenny was thrilled at the promotion, but sad to lose her roommate and best friend. But things had been getting more serious between her and Mike, and perhaps an engagement may be in the future. She turned to Alison. "I never asked you about Carolyn. What happened? She must be furious to be replaced by Henry and me."

"Don't worry about her. The network offered her another job. One without kids." Alison laughed. "She just didn't have the personality for this show, but she's an organized producer. And Thea will be going with her."

"I can't wait to work with Henry and keep the energy alive you've instilled in the show. And besides, there will have to be some meetings with our consultant. But I am going to miss you terribly!"

"Me too," agreed Alison, hugging her friend with an affectionate force.

"Congratulations," said a voice behind Alison. She released Jenny and found Jake gazing down at her. "Thank you. I was going to tell you, but we never had a chance to talk."

"I know. How about in an hour I meet you at the estate? In the library?"

"Perfect. I have to clean up in there any way."

"I'll see you then." As Jake walked away, his heart was racing. She had made a decision without him. Now he was confident he wouldn't interfere with her future dreams when he let her know.

Jenny shook her head. "I can't believe you two haven't talked yet. This untouched, ravishing chemistry is driving me crazy!"

"You and me both!" They laughed. "I made up my mind to follow my heart and work with these orphan and foster kids. It felt right, and I will still have time to write. If Jake is interested in a relationship, he better let me know. I've made my move." Alison felt strong and determined.

"You go, girl!" Jenny was happy for her friend. "Are you sure you don't want any help breaking down the office? Mike and I could stay and leave in the morning."

"Absolutely not. You have time to make it back to the city and have a relaxing Christmas Eve. I can stay if needed."

"Maybe there's someone who could help you." Jenny winked at her.

Alison hugged her once more. "I'll be back in the city after Christmas. We'll have plenty of time to talk. I love you!"

"Love you too! And Merry Christmas." Jenny briskly walked away in search of Mike.

***

As Alison entered the estate kitchen, Maggy stood there making a cup of tea. "There you are. The successful New York producer. Congratulations!"

"Thanks, Maggy," Alison replied, fondly. "Couldn't have done it without the whole team."

"Yeah, but I recognize a mastermind when I see it. And you've inspired me. I understand why you made the decision to make the move. Perhaps I can help *Hands-On Beyond* in Los Angeles. We'll chat in the new year."

"Sounds great. I want to reach as many kids as possible."

"Looking for Jake?"

"We said we'd meet in the library."

"He just took some tea in for you two." Maggy smiled. "We never got to talk, but I guess you didn't need it. You knew all along what you wanted to do."

"I guess so. It just took some serious contemplation amidst a flurry of confusion." Alison laughed.

Alison slowly walked towards the library, conscious of each step she took. She stopped only to fix her hair in the mirror in the hallway, but as Jake came into sight, all trepidation melted away. "Hi."

Jake could feel his temperature rise gazing at her. His heart had opened wide these last few weeks and the intensity of his profound loss had diminished to the point where he could see a future for himself again. He knew Clara would have wanted the same thing for him and for Annie. His feelings for Alison were unexpected, yet he had to be sure she was ready to leave New York. He couldn't do a long-distance relationship and Annie was his priority.

"Hi. Thanks for coming. I guess we're finally going to have our talk." He laughed.

Alison took a step closer. "Yes. And you might be seeing more of me."

Jake approached, then reached out his hand, taking hers. "Does this mean you'll be available for a date?"

Alison gazed tenderly into his eyes. "I think it could be arranged."

"I didn't want to interfere with your dreams, Alison. When my uncle told me about the promotion, I pulled back. And I'm sorry," he said, attentively awaiting her reaction.

"I wondered what happened." All worry from the previous uncertain days was slipping away, and all she wanted was to be taken into his arms.

As if reading her mind, Jake reached out and pulled her close. "My feelings are real, Alison. I've fallen in love with you."

"You won my heart weeks ago, Jake Sanders."

Jake's lips softly eased into hers. First, gentle, then slowly with a passion of their long-awaited love exploding into an irresistible, deeper kiss. Alison allowed herself to completely surrender into Jake's tender caress, knowing she had at last come home.

As they gradually pulled away, Jake's unwavering gaze communicated his clear intentions for Alison. "Can you stay with us for Christmas? Your parents too?"

Alison knew she wasn't ready to leave Jake quite yet. Her parents would happily understand. "I would love to."

"I already talked to Uncle Jim, and he insisted your parents move over here for as long as you can stay." Jake searched her eyes for a response.

Alison smiled. "I think it could be arranged. They were secretly hoping something would happen with us."

"Yes, Alison, something definitely is happening between us. And I am not going to let you down. You'll see." Jake's assurance was strong.

"I'm all yours, Jake." Alison's entire being quivered with anticipation.

Jake took her in his arms once more, kissing her tenderly, then wrapping his arms tightly around her. "I'll never let you go," he whispered.

Alison gave thanks her prayers had been answered. Better than she could ever have imagined. Looking out the window over Jake's shoulder, a falling star fell against the evening sky, and she knew her wish had been fulfilled. After all, it had been written in the stars.